McKnight, A. M., author.
Goslyn county

2015
33305248331872
mi      08/12/21

*'NTY*

A.M. MCKNIGHT

2015

This book is a work of fiction. Resemblance to persons, locations, or characters real or fictional, living or deceased is entirely coincidental and unintentional.


Cover Design: CreateSpace
Cover Badge Image by: Keith Bruce (Kbkgraphx)| Dreamstime.com
Copyright© 2015 by A.M. McKnight
ammcknight.wordpress.com
facebook.com/ammcknightbooks

The publisher and author acknowledge the trademark ownership of all trademarks, service marks, and word marks mentioned in this book.

All rights reserved. No part of this publication may be reproduced or transmitted in any form or by any means, electronic, mechanical, or digital, including photocopying, recording, or otherwise, or by any information storage or retrieval system without the prior written permission of the copyright holder.

# PROLOGUE

Thirty Years Ago.

*Wow, it's hot out here,* Pat thought. The heat circled her ankles and hovered just above the asphalt driveway leading up to Ollie's garage. The shrubs in front of the house were as dry as dust and had turned as brown as Pat's skin. She said aloud, "I hate summer," knowing it would get a rise out of Ollie.

"You're crazy, girl! No school, no waking up early! I love summer!" Ollie grabbed the basketball from Pat and threw it up at the net and backboard above the garage door.

Pat snapped back, "You love it *this* year 'cause you're not stuck in summer school for three weeks!"

Ollie knew that was true. Everyone who knew Olivia Ann Winston also knew the Winston family motto--*Education never goes on vacation.* That motto was created and enforced by Mrs. Selma Ann Winston, Ollie's mom and head of the Math Department at Lincoln Middle.

Twelve-year-old Ollie thought it was the corniest thing she had ever heard and would cringe whenever her classmates mimicked her mom saying it.

"So tell the truth," Pat asked as she chased down Ollie's missed shot, "how did you get out of going to school this summer?"

Ollie wiped the sweat from her brow and gestured for Pat to throw her the ball. She threw it up at the net again. "Score, two points," she said.

"C'mon, tell me," Pat pretended to beg.

"All right. It's no big deal. My mama said I didn't have to go if I promised to go to the library once a week and check out a math book. I already finished two books."

"Really?! Your mama's way too easy, Ollie. Everybody knows you like to read boring numbers stuff anyway."

"I know, and I told her it was a good way to keep my brain from taking a vacation."

They both laughed at Ollie's jab at her family motto then headed to the back of Ollie's house. The shaded back porch swing was their favorite place to sit.

"My mama won't let me check out books by myself," Pat said. "She won't even let me use my own library card. I have to use hers."

"Well it's your own fault. You shouldn't have told her about that book I showed you."

Pat stared into space as she remembered sitting next to Ollie on the reading room floor in the public library. She had listened as Ollie read from an old, African love story. The book had a drawing of the characters--two young, pretty, black women holding hands.

Eleven-year-old Patrice Lynn Henley had heard about those kind of women--the kind her other friends called nasty names that she wasn't allowed to repeat. But it was the first time she could really imagine two women holding each other the same way that her mom and dad did.

"Hello, Earth calling," Ollie said as she waved

her hand in front of Pat. "You daydreaming, girl?"

"Oh, sorry."

An awkward silence followed.

Ollie rose from the swing and dribbled the basketball several times. She was bracing herself for what she knew her best friend was going to ask because she had asked it before.

Pat kept rocking quietly, trying to gather the courage to speak. Ever since she and Ollie learned about the "birds and the bees," she had noticed the way Ollie would act around certain girls--the girls Ollie called the "really pretty tomboys." She would tease Ollie about her blushing like a love struck puppy whenever they watched the Lincoln girls' basketball team play. Ollie always denied it and brushed it off as Pat just being silly. But there was no fooling Pat.

"Do you like girls, I mean, do you like girls the way boys like girls?" There, she asked it.

Ollie pretended to ignore her and kept dribbling but suddenly stopped as if she was struck by a sad thought. She moved to the edge of the porch and sat on the top step.

Pat got up from the swing and joined her.

"My brother thinks you like girls," Pat said, "and he says you act like a boy."

"I don't care," Ollie said softly. "Your brother's just jealous 'cause I kicked his butt in football. Why are you asking me that anyway?"

"Cause my mama says you might be a lesbian, but it's just a phase you'll grow out of."

"What!" Ollie yelled. "Why do you talk to your mama about me?!" Ollie hung her head the second she saw the look on her best friend's face.

Pat, looking embarrassed and hurt, didn't speak.

Ollie quickly stood and threw the basketball into the open backyard where it hit a stack of firewood and bounced right back at her. She sprinted to meet it and slowly came back and sat next to Pat.

"I'm sorry, Pat."

They sat without speaking for awhile.

Ollie then asked, "If I did like girls, would it matter? Would we still be best friends?"

"I don't know," Pat said. "Would we still be best friends if I told you I like Eric Rice?"

"Are you joking, Pat? 'Metal Mouth' Eric Rice?!"

They both broke out in laughter and bumped shoulders.

"You're so goofy," Ollie said. "C'mon, let's play one more round before we go to the pool."

Ollie jumped down to the bottom step and waved for Pat to follow.

"Okay. But I'm not chasing down your missed shots," Pat said.

"What missed shots?" Ollie dribbled the ball between her legs. "Watch me go ten for ten. It'll be swish and nothing but net."

# CHAPTER ONE

Present Day.

"Ollie, if you don't stop banging on my TV, I'm gonna chase you out of here with my broom!"

Olivia Ann Winston looked at her grandma and shook her head. "Grandma, this used to be a TV. Now it's just a heavy block of junk. Look at it. There's no color, the picture won't stop jumping, and the light on the converter box keeps blinking." Olivia leaned against the huge floor model set and straightened the crooked antenna. The faux wooden side panels were peeling, and the cardboard backing had warped around the edges.

Grandma Rita May Jones didn't mind. She loved her TV. It matched well with her old-school style of knee-high stockings and a closet full of pinstriped housedresses. She still used a pair of curling irons heated on top of a gas stove pilot to do her hair, and she swore she could bake a loaf of bread better than any brand found in a grocery store.

"Dear child, it's a black and white set," Grandma Rita said, "and you have to turn the knob at the bottom to fix the picture. And as long as I keep getting my soap opera, I don't care about a blinking light."

"Where's the flat screen I bought you?" Olivia asked.

"In the hall closet. Now please turn off *my* TV and scoot out of here with those mums and daffs!"

"Yes, ma'am." Duly scolded, Olivia grabbed an armful of the potted yellows and whites and marched out the back door and into the community garden. Digging and planting was always on the weekend schedule at Grandma Rita's house. And with the Sun beaming down on an early Spring Saturday, every neighbor within a four-block radius was expected to pitch in.

Olivia had to admit that gardening was a welcome relief from investigating burglaries and armed robberies. She often thanked her grandma-- when she wasn't complaining about the work--for starting the garden and for having it in her backyard. People were at their best when they had a common goal.

A mostly black community with its roots in farming, Goslyn, Virginia lay just south of the State's Capital. The once small, close-knit county had grown rapidly in the past two decades and boasted a population of just over fifty thousand. But the county's crime stats had grown as well, and the latest offenses included several break-ins and rumors of a meth lab. Time had brought many changes, and many of the longtime folks of Goslyn no longer recognized their community and longed for days gone by.

"All right, Grandma, I planted the mums and daffs," Olivia said as she returned through the back screen door. "What's next?"

"That was fast."

"Well you've made me do this for years. I think I've got the hang of it by now." Olivia raised her brow at her grandmother.

"Next are the sweet potatoes." Grandma Rita ignored the sarcasm and pointed to a large tray of shoots sitting on the floor just to Olivia's right. "Be careful pickin' 'em up. Just sow 'em like I taught you in that row Harold already tilled up by the tool shed."

"Hey! No fair, Grandma!" Olivia looked at her elder thumbing through a magazine at the kitchen table. "You're in here chillin' while I'm getting dirty." She pointed to the grass and dirt stains on her old Levis and faded Lincoln High T-shirt.

Now forty-one and standing five-eight with a slim, toned figure, Detective Winston always felt like a school kid, unsure and awkward, around the woman who helped raise her. Grandma Rita stood a slightly bent five-four, but her personality was straight and strong. Her confidence was earned in her early years as a southern black woman widowed by the Korean War. Now in her late eighties, Rita May Jones was still a strikingly beautiful, dark-skinned woman, just like Olivia's mom and just like Olivia.

"Hush, child," Grandma said. I'm collecting ideas for the garden. Besides, I already picked a pot of string beans and planted a row of tomatoes all before you rolled out of bed this morning. Now get out of here with those shoots!"

Olivia groaned, pretended her feelings were hurt, and carefully lifted the tray and backed out the door. Just as she turned around, there stood Harold Brooks with a shovel in one hand and a head of cabbage in the other.

"Hey, Detective, Lady of the house givin' orders again?"

"Morning, Mr. Brooks. Yes, the gray-haired

taskmaster is at it again."

Long retired from the post office, the brown-skinned eighty-year-old Mr. Brooks stood six-foot-two and took pride in not looking a day over sixty. He wore a neatly cut mini-afro with a large, gray patch just off center.

"Let me guess. Sweet potatoes, right?" he asked as he nodded at the tray in Olivia's hands.

"Yes. And let me guess. Coleslaw for Sunday dinner?" Olivia nodded at the cabbage head.

"Indeed. It'll go perfect with your grandma's famous roasted turkey." Mr. Brooks looked past Olivia and tried to see through the screen door.

Though she and Mr. Brooks were a generation apart, Olivia always sensed that he understood what it was like to be considered different by some. Just a guess on her part, but the detective thought maybe Mr. Brooks was gay. He never married despite many attempts by a few local widows. And he never spoke of any love interests despite Olivia's occasional attempts to coax a name out of him.

"She's right inside," Olivia said as she stepped around him and headed to the garden.

"By the way, thanks again for coming to the neighborhood watch meeting." Mr. Brooks turned slightly and looked over his shoulder.

"No problem, Mr. Brooks. Thanks for inviting me," Olivia said as she turned to face him.

"Oh, and I heard you met Maureen." Mr. Brooks winked as the name rolled off his lips. He didn't bother waiting for a response as he quickly disappeared behind the screen door.

*Maureen?* Olivia's eyes widened. *How in the*

*world does he know…*

***

Olivia grumbled to herself as she knelt down in the dirt, "This is starting to feel like a second job." She hoped Grandma Rita didn't have anything else she wanted done.

It was almost noon and many of the neighbors were present and hard at work. Mrs. Thompson was tending to sprouting potatoes. Mr. Allen and his six kids were pulling weeds from around the red peppers. Mrs. Allen--pregnant again--was watching and giving instructions. Mr. Jackson was across the yard spreading mulch around the azaleas, and members of the "biz wiz" club had started sowing new rows for melon seeds.

Olivia finally planted the last shoot.

"Good morning, Professor Winston," said a sleepy-eyed twenty-year-old girl who had walked up to Olivia.

"Good morning, Nicki." From the bags under the girl's eyes, last night must have been rough. "Long night again?"

"Yes, ma'am. He's still not sleeping through the night," the single mother said.

"And imagine, only eighteen more years to go," Olivia joked.

"Sorry for turning my assignment in late, Professor. My internal clock is all messed up."

"Don't worry about it. You did a good job."

"So where can I start?" Nicki asked as she looked around the garden.

"How about by saying hello to my grandma first? Then we'll put you to work." That got a big smile.

Off went the young mother who, Olivia knew, would hear some words of wisdom from Mrs. Jones and, perhaps, a bit of gossip from Mr. Brooks.

Olivia, with her lieutenant's permission, spent every other Wednesday night in Richmond teaching basic math through trigonometry to young adults at a community college. She thought the class was a good way of helping many students who didn't get the attention they deserved while in middle and high school. It was also a way of showing her mom that her degree in mathematics wasn't wasted. She could still see the look on Selma Ann's face when she told her she wanted to be a police officer. It was that look that said, "Lord, will this child ever do what I want her to?" Mama Winston's plan was to have her daughter one day head the math department at a distinguished, historically black college or university.

But Olivia didn't have the same passion as her mom did when it came to teaching. Instead, an ordinary field trip to the local police department over twenty years ago set Olivia on a path she knew she wanted to follow. She entered the Police Academy straight out of college. After ten years in uniform, she made Detective.

Olivia's cell phone rang. *The lady's always on time,* she thought. She wiped her hands on her jeans and pulled her phone off her belt. "This is Detective Olivia Ann Winston of Goslyn PD, Crimes Against Property and Persons Division. How may I help you?"

"If you weren't my child, I swear …," said the

warm voice of Mrs. Winston.

They both laughed.

"Good morning, Mama. How are you?"

"Just fine, thank you. What are you planting this morning?"

"Sweet potatoes. What poor child are you punishing with the multiplication table this morning?"

"Hey, I don't punish. I empower, young lady. Look at how you turned out!" She had Olivia there.

For the last two months, Olivia had been house-sitting for her mom who was in Haiti with several other retired teachers. They were helping to re-open the schools that had been devastated by the latest round of bad weather. Mrs. Winston, now in her sixties, was a lifelong educator who believed knowledge not only gave you power, it also obligated you to lend a hand to those in need.

"So anything new going on?" Mama asked.

"Not a thing. I replanted your rose bushes as you requested, and Mr. Johnson repainted the front porch columns."

"What about the floors?"

"Mr. Johnson gave them a good sand and polish. Everything looks brand new. Anything else, Boss Lady?"

"Ollie, you know how much I love that house."

The whole world knew how much Selma Ann Winston loved her home. Second to Olivia, it was the best gift she had received from her husband, John. It was a beautiful three-bedroom brick rancher built from the ground up by the late Mr. Winston. Rose bushes and shrubs surrounded the house. A gorgeous red cedar swing was on the back deck porch, and the backyard view extended for a clear half-acre, giving a perfect view right into Grandma Rita's backyard garden--because Mr. Winston knew mother and daughter liked to stay close.

"How was your week?"

"Nothing exciting, just the same old police work."

"Do I want to know the details, Ollie?"

"Oh, Mama. No one has shot at me, and I haven't had to shoot anybody." Olivia tried to put her at ease.

"Okay. By the way, thanks for the photos you *finally* sent. The kids think you're beautiful, and the girls really like your hair. That style is called 'twisties,' right?"

"Yeah, Pat talked me in to getting them."

"That reminds me. I hear you have a special friend named Maureen."

"Where did you hear that?!"

"Never mind where I heard it, just fill me in."

"Sorry, Mrs. Winston, but we have a bad connection. I think I'm losing you." Olivia held the phone away from her ear.

"Very funny. Okay, be that way. I'll let it go, for now. Tell your grandma I'll call her tomorrow night. I love you."

"I love you too, Mama." Olivia flipped the phone shut and laughed out loud. *It's good to be loved.*

# CHAPTER TWO

"Good morning. Henley-Rice & Associates, this is Justine. How may I help you? …No, sir, Mrs. Henley-Rice is in a meeting until noon today. May I take a message? …All right, I'll let her know she can reach you after three o'clock. Have a good day."

Justine Mabry rose from her seat and maneuvered around balls of bubble wrap that littered the office floor. New laptops had arrived that morning, and the tech associates had torn into the boxes like kids on Christmas Day. They left trails of packaging Styrofoam from the front door to the dozen cubicles lining the walls of the spacious rectangular office.

"Hey, Lisa, cover for me. I need to run to the little girls' room."

"Again?!" Lisa frowned at the extra large cappuccino sitting on Justine's desk. "You drink enough coffee for the both of us." She quickly put on a headset.

"Yeah, I know. I'll be right back."

The phone rang. "Henley-Rice & Associates, this is Lisa. How may I help you?"

"Good morning, Lisa. How are you?"

"Hello, Olivia. I'm good. And you?"

"Fine, for a Monday morning. Do anything over the weekend?"

"You know me, Olivia. My weekends are made for outlet shopping. Williamsburg should give me a key to the city. I know you were a good granddaughter and did that garden duty."

"I'm trapped for life, Lisa, with no way out. Is the cranky computer geek in? I've got some detective work for her."

"Officially, she's in a meeting. But she's probably asleep after waiting in line all night to buy another iPhone."

"Okay, can you let her know--"

"Oh, hold on Olivia, the 'Data Queen' just poked her head out of her office. It's Olivia," the veteran receptionist said as she pointed to her headset.

Pat Henley-Rice put the phone to her ear. "Well, well, if it isn't the detective who couldn't find her way downtown last night."

"I love you too, you geek. But you didn't seriously think I would spend the night on a cold sidewalk waiting to buy a phone, not after eating a hot meal at Grandma's?"

"Yeah, yeah, I know where Eric and I rank on your list of priorities."

"You rank just below Sunday dinner and my warm bed."

"All right, all right." Pat wiped the sleep from her eyes. "So what's going on?" She untangled the phone cord, walked over to her office window, and opened the blinds.

"I need your expertise again," Olivia said. "I'm working on some recent burglary cases."

"Anybody we know?"

"No, thankfully. It's those quick tax refund services. Someone broke in and stole the laptops and just about all the paper files containing the clients' identity info. We don't have any leads, not even the usual suspects."

"Never trust your social security number to a business located next to a liquor store," Pat sniped and opened up her new laptop.

"I know, but some people don't have a choice, Pat."

"You're right. How can I help?"

"I know identity info is usually sold over the Internet. So I need to know if any of your tech friends have heard about these recent break-ins."

"I've got some sources I can check. There's always somebody bragging on the Net about something they shouldn't have done. But remind me again why you're not using the fine resources of Goslyn PD for this?" Pat knew the answer but loved hearing it from Olivia.

"For the hundredth time, I quote, 'The Goslyn Police Department still does not have a division capable of addressing certain cyber-based crimes.' There, you happy?"

"Very. I never get tired of hearing that." About a year ago, Henley-Rice & Associates had entered a bid to act as consultant for the Department's proposed Internet-based crimes division. A competitor had won the bid, but the Department still didn't have its new division, and the local newspaper had made it a front-page story.

"Enough shop talk. Did you guys really spend all night outside?"

"Of course we did. I freely confess my addiction to iPhones, iPads, iPods and--"

"All right, I get it. What about the twins?"

"They were at the in-laws' being spoiled

rotten."

Though Olivia loved to give her best friend a hard time, she was very proud of Pat. Henley-Rice & Associates was a top-rated IT service provider for several local companies and had recently updated the County's Public Works database. Mrs. Patrice Henley-Rice had grown from a scrawny teen into an attractive and nerdy woman who relished all things computer. Her caramel colored skin went perfectly with her shoulder length braids, and her five-foot-six stature belied her skills as a black belt.

"We still on for Thursday after work?" Olivia asked.

"Absolutely. I need time away from Eric and the twins at least once a week. Between his freaking out about taking the Bar Exam and all of the boys' after-school activities, it's a wonder I have sanity to run this place." Pat made a wild hand gesture at the walls of her office.

"Okay. I'll swing by around six thirty, and we'll do Chinese at the mall."

"Sounds good. I'll tell you about your godsons' latest bad behavior, and you can tell me about somebody named Maureen."

"What?! Not you too!"

"Just be ready for an interrogation, Detective. Bye."

Pat got up and rubbed her neck with a loud moan. "Justine, an aspirin, please! I'm getting too old to be sleeping on concrete with folks half my age."

Justine sprinted in with a pill bottle while trying to hold her headset in place. She sprinted back out to catch the next call.

"What some people will do for a simple phone," Lisa said as she brought in a coffee pot and mug. She filled the mug and handed it to Pat.

"Look who's talking, the woman who drove through a hail storm for a jewelry sale."

"You got that right. So what's up with Detective Winston?"

"She wants us to be Internet snoops again, 'Dr. Watson.' " Pat took a big gulp from the mug. "Ahh, Nature's best drink ever."

Lisa knew her boss loved it when Olivia asked her to help with an investigation. It was like a big sister relationship that Lisa enjoyed watching.

Over ten years ago, Lisa Kelley answered Henley-Rice & Associates' ad in the paper for a part-time receptionist. She was working as a 9-1-1 dispatcher at the time but was becoming burned out. On the day of the interview, the new office was in chaos--phone lines ringing, associates complaining about office space, and computer equipment stacked to the ceiling. Lisa went straight to the phone, put on a headset, and got to work handling every kind of caller--from those looking for the previous tenant to those wanting to order a pizza. By the end of that first day, she had the job.

In those quick ten years, Pat had repaid Lisa's support not just in wages but also by teaching her almost everything she now knew about computers and the Internet. Together, through hacker sites, blogs, and chat rooms, they could find out anything about anybody.

"What are we hunting for this time,

'Sherlock'?" Lisa asked.

"Identity thieves, my friend."

"Ooo, I'll call home and let Dan know I'll be working late."

"Just don't blame it on me this time," Pat said. "You've got Dan thinking I'm a computer junkie with a hard drive for a heart." She tossed an aspirin into her mouth, took another big gulp, and turned to her laptop. "All right, let's fire up this new toy and do some sleuthing."

# CHAPTER THREE

"Special Agent Jeffries will see you now, Mr. Lewis." Carol Taylor looked up at the heavy-set man who had been standing in front of her desk for the past ten minutes pacing in a circle. She nodded to the office door.

Bertrand Lewis swallowed hard and felt his Adam's apple twitch. He took two steps toward the door then turned back and picked up a large briefcase he had left next to Carol's desk. He turned to the door again but suddenly froze.

"Where's the men's room?" he timidly asked.

"Just go out the door and make two rights."

Carol walked into Maureen's office and said, "There goes a ball of sweat. Take it easy on this guy. He looks like he's about to pass a kidney stone."

"Such a lovely image you just put in my head," Maureen said. "If he's not back in five minutes, I nominate you to go knock on the bathroom door."

Five minutes later. "Here he comes." Carol headed back to the front desk. "Please go right in, Mr. Lewis."

IRS Special Agent Maureen Jeffries stood and extended her hand to the nervous man. After feeling his damp palm, she immediately regretted being civil. She had done hundreds of these interviews, and yet the routine never got old.

"Ma'am, I know there're some issues with my prior tax returns...but...you see I..." Bertrand stopped in mid-sentence as he switched his oversized briefcase from one hand to the other.

19

*He really does look like he's about to pass a kidney stone,* Maureen thought.

A brown-skinned man with a head full of disheveled, white hair, Bertrand also looked like he had slept in his suit.

Maureen directed him to a chair opposite her side of the desk. She remained standing. It was an old tactic the veteran agent liked to use with hard cases. She would slowly walk to the other side of her large office, retrieve big bound copies of the tax code, and place them on her desk next to a folder conspicuously labeled with the taxpayer's name. This move usually got her guest to understand that this was not going to be a brief meeting. To her surprise, Bertrand Lewis came without legal counsel. He was either totally cocky or totally clueless.

Maureen took her seat, opened the folder, and said in a very serious tone, "Mr. Lewis, you've had a string of bad luck recently, and I'm not referring to your unfiled personal returns." She stared at her guest as he took a deep breath and cleared his throat.

"What can I say, ma'am? Either somebody hates me, or I'm cursed." Bertrand tried to laugh but hiccupped instead.

"All three of your tax refund locations were burglarized last month. I would say there's definitely something working against you."

Bertrand seemed confused by the agent's comment. "Uh...Ms. Jeffries...I have cooperated with local authorities, and I have directed my employees to do the same."

"Have you notified your customers of their personal information being stolen and offered them any credit protection services?"

The rotund man twisted his lips and seemed offended by the question. "Yes, *Ms*. Jeffries, my company's general counsel has notified all concerned parties." He briefly returned her stare.

A recent investigation aired by *60 Minutes* had embarrassed the IRS and made several of Maureen's colleagues look lazy if not incompetent. Apparently, identity thieves were raking in huge amounts of money by filing fraudulent tax returns and receiving refunds. Bertrand Lewis' sloppy handling of client data, a barely trained staff, and a cheap security system had only made the fraud much easier.

Despite the bad publicity, Special Agent Jeffries was still proud of her nearly twenty years of service with the Agency. Straight out of high school, she worked in an admin support position for two years with Richmond PD. She then obtained an accounting degree and became an entry-level agent with the IRS. Four years later, she entered her current position in the criminal investigations unit. Some weight lifting and a steady four-mile run every evening helped her maintain her five-nine athletic build, and a good pick-up game of basketball didn't hurt either.

"And ma'am, I'm part of this community too," Bertrand went on, "and I'm stunned by what happened."

Maureen caught Bertrand eyeing the picture she proudly hung on the wall directly behind her. It was a photo of her accepting a community service award from a local LGBT organization. She noted the slight sneer on his face as he pulled out a handkerchief and wiped the sweat from his hairline.

"Mr. Lewis, you were asked to come in today because dozens of your company's recent customers had tax returns fraudulently filed under their names and social security numbers." She waited for a response.

Bertrand tucked the soiled handkerchief back into a wrinkled pocket and said, "Believe me, ma'am, if I had any information about who broke into my locations, I would gladly tell you. But like I told the police, I don't have a clue."

Special Agent Jeffries didn't believe a word he was saying. But as long as he was in the mood to talk without a lawyer, she intended to squeeze as much out of him as possible.

*** 

Maureen rubbed the back of her neck and sat on the edge of Carol's desk. She was finally done with her guest who made a beeline for the men's room the second he left her office. "Why do I feel like I need a shower?" she said.

"Because you spent the whole morning talking to a man who was feeding you crap and sweating all over your desk."

"You paint such lovely images, Carol."

"Thanks. It comes naturally."

Maureen looked at the clock on Carol's desk. "It's almost one thirty. Have you had lunch yet?"

"Not yet. Jackie's running a little late, but she'll be here soon to cover for me."

The phone rang which seemed to give Maureen an instant boost.

"Special Agent Jeffries' office. How may I help you?" Carol listened for a moment and said into the receiver, "Hello again, Detective Winston."

Maureen was up and back at her desk before Carol could finish.

Carol placed the call on hold and poked her head into Maureen's office. "Well, shut the front door! If you had jumped any higher, you would've hit the ceiling."

"Back to work, you slacker," Maureen joked. She picked up the receiver, pushed the line button, and leaned back in her chair. "Hello, Detective Winston. How are you?"

Olivia thought, *I just got better.* Aloud, she said, "Not bad. How are you?"

"I had an interesting morning with Bertrand Lewis," the agent said as she slipped off her loafers under her desk.

"That's why I'm calling. Did he have any leads on who might've done the burglaries?"

Maureen thought, *You mean you're not calling just to talk to me?* "He pleaded total ignorance. But I suspect it's money related."

"How so?"

Maureen flipped through her Lewis file. "His profit and loss statements for the last three years show declining but still okay revenue streams. However, the bank statements for the same time period don't show any substantial deposits other than enough to cover payroll. But even that dropped off. So I'm thinking he was burning through cash as soon as it came in the door--probably on gambling."

"Why do you think it's gambling?"

"I could pretend it was a good guess on my part, but it was all the poker chips that fell out of his briefcase he knocked over when he ran to the bathroom for the third time." Maureen stood up and stretched.

"So maybe we're looking at a gambling debt gone bad?" Olivia asked.

"Maybe. There was a large deposit of a hundred twenty thousand dollars about ten months ago. About half of that was eaten up by payroll while he sent the rest to us to apply toward back taxes. So--"

"So where does a man with a failing business and a bad gambling habit get a lump sum of a hundred twenty grand?"

"The answer may break both our cases." Maureen brushed her hand across her dark-brown cheek and ran her fingers through her short, curly fade. "Of course, Mr. Lewis claims the money was earned by hard work and dedicated employees."

"You got more than I did," Olivia said. "When I talked to him, all I got was something about him being cursed and his insurance company dropping him. The employees at each location seemed up-front. But they didn't know much about Lewis' financial situation. As long as their paychecks cleared, everything was fine."

Maureen heard several beeps and what sounded like a microwave starting.

Olivia continued, "We got nothing on the security video either--images were too grainy. But we're still running all fingerprints through our system."

"Those fraudulent refunds were routed to untraceable bank accounts in Atlanta," Maureen said as she slipped her shoes back on. "I've got calls in to our office there. Also, Atlanta PD told our guys that some local thugs were making noise about free tax money. I think I may need to take a quick trip down there this week."

"Now there's an Atlanta connection?" Olivia asked.

"Could be, Olivia." Both were silent for a moment. "Sorry, I get a little slow when I'm hungry."

"No problem, Maureen," Olivia said. "Your cyber guys working the Internet angle?"

"Yeah, but they say it's like searching for a dime in the ocean."

"We may get lucky on our end. I've got a friend who's very good at hunting for info on the Net. So go get some lunch, and I'll be in touch again.

\*\*\*

Olivia waited for the microwave to count down. As she leaned back against the counter and read the latest postings on the break room bulletin board, she wondered what Special Agent Jeffries was having for lunch and if she had a favorite dish. "I've got a silly crush," she mumbled and laughed at herself.

The microwave beeped, and the smell of roasted turkey filled the room when Olivia popped open the microwave door. She blew on the hot string beans and sprinkled them with black pepper.

Lunch in hand, she went back to the squad room where she found her partner at his desk. Marcus Rowland sat opposite her and was about to dig into veggie lasagna his wife made once a week at his request.

"Boy, that smells good," Olivia said as she sat down. "When is Phyllis going to give that recipe to my grandma?"

"Never, my friend. She guards it like she guards her checkbook."

"Can you blame the woman? You buy enough tools to open your own car repair shop."

"A man's gotta have a hobby," Marcus said before cramming a fork full into his mouth. "Mmm, now I remember why I love that woman." A bite of garlic bread was next.

Marcus Rowland, in law enforcement for nearly thirty years, had been Olivia's partner for the last seven after transplanting from D.C. Besides a known obsession with drill bits and overpriced pliers, Marcus was also obsessed with 1970s "shoot first then take names" blacksploitation films. And Olivia loved to kid him about how he worked to look like *Shaft*--with a tightly trimmed afro and a matching mustache, minus the bellbottoms and turtleneck. Thankfully, Detective Rowland's work as a cop was better than his taste in movies.

"You're humming," he said.

"What?"

"You were humming. Either Mrs. Jones put something extra in that bird, or you just talked to a certain somebody."

Olivia tried to give Marcus a fake mean stare but was too busy enjoying the bacon bits on her string beans.

"Have you asked her out yet?"

Olivia choked. She grabbed a napkin before green stuff flew everywhere.

Marcus snickered. "I guess that's a no."

Olivia wiped her mouth and took a sip of water. "You did that on purpose, you tool freak."

"I'm just very observant, Detective."

"There's nothing to observe. We're just keeping each other updated."

"Right. Does she have a girlfriend?"

"What?! How would I know that? Just eat your lunch."

"Okay, okay." But Marcus wasn't done. "What kind of gun does she carry?"

Olivia threw her hands up in frustration. They both started laughing so loud that it caught the attention of everyone in the squad room.

"You guys are having too much fun," a uniformed officer said on her way to the copy room.

"Can we please get through lunch?" Olivia asked.

Marcus pulled out the Lewis burglary file and logged into his computer. "Quick update?" he asked after another bite of bread.

"Sure," Olivia said before a scoop of coleslaw.

Marcus thumbed through the file. "So far, all fingerprints belong to employees, and no one has a criminal record other than a few misdemeanors-- none involving theft." Marcus pulled up more information on his computer screen. "Bertrand

Lewis appears to be clean--no criminal record, no outstanding warrants. But there was an incident some time ago. Looks like Mr. Lewis gave an eyewitness statement in a fight that broke out at a private poker game."

"No surprise there," Olivia said. "According to Special Agent Jeffries, he may have a bad gambling habit but made a six figure deposit almost a year ago."

"Then we should have a chat with Vice," Marcus said, "to see if their contacts know anything about this guy and his gambling buddies."

"Good idea." Olivia cleared her screen saver and made a note in the system.

Marcus also made a note in the paper file. "What else?"

"Maureen, I mean, Special Agent Jeffries," Olivia ignored the smirk from her partner, "said there may be an Atlanta connection because some of the tax refunds were deposited down there."

Marcus leaned back in his chair and put his hands behind his head, a position Olivia called his "thinking pose."

"What?" Olivia asked.

"Does it make sense for a thief to break into a business to get identity info that he could've stolen in seconds by just hacking into Lewis' electronic filing system?"

"What makes you think our bad guy knows how to hack?"

"I don't. But that info got on the Atlanta streets really quick. So I'm thinking there's at least one pro involved, at least on the Atlanta end. And any pro these days wouldn't be relying on break-ins to get info. He'd just tap right into a company's system by using the Net."

"I follow you. Pat's checking with some of her sources to see if there's any noise about the break-ins."

Marcus, who trusted his teenage sons with his car more than he trusted the world-wide-web, grunted and made more notes.

***

Olivia rubbed her eyes and logged off her computer. "It's almost five o'clock," she said. "I need to swing by my place and pick up my workout clothes. You coming down to the gym after work?" Olivia always asked and always got the same answer.

"I'll be there in spirit," Marcus said. The closest Marcus ever got to the Department's gym was when he passed it on his way to the Department's shooting range.

"What do you have against working up a good sweat?" Olivia asked.

"I prefer to do my sweating in a sauna instead of on a gym floor," Marcus said, "and hit a bulls-eye instead of a punching bag." He patted his gun holster.

Olivia laughed. "See you later, 'Shaft'."

# CHAPTER FOUR

Chief Roy Anderson frowned as he looked out his office window and watched the familiar figure walk across the parking lot. He could feel his blood pressure rise and the top of his dark baldhead get warm. The sight of Olivia Winston always brought back bitter memories--memories that reminded him why he didn't like her. He took a deep breath and scratched his solid gray mustache.

Lieutenant Nicole Beal sat at attention and brushed a stray dreadlock back behind her pierced, brown ear. She tried not to look as annoyed as she felt. She hated these five o'clock meetings that were usually about nothing that couldn't wait until the morning, and they always made her late getting her kids to soccer practice. She was tempted to fish a stick of gum out of her purse to kill her cigarette craving.

The chief watched Olivia leave in her truck. He then sat at his desk and wiped the top of his head with a handkerchief. "How did your meeting go with the IRS agent?" he asked.

Lieutenant Beal groaned internally. She knew where this was going, and she wasn't in the mood to play along. Unlike her boss, she had no interest in trying to impress the Feds or anybody else when it came to her detectives. She knew the community respected her department and that included the local politicians who controlled the county's budget.

"It went fine, sir. I promise you we didn't come off as a bunch of hicks who can't handle a burglary case," she said.

Chief Anderson opened a side drawer of his desk and took out a neatly folded blueprint. He slid it across the desk to the lieutenant. "That *will* be the future of Goslyn PD in another three years--a state of the art emergency response center with all the latest bells and whistles."

"Yes, sir. And I know it depends on the Board of Supervisors convincing Homeland Security to foot most of the bill."

"Exactly. So you understand why I'm concerned about our image. I don't want to give this IRS agent any reason to badmouth us back to her superiors." The chief put the blueprint back in the drawer and took out a prescription bottle from another. "This is no longer some rinky-dink little county with a sheriff and a few sidekicks," he continued. "We have a chance to make Goslyn PD a major hub in law enforcement, and I plan to make sure it happens."

"Sir, it looks like your standard break-ins. It's nothing my detectives can't handle." Lieutenant Beal watched a slight scowl form across the chief's face as he briefly struggled with the safety cap on the bottle.

Chief Anderson poured one pill into his hand and swallowed it dry. "Any particular reason you assigned Detective Winston to this case?" he asked as he fiddled with getting the cap back on the bottle.

*Damn, when is this man gonna stop scrutinizing Olivia?* Lieutenant Beal knew enough of the history between the two to know that Chief Anderson was carrying a big chip on his shoulder when it came to one of her top detectives. Though she never heard him badmouth Olivia or her work, the lieutenant was well aware that the chief paid more attention to Olivia's cases. Lieutenant Beal got the feeling Chief Anderson was waiting for Olivia to slip up.

"The case was assigned based on workload, sir. Detectives Winston and Rowland had room on their plate after wrapping up a vandalism case at the recycling center."

Chief Anderson didn't have a good reason to object to the case assignment, and Lieutenant Beal knew it. She watched him fight back a frown, though unsuccessfully.

"All right. I trust your judgment," he said.

He sounded disinterested to the lieutenant, but she knew he was interested to the point where he expected a briefing twice a week.

"I'll follow up with you tomorrow. Have a good evening, Lieutenant."

Lieutenant Beal didn't hesitate leaving. Halfway out the door, she dug a stick of gum out of her purse and took the stairs instead of the elevator down to the first floor.

***

Chief Anderson walked back to the window and looked out at the parking lot again. He was pleased with how quickly Goslyn PD had expanded with him at the helm. He had been the chief for nine years after having held all ranks within the Department, including detective. He was an ambitious man with high expectations of himself and those under his command.

Originally with Memphis PD, he had moved to

Goslyn forty years ago after his first divorce. He felt the breakup was a personal failure on his part, and he wanted a fresh start somewhere new. Goslyn, in the mist of a growth spurt at the time, gave him the perfect opportunity, professionally and personally. He joined the patrol division and started a relationship with a secretary who worked in the Commonwealth Attorney's Office. By the end of his fifth year, he was married again and had become a father. From there on, his goal was to help build a police force that he would one day run. He achieved that goal but neglected his wife in the process, and the marriage had recently ended after a long separation.

The chief continued looking out the window and watched as a young, uniformed officer exited the building and stood next to a cruiser. The young man reminded him of his son, Clifford Anderson. He also reminded him of the frustration and disappointment he felt as a parent who was at odds with his only child.

He turned away from the window and unlocked the top drawer of a file cabinet where he kept an aged bottle of brandy and a glass engraved with his initials. Both were an old birthday gift from Clifford. Underneath the bottle and glass was a tattered Internal Affairs folder that summed up the story of his son's career.

The chief poured himself a drink and placed the folder on his desk. He knew the contents by heart yet was always tempted to read it whenever he thought of his son. He sat down, opened it, and read the familiar reports and statements. Every word was a reminder that he wasn't the father he wished he had been.

Former police officer Clifford Anderson now resided on the west coast where he ran a chain of successful martial arts schools. Before life events had led him away from Goslyn, he was a rookie riding street patrol with Olivia Winston as his senior partner. The two quickly bonded over their love of trucks and Chinese food and spent many weekends together with Pat Henley, Olivia's IT friend, as Clifford helped Pat advance through her karate belt levels.

The bond grew tighter after a domestic disturbance call landed Clifford in the ER with a broken rib and tied Olivia to temporary desk duty after punching the intoxicated husband who had attacked Clifford.

The partnership, however, was short-lived. By the middle of his second year of patrolling with Olivia, Clifford knew something was wrong-- something that made him afraid to get out of bed in the morning and even more afraid to put on his uniform. He told his dad, but Roy Anderson, just promoted to Deputy Chief, didn't have a sympathetic ear for anything that could disrupt his son's career. He wanted Clifford to move through the ranks just as he had done. To him, Clifford just needed to take some vacation time and consider getting a new partner. Roy had reservations about his son being paired with an openly gay officer. He thought it would be a distraction and take away from Clifford's focus.

But the problem couldn't be solved by taking

time off, and Clifford wouldn't think about leaving Olivia. He had confided in her, and she had covered for him several times when he felt too paralyzed by fear to show up for roll call. She convinced him to see a therapist who diagnosed him with having a panic disorder.

Clifford didn't share the diagnosis with anyone other than Olivia. He thought he could handle it with private counseling and medication. But the stress of police work proved too much, and it all came to a head on a late summer evening when he and Olivia responded to an armed robbery call. The suspect had run into an empty church and taken a shot at a janitor who was working inside. Olivia instructed Clifford to cover the rear entrance as she went through the main doors. But Clifford never made it to the rear. At the side of the church, he froze and crouched in panic next to a dumpster with his gun still holstered. The janitor escaped out of a side window, spotted Clifford, and rushed toward him for help. Clifford, thinking the janitor was the suspect, attempted to draw his weapon but dropped it before he could take aim. The gun discharged, and the bullet grazed the janitor's leg.

Inside the church, Olivia exchanged fire with the suspect before he ran out the rear. She radioed Clifford but didn't get a response. She chased the suspect around the side of the church where she saw him run toward Clifford and the janitor who was on the ground. Clifford couldn't move as the suspect ran right passed him. When Olivia yelled a halt command and gave chase, the suspect turned and fired a wild shot. The bullet ricocheted off the dumpster and hit Olivia in the right side of her Kevlar vest, knocking her down and momentarily unconscious. A backup unit later caught the suspect fleeing in a stolen vehicle halfway across the county.

An investigation of the shooting led to the Department declaring Clifford unfit for duty, and he was placed on indefinite leave. But Clifford, too ashamed to face his fellow officers, resigned from the force. Olivia gave a statement to Internal Affairs in which she admitted to knowing about Clifford's condition and covering for him. Internal Affairs initially didn't find any fault with her conduct. But Roy, as Deputy Chief, demanded she receive a written reprimand and a suspension for failing to tell a superior about his son. He claimed Olivia's conduct showed poor judgment that put her and the public at risk. He further demanded she be placed under close supervision of another senior patrol officer. Internal Affairs supported the written reprimand but not the suspension or the supervision, and the decision was backed up by the then Chief of Police.

Olivia was allowed to return to patrol with a new partner where she remained until she passed the Detective's exam a year later.

Chief Anderson closed the folder and finished off his brandy. The entire matter still made him angry--angry with Clifford for not being tough enough and angry with himself for not being able to take control of the situation. But his resentment toward Olivia outweighed that anger. He resented her for being his son's confidant when it should have been him. And he felt upstaged by her when she was allowed to return to duty after receiving what he saw as a slap on the wrist.

He turned to his computer and started to compose an e-mail to Clifford but stopped because he really didn't know what to say. They only communicated when pressured to do so by his ex-wife who usually played the intermediary between the two.

"All right," he mumbled to himself. "Enough of this trip down memory lane." He wiped the glass clean and put it back in the file cabinet along with the bottle and folder. There were plenty of things to do before he ended his day. He turned back to his computer and dealt with his first priority-- scheduling his next follow up with Lieutenant Beal.

# CHAPTER FIVE

Bertrand Lewis yelled into his cell phone, "Bobby, you idiot! Call me back, right away!" He tossed the phone onto the passenger seat of his Cadillac. The meeting at the IRS had left him feeling raw and exposed. Another three and a half hours with his accountant had made it even worse. He felt like throwing up as he sat in his pharmacist's parking lot.

"Damn it! How did things get this bad?" he said as he sat slumped in the front seat, rubbing his gut and raking his fingers through his hair. His phone vibrated. "Hello?"

"Hey, it's me."

"Bobby, what the hell did you do?!" Bertrand screamed at his cousin and attorney. "I've got government badges crawling all over me!"

"Take it easy, cousin. We haven't done anything wrong. They're fishing in an empty pond."

"What?! What the hell are you talking about...empty pond?! My ass is on the line here, and you're talking like some idiot in a movie! Where are you?!"

"Bert, just calm down. I'm at the office."

Bobby was lying, and Bert knew it when he overheard the OTB announcer in the background call for the next race.

"Bobby, I'm tired of paying you to do nothing but play the ponies! Now what the hell happened?!"

"Listen to me, Bert. Burglaries happen all the time. We've covered all our bases. We cooperated with the local cops and the insurance company, and we sent notices to all the customers. Just relax, okay?" counsel offered as his best advice.

"Relax?!" Bert barked into the phone. "I've been doing business in this county for years, and now it's all shot to hell! I want some straight answers from you. Does this have anything to do with that loan we took out from your so called friends?!"

"Hey, it's a little late to be asking questions, cousin."

Bert knew by Bobby's response that it was connected to that one desperate decision.

"Holy Mother Mary, how did I get into this?" he asked aloud. He leaned his head back on the headrest, again trying to keep down churning stomach acid.

"I warned you about the risks," Bobby said. "We got no choice but to ride it out."

It *was* a desperate decision by Bertrand: relying on a loan shark to cover payroll and delinquent taxes.

Bertrand's world for the last several years had been on a steady roll downhill, all due to an expensive gambling habit he shared with his cousin Bobby. Years ago, he could have walked into any local bank and easily walked out with a decent line of credit. But that was out of the question starting three years ago when he thought it was okay to use company revenues to finance nightly poker games. Then came the all-day poker games that left no time to care about company business. He was only good at winning the small pots--just enough to pay his mortgage, keep the lights on, and keep him chasing after that one big win.

"I didn't think being a few days late would make them jack-up my business," Bertrand said. "Bobby, Bobby, you still there?"

"Yeah, I'm still here," Bobby said. "Listen, cousin, you know we were more than a few days late--more like a few months. There's nothing we can do about it now anyway. They obviously didn't feel like waiting for us to make good on the loan. So they took something worth more. I don't know about you, but I'd rather deal with some break-ins than have my jaw broken or my kneecaps busted." Bobby then went on and on about helping to rebuild the business and spending more time with family.

Bertrand zoned out as he thought about the day he had met his cousin's "friends." At first glance, Bertrand figured there was no way these two were muscle for a loan shark. One smelled of stale beer and the other had the telltale signs of being a "meth head"--that half-zombie, half- juiced-up look--and a body odor that made Bertrand gag. He should've backed out of the deal right there and sold what was left of his business and crawled into a casino somewhere in Atlantic City.

But it was hard giving up on something that was all his. So he listened to them sputter out the details: he would get a phone call telling him when and where to pick up the money and how to make his repayment. The rate was thirty percent with the full amount due in ninety days by cash only, and he would not meet or speak to the "lender."

Twenty-four hours later, the call came. He was instructed to pick up the money that night from a locker at the Amtrak station using a combination left in his home mailbox. At the end of three months, one of Bobby's "friends" would show up to collect. End of instructions.

Bertrand sighed and rubbed his forehead as he heard his cousin rambling. "Shut up and listen, Bobby," he said. "You're my lawyer, for what it's worth. So I'm done talking to anybody with a badge. I'm putting you in the hot seat from now on. I'm going home and empty my bladder. Damn kidney stones are killing me."

At the end of the call, Bobby Lewis hung up and mumbled to himself, "Freaking jerk. Never do business with family." He checked his voicemail and listened to messages from other clients who were just as loud and demanding as his cousin. Instead of returning calls, he placed another bet and settled in for another long day at "the office."

# CHAPTER SIX

"Stay in the right stance and lower your chin. Now jab...again...now left hook. Speed it up...jab...now hook. Move your feet to the left. Left! C'mon, tough girl, speed it up! Work off that coleslaw!.. All right! Time!"

Olivia collapsed on the gym mat. Her T-shirt and shorts drooped from the weight of her sweat, and she tried to remember if she had any Ben-Gay in her locker. Her sparring partner could hardly keep his balance as he bent over and sucked air. They had survived another ten minutes of torture.

"On your feet, tough girl," said Sergeant Ivan Kurz, better known as Sergeant "Make It Hurt."

Olivia gave a sarcastic salute and pulled herself up off the mat. "I hate you so much," she managed to garble through her mouthpiece.

"Do I look like I care!" the sergeant snapped back. "You, rookie, hit the weights for the next ten minutes!"

The young man acted as if he were just granted clemency and staggered off the mat.

"All right, Detective, you know the drill, two quick rounds with me before I let you out of here." Sarge put on his headgear followed by his chest and foot pads.

Olivia put on her pads after slipping off her sneakers and boxing gloves. This was always bareknuckled training. "Where's your mouthpiece?" she asked.

"Why? You think you gonna land a shot, tough girl?" Sarge was a thick two hundred pounds and a couple of inches taller than Olivia. As the Department's toughest physical training instructor, he prided himself on intimidating rookies and embarrassing veterans in the gym. "Ready?" he asked.

They took positions facing each other on the mat and entered the fighting stance--fists at chin level, elbows close in, head up, and right leg back with heel up.

Olivia nodded. Sarge lunged at her with a straight right punch. She blocked it with her left forearm and countered with a right palm heel strike aimed under his chin. He grabbed her right wrist before her blow could land and pulled her forward. She threw a left elbow as she flew into his chest. Sarge stumbled back but grabbed the side of her chest pad with his right hand and quickly regained his balance. Olivia chopped at his wrist with her forearm and threw a quick front kick. It landed just below his pad, and he released her wrist.

Sarge then rushed at her with both hands aimed at her throat. Olivia twisted her body to her left, swung her right arm up, and came down hard with an elbow across Sarge's forearms and followed with a quick right elbow to his head. He fell forward and grabbed at Olivia's legs before she could throw a knee. Sarge knocked her off balance, and they both went down on the mat.

They grabbed each other, each trying to get top position. Both threw short knee strikes and jabs. Sarge was trying to straddle Olivia, but she went in to the "back on ground defense position"--knees up, hips moving, ready to strike a kick. Sarge managed to use his weight to press down on Olivia's knees with his chest and landed two short hammer punches to her abs. Olivia almost spit out her mouthpiece. Sarge threw punches to her head, one just grazing her right jaw, two hitting her forearms she was using to shield her face. Olivia pushed him up with her left knee and threw a right kick that caught the left side of Sarge's head. He rolled off, and they both jumped to their feet.

"Had enough, tough girl?"

"Rethinking that mouthpiece, Sarge?" Olivia asked as she adjusted her foot pads.

Sarge was rethinking it as he mumbled something unintelligible. He managed to say, "Round two."

They entered their fighting stances again, and Sarge gave the nod. Olivia landed quick left kicks to Sarge's right thigh and to his right side. Sarge winced but lunged forward and countered with a left knee hard to Olivia's right inner thigh. She stumbled backward, and he rushed in and put her in a headlock. Olivia instantly struck at his groin with one hand and reached up with her other to push up at his nose and cover his eyes. Sarge tried to hold on, but he couldn't see. As he released her, Olivia rose up and caught him square in the right jaw with a right punch. Sarge went down on his back, and Olivia's instincts told her to pursue. She did and landed a chopping stomp straight down on his mid-section.

"Ough!" Sarge quickly gave the timeout signal. The round was over.

"You all right, Sarge?" Olivia mumbled out

past her mouthpiece.

Sarge gave a thumbs-up as he caught his wind.

Olivia staggered around the mat, still feeling the adrenaline buzz.

Sarge gestured to her to give him a hand up. He stood and removed his headgear. That right shot was leaving a mark.

He took a couple of deep breaths and said, "*Kol hakavod*, my friend, good job." He patted Olivia on the shoulders. "But we need to put some more steel in those abs of yours and work on your balance. I'll make you a Krav Maga warrior eventually."

Olivia took out her mouthpiece and tucked it in her sweats. "*Toda*, Sarge, thanks," she said. She pulled off her gear.

They dropped everything in a basket, toweled off, and headed for the gym's bleachers. Both lay out on a tier and took several minutes to cool down. Olivia started to think about Maureen.

"Sarge, you and Robert met when he was working for the Department, right?" she asked.

"Yeah, he was with homicide, and I was on street patrol."

"Did you work any cases together?"

"I was a first responder on a fatal shooting assigned to Rob. Why? What's up?"

"Just curious." Olivia tried to sound innocent, but it didn't work.

"Oh, no you don't." Sarge set up and faced her. "You're not leaving me hanging like that. Spill it, tough girl, or drop and give me ten!"

"You're a brute, you know that?"

"Answer the question."

Olivia hesitated as she sat up too. "I was thinking about asking someone out, but we're sort of working a case together," she said.

"Someone in the Department?"

"No. She's with the Feds. She's investigating a tax fraud that's related to my burglary cases."

"Is she gay and single?" Sarge asked.

"Actually…I don't know. I only met her in person once when she came here to brief us. We've talked on the phone a couple of times since then."

"And your gaydar wasn't working when you met her?"

"My gaydar has been out of whack ever since I heard the word polyamorous."

Sarge slapped his knee and roared with laughter. "Olivia, I don't need to tell you that the investigation comes first. But I don't see any harm in asking her out to discuss the case and easing into a personal conversation. You may be surprised at how far you get."

Olivia thought about it but wasn't too confident. "Maybe, Sarge. I'll let you know how it goes. How are Robert and the girls?"

"They're good," Sarge said with a big grin. "Being a stay at home dad has turned him into a pushover. Those little devils have him wrapped around their fingers."

"Good to hear. I'm hitting the showers and the Ben-Gay."

Sarge looked at the wire-covered clock on the gym wall. "It's only seven o'clock."

"Perfect time for dinner," Olivia said.

"Hey, take it easy on your grandma's coleslaw.

I'm trying to build a warrior, remember?"

"Right. I'll keep that in mind, you brute. See you later, Sarge."

*Ease into a personal conversation,* Olivia thought as she headed for the locker room. *I swear if she tells me she's polyamorous, I'm joining a convent.*

\*\*\*

"…Yes, I'd like to place an order for pickup…I want the steamed chicken with mixed vegetables, brown sauce on the side, and one spring roll…Winston…Ten minutes?…Thanks." Olivia flipped her phone shut and was about to pull out of the gym's parking lot. She loved ending a long day with one of her favorite dishes. The workout had left her hungry and sore.

Her phone rang just as she started her truck.

"Hey, Marcus, you still up in the squad room?"

"Hangin' around until Phyllis picks me up. The boys have my car."

"What's up?" Olivia asked.

"We got some feedback from Vice. Word from the gambling crowd is that Bertrand Lewis was in deep you-know-what with some local fellas. Vice couldn't pry any real names out of their contacts, but they got two nicknames--'Malley' and 'CJ'. "

"Malley?"

"Yeah. Spelled M-A-L-L-E-Y."

"What else?"

"Vice hadn't heard of these guys. So I ran the names through the central system. No hits on Malley. But you wouldn't believe how many knuckleheads nicknamed CJ have criminal records."

47

"Try me."

"Nineteen and that's after I weeded out the usual suspects we already questioned. All have theft convictions."

"Nineteen possible suspects." Olivia thought about dinner. "Okay. I need to eat something and ice down my knees and a few other places."

"You let 'Captain Crazy' beat you up again?" Marcus asked.

"It's Sergeant 'Make It Hurt'."

"If you say so. I'm sticking with the sauna."

# CHAPTER SEVEN

Maureen circled the park one more time before heading home. Running helped to clear her head so she could sort out details of the cases waiting for her at work. Despite the workload, she thought about tacking on a personal day to the coming weekend. She wanted to spend more time with her aunt and uncle in Goslyn. "And maybe see Detective Winston," she said aloud as she approached a crosswalk.

When she first met the detective and her partner, she immediately recognized Olivia from years ago. They'd never met, but Maureen would see the then young girl just about every morning during their high school years. She would watch from a backseat window as the pretty stranger walked to the neighborhood school. Maureen instead was bused across the county. It was the confident, slightly tomboyish walk that caught young Maureen's eye.

She still vividly remembered the day her school bus was stuck at a broken traffic light long enough for her to watch the young girl walk three blocks and disappear into the school building. It wasn't until her last year of high school that Maureen found out the girl's name when someone showed her the Lincoln High yearbook. It was Olivia Ann Winston. Those days, as well as many others, had helped an adolescent Maureen realize she was gay.

She reached her front porch and checked her watch. "Not bad for a middle-aged chick." Just then, her sister pulled up in the driveway. Maureen sat down on the front steps and untied her sneakers.

"What brings you by?"

"Dinner," Gloria said as she held up a bag. "But I'm just dropping off. It's a 'Thank You' for looking over my salon's books."

Relying on physical appearances alone, a stranger would never guess that the two women were related. Gloria described herself as being naturally curvy with an afro that accentuated her full-lipped and wide-eyed features. And her wardrobe always included five-inch heels.

Gloria leaned down to hug Maureen but abruptly pulled back when she saw her sweaty T-shirt.

"Peyew, you stink!" she said.

Maureen sniffed. "That's what happens to people who exercise. You should try it sometime."

"Please, I get enough exercise doing hair all day and chasing behind a two-year-old. Here's one of those big taco salads I know you like." She handed Maureen the bag.

"Perfect timing." Maureen got up and unlocked the front door. Gloria followed and headed straight for the stash of chocolate that Maureen kept in a kitchen drawer.

"You got plans this evening?" Gloria asked as she unwrapped and tossed a Hershey's Mint Kiss into her mouth.

"You must be joking," Maureen said. "It's Monday, the hardest day of the week. I'm going straight to bed after dinner."

Maureen left her salad on the kitchen table, sat in the living room's recliner, and kicked off her sneakers. Gloria followed and kept eating.

"I'm heading back to the salon," Gloria said and checked the time on her cell phone. "I've got some clients who need their hair done for a wedding tomorrow. Oh, before I forget, Daddy called and wants you to check the attic for his golf clubs."

"Those old things? He's better off buying a new set."

"He says they're his lucky clubs, and he wants you to ship them if you find them."

"Right. So lucky that he refused to use them again after I beat him in nine holes." Maureen slouched back in her recliner and removed the bandana from her hair.

Her dad had recently retired to Florida after decades with the State Auditor's Office. Maureen had convinced him to sell his Richmond home to her and purchase one in an Orlando senior citizens community. He'd been reluctant to leave his girls, but Maureen and Gloria knew he deserved to enjoy himself after he had made so many sacrifices for them.

The Jeffries had separated when the girls were pre-teens. The sisters lived with their mom in Goslyn during the school year and stayed with their dad during the summers. Mrs. Jeffries died a year after Maureen had finished high school and Gloria had opened her salon. It was a big adjustment not having a mom around to talk to about "girl stuff." But Mr. Jeffries had done his best--cramming with Maureen for her accounting exams and acting as the salon handyman on weekends as Gloria worked to build her clientele.

Gloria's cell phone beeped. "Hello?...Hey, Ms. Rogers...Around eight thirty?...Sure. No problem. I'll see you then." Gloria dropped her cell phone into her purse. "The wedding party's running late, so you have to entertain me for forty-five minutes."

"You can entertain yourself," Maureen said. "I'm going to straighten up my weights then take a shower." She got up and went out a side door to an attached garage. Gloria grabbed a handful of the chocolate Kisses from the kitchen and followed.

"I talked to Aunt Lena yesterday," Gloria said. "She asked me to come down this weekend to help replant her garden. Wanna come?"

"Sure, I was planning to go anyway." Maureen lifted the dumbbells, placed them back on their racks, and pushed the weight bench into a corner. "You do know Aunt Lena will find a million other things for us to do when we get there?"

"I know. She still misses Mama so much and likes having us around."

"Help me move this stack of weights," Maureen said as she pointed to several ten-pound plates on the floor.

"Hey, I'm a stylist. My hands are precious."

Maureen ignored her and lifted the plates herself.

"Anything going on besides work?" Gloria asked.

Maureen asked, "Do you remember hearing anything about the Winston family when we lived in Goslyn? I asked Aunt Lena, and she thought the name sounded familiar."

"Winston ...Winston," Gloria said and tilted

her head. "No, don't recall...wait...I remember a Mr. Winston. He helped Uncle Frank remodel Mama's kitchen years ago." Gloria sat down on the weight bench that Maureen had pushed into the corner. "I remember him working with Uncle Frank on the cabinets at the house one day. Mama asked him if he could build her some bookshelves for the living room. He asked for a piece of paper to do some sketches, and I remember giving him a sheet from a notebook I had just bought for my first cosmetology class." Gloria peeled the wrapper off another Mint Kiss. "He drew these gorgeous designs," she said, "and I remember staring at the paper and being amazed at how perfect they looked." Gloria seemed lost for a moment in a peaceful thought before tossing the chocolate into her mouth. "I think I kept that sheet of paper on top of my dresser for weeks."

"We never had bookshelves in the living room," Maureen said.

"I don't know what happened after that, but you know Mama was always talking about fixing or remodeling something around the house. What's up with the Winstons?"

"I'm working a case with a detective in Goslyn--Olivia Winston. She grew up there, and I was just curious."

"And?"

"And what? I'm just 'conversating' with you." Maureen headed back into the house with Gloria right on her heels.

"You never ask about *anybody* without a reason, and 'conversating' ain't even a real word.

So something's going on!" Gloria grabbed the entire bag of Mint Kisses from the kitchen, plopped down on the living room couch, and waited for an answer.

"Shouldn't you be leaving?"

Gloria dug through her purse to check her cell phone. "No. I got thirty minutes. So talk!"

Maureen sat back in her recliner, and her big sister threw her a piece of chocolate. As Maureen unwrapped the candy, she said, "I remember Detective Winston from my high school days, and I was thinking about asking her out." Maureen popped the chocolate into her mouth.

"What's stopping you?" Gloria asked.

Maureen sighed and gestured for Gloria to throw her another chocolate. "It could make things uncomfortable between us because of the case--you know, trying to stay professional while getting to know each other personally."

"Hey, genius, you're an investigator. I'm sure you can figure out how to talk about personal stuff and still do your job. Besides, it's time you started dating again. Celibacy must be boring you to death."

"I'm not celibate, you nut!"

"Really? When was the last time you went out on a date? And I don't mean those lame after work parties with your co-workers."

Maureen didn't know what to say. It was years since her last real date, and that was a waste of time. Her date expected a quick hook-up while Maureen was hoping for some interesting conversation. Both were disappointed.

"You know, sis, life still goes on after Denise," Gloria said as she got up and took the bag of candy back into the kitchen.

"Yes, it does," Maureen said softly.

"Ask the detective and keep me in the loop. I'm leaving, and you still stink. So no hugs."

They both headed for the front door.

"I'll call you about this weekend," Gloria said.

"I'm going to Atlanta sometime this week, so call my cell phone or e-mail me."

Gloria rushed out to the car and pulled off.

Maureen locked up for the night and undressed for the shower as she thought about Olivia. *It has been a long time. Why not ask her?*

# CHAPTER EIGHT

"Listen, you fat bastard! You think you better than Malley? You think you can dis him like dat?" CJ was enraged. He slung a plastic trash can against the wall, and Bertrand Lewis' framed business license came crashing to the tax office floor. "I'll break your arm if you don't come up with dat fuckin' money!"

Bertrand had sweated clean through his suit and couldn't focus his right eye. His right ear was still ringing from the last slap that drew blood, and a sharp pain was shooting down the back of his neck. He didn't know if he should yell for help or pretend to pass out.

"Where's the money?!" CJ yelled as he grabbed Bertrand by his tie and pinned him with a left forearm against a file cabinet. "Where's the money?!" he yelled again, this time flashing brown-stained teeth.

Bertrand caught a whiff of that awful body odor, a smell that made his stomach flip. He looked into the addict's dilated eyes. *Christ, this lunatic's going to kill me.*

"I'm telling you the truth," Bertrand struggled to spit out. "I'm flat broke. My business is broke. I used everything I had to…" He went silent when he saw CJ raise the steel pipe in his other hand.

CJ lowered his forearm and shoved one end of the pipe underneath Bertrand's chin. "You owe dat money, so I don't give a damn about you being broke."

"But I thought everything was settled with the

break-ins, right?" Bertrand asked.

"It ain't settled," CJ said. He grabbed Bertrand by the collar, led him to the back of the office, and shoved him down into a chair. "The money! Where's Malley's money?!"

"Okay, okay. All I've got is what's on me." Bertrand pulled a leather wallet out of his back pocket and handed it over. "And I have my watch." He slid it off his wrist, and it fell to the floor. "And I have my gold ring." He tried getting it off his finger, but it wouldn't budge.

CJ struggled to get the wallet open with one hand while holding the steel pipe in the other. He backed up, dropped the pipe, and tore open the leather.

"Twenty bucks! Sonofabitch! You kiddin' me, man!" CJ shoved the money in his pocket and picked up the steel pipe.

Bertrand knew he had to think fast. "Listen to me!" He swallowed hard and rubbed his right eye, but it still wouldn't focus. "I have some money in my car, in the trunk. It's in a petty cash box I take to poker games. You can take all of it." Bertrand didn't know if the lunatic had heard a word he had said. He watched as CJ just stood there breathing heavy and staring at him.

CJ staggered back and forth. "Give me the keys," he finally said.

Bertrand scrambled the keys out of his pocket and tossed them to CJ.

"Where's the car?"

"In the alley out back, straight out the back door."

CJ grabbed Bertrand by the collar and pulled him up and toward the back exit.

But Bertrand stumbled and went down on his knees. His legs had gone weak and a knifing pain shot through his chest.

CJ left him on the floor and went out the door.

Once alone, Bertrand struggled to his feet and tried to catch his breath. He checked his pockets for his cell phone. *Damn, where is it?* He staggered over to a desk, reached for the landline, and hit 9-1-1. He collapsed after hitting the last digit.

"Nine one one dispatch, what's your emergency? Hello? Sir? Ma'am? What's your emergency?"

*** 

CJ tore apart the trunk of the Cadillac right down to the spare tire. No cash box. He opened the rear door and looked in the back and underneath the front seats. Still nothing. "I'll kill that lyin'…" There was the box, on the front passenger side. He grabbed it and ran back into the office.

"Where's the key to the box? Hey, get the hell up and…"

Bertrand was out cold with the phone receiver still in one hand and his other hand clutching his chest.

CJ could hear the dispatcher on the other end of the line, *"Sir? Ma'am? A unit is on its way. All units in the vicinity of Patterson and Glenside be advised we have an unresponsive party at the following location …"*

CJ slammed the box down on the floor and out flew poker chips and half-smoked cigars. No cash, not even a dollar. He could hear sirens approaching and started to panic.

"Man, think. Where did I park the fuckin' van?"

Blue lights flashed out front as he ran out the back and down the alley. Still trying to remember which way to go, he took the first right and tried to disappear into the early evening foot traffic.

***

"Why do you always order the same thing?" Pat asked as she browsed through the menu.

"Because I like the same thing," Olivia said and waved 'hello' to the restaurant owner who was wiping off the bar stools.

"Why do we always sit at the same booth table?"

"Because I'm a creature of habit. Now make up your mind."

"I'm going to try the Bang Bang Shrimp this time…," Pat flipped over the menu, "with a wonton soup…a large vegetable fried rice…and a cherry ice tea."

"What, no room for dessert?" Olivia joked.

"I haven't eaten since breakfast."

"Are things that busy at the office?"

"Indeed. Knock on wood." Pat tapped the table. "I'm thinking about hiring another associate. Half of my clients either downloaded a virus or forgot their passwords."

The waiter brought a bowl of fried noodle chips and took their orders.

"Speaking of computer stuff," Olivia said after the waiter left, "Mama e-mailed me some pictures and sends her love to everyone."

"How is Mama Winston?"

"Still Mama Winston."

"Enough said."

They laughed and nibbled on the noodle chips.

Dinner arrived quickly, and Olivia had her usual steamed chicken with mixed vegetables, brown sauce on the side, and one spring roll.

"This tea is really good," Pat said after drinking half and raising her glass to the waiter for a refill. "Oh, I got something for you." She pulled several sheets of paper out of her laptop carrier. "Lisa, a.k.a 'Dr. Watson', snooped around some chat rooms and found stuff on a hacker. He could know some folks here in Goslyn." She shuffled the papers around on the table and handed a highlighted page to Olivia. "Take a look at that."

"Looks like a conversation between 'cleverman02' and 'WRsouthbound95'," Olivia said.

"Right. Start reading halfway down."

Cleverman02: *Hey man U still wastin' time with those clowns up in Goslyn? Family or no family, them boys gon' get U snatched up by 5-0. Ain't U already makin' mad money flippin' that ID shit on the net & dumpin' it on the street?*

Olivia kept reading:

WRsouthbound95: *I hear U man but tryin' to get those fools back on track in the money game-- sometimes U gotta break some off for family. I be killin' it on the net shit so I can throw a few bones up north*

Olivia looked up at Pat who was sharking down her Bang Bang Shrimp. "You and Lisa have done it again. Any idea how I can find out the real names of these guys?"

"Sorry, Detective, we hit a dead end on that. We tried to track them through their IP addresses but got nothing."

"I really appreciate it, Pat, and tell Lisa an Outlet gift card is coming her way." Olivia bit into her spring roll and thought about passing the information on to Maureen. She smiled, which caught Pat's attention.

"What?" Pat asked with a shrimp in one hand and a fork full of rice in the other.

"Nothing. Just wondering if I'll have to roll you out of here."

Pat laughed and launched in to her usual complaints about the boys misbehaving at school, about Eric leaving dirty clothes on the bathroom floor, and about her parents calling every weekend from Ohio to complain about her not calling them.

Olivia talked about how hard Grandma Rita worked her in the garden, about her workouts with Sergeant 'Make It Hurt,' and about work.

Olivia often wondered what it would be like to have a wife--a partner to wake up with each morning and to end each day. But she thought her idea of a relationship was outdated compared to what seemed to be the norm nowadays--online dating, speed dating, and hook-ups. Her experience in law enforcement made her leery about meeting someone online or at a one-minute get-to-know-you session. And she just wasn't in to casual sex.

Instead, she wanted an honest relationship that would grow in to a commitment.

She had been in love before. That love began during her first year with the Department and lasted for nearly four years. She had met Kendra, a magistrate in Fredericksburg, while attending a regional law enforcement conference.

Kendra made the first move by asking Olivia out for drinks at the end of the conference. Olivia didn't drink, so they settled on an early dinner. From there on, they traded phone calls and alternated driving up and down I-95 to see each other on weekends. They eventually met each other's families and friends and talked about living together. Olivia even considered applying for a position with Fredericksburg PD.

But a simple discussion one day about having a civil ceremony left Olivia blindsided. After three and a half years, Kendra wasn't ready to "officially" commit. In fact, she was thinking about dating other people.

It wasn't the confession that hurt Olivia the most. It was realizing Kendra didn't think enough of their relationship to say how she was feeling.

Olivia stayed with Goslyn PD, and Kendra applied for a court position three hours away in Roanoke. They spoke to each other for the last time the day before Kendra started her new job.

Olivia put down her fork and sighed. Thinking of Kendra always killed her appetite.

"I'm done," she said as she pushed her plate away.

"I'm stuffed." Pat asked the waiter for a to-go

container and finished off her tea. She then asked Olivia, "So Detective Winston, who's Maureen?"

Olivia froze like a kid caught with her hand in the cookie jar. She tossed a napkin to Pat.

"Wipe the sauce off your mouth, Ms. Piggy."

"Don't change the subject. C'mon, tell me?" Pat pretended to beg, just like when they were kids.

"She's the IRS agent who's working the tax fraud angle on my burglary cases."

"Keep going, keep going," Pat insisted.

"There's nothing else to tell. We met once, and we keep each other updated. That's it." Olivia leaned forward and rested her elbows on the table. "How'd you know about her anyway?"

"Eric told me. He heard it from Mr. Brooks one day at the old barbershop on Main. No matter how much this county grows, Mr. Brooks still manages to find out other people's business."

"Apparently!" Olivia said.

"Anything going on between you two? Are you interested in her?" Pat also leaned forward.

Olivia didn't know how to answer.

"Ollie, you just hesitated and that means you *are* interested. Well, about damn time!" Pat shouted out to the surprise of Olivia and the other patrons. Pat lowered her voice. "Finally, you can throw away that vibrator I know you're hiding in your closet."

"Pat," Olivia whispered, "will you stop embarrassing us?" She blushed and gestured to the waiter for the check.

Pat laughed loudly and threw the napkin up in the air. "Have you asked her out yet?"

"I'm thinking about it."

"Do it or I'll find out her e-mail address and do it for you."

"You're crazy."

"Yes, I am." Pat became quiet as she sat back and played with the straw in her glass. Then she said, "Ollie, sometimes your first love doesn't turn out to be your only love or your best. You have to stop reliving your disappointment in Kendra."

Olivia smiled at her friend. "You know, you *are* as smart as you look, you geek."

"Of course I am." Pat pretended to pat herself on the back.

"Let's go. I want to walk through the mall before dropping you off."

\*\*\*

"C'mon, c'mon!" CJ kept turning the key and banging on the dashboard. The engine choked and smoked each time he stomped on the gas, and a burnt oil smell started to seep up through the floorboard.

It was just before dusk, and rush hour traffic had long cleared by the time he remembered where he had parked the van--behind a convenience store two blocks down and across from the tax office. His plan was to collect the money from the deadbeat Lewis, hightail it back to the store to pick up a forty-ounce for Malley, and then find his drug buddies to buy a fix. But CJ's mind had faded along with his high. The only thought pressed into his brain at the moment was of the old man out on the floor and cops at the office front door.

"Turn, baby!" The engine bucked with enough

force to shake the whole van. CJ jerked the gearshift, and the van bolted straight ahead. He yanked the steering wheel, sped around the building and into an intersection just as the light turned green in his favor.

"Don't speed, just take it easy," he told himself.

He turned onto a side street and tried to remember which back roads would take him toward the county line and into the woods.

He smacked the steering wheel. "Malley gon' kick my ass!"

He stayed on the side street for almost a mile until he realized it was about to merge into a major intersection that would put him right out in the open. Somebody could have seen him coming out of the alley or pulling out from behind the store. He couldn't take the chance.

*Think. Think.*

\*\*\*

The cashier kept wringing her hands as she talked to the lead officer, "...Then I saw all the flashing lights and saw the ambulance. I came outside and saw this skinny, light-skinned man-- about your partner's height--come across the street and duck behind the store here." The cashier nodded at the building. "At first, I was busy trying to see what all the commotion was about. Then a dark green van came from behind the store, and I barely saw the same man inside. He looked kind of freaked out and--"

"Ma'am, which way did the van go?" the officer asked.

"It went down the street here." She pointed

straight ahead. "Then it turned right on Patterson."

"Can you describe the van, ma'am?"

"An ole' beat up one. The back doors and bumper had big dents, and tape covered a crack on one of the back windows."

"Could you see the license plate?"

"I don't think it had one, officer."

The officer asked the cashier for her contact information then allowed her to rejoin the crowd that had gathered.

"This is unit forty-seven. We've got a description of a suspicious vehicle near the location, over."

"Go ahead, unit forty-seven."

\*\*\*

CJ had pulled over to let several cars pass. He was losing daylight and needed to focus and get his bearings. He wanted to make a U-turn to double back a block and cross over several side streets so he could work his way around the intersection.

He made the U-turn, but the van started jerking like it was about to cut off. He pressed the gas, and the van jerked again, but the engine kept running. He hit the gas one more time and was about to turn right when he spotted a police unit coming straight at him.

"Don't panic, just keep moving," he mumbled.

He made the right and watched out the rearview mirror. Three seconds. Five seconds. Ten seconds. He exhaled as he rolled right through a stop sign.

The police unit appeared in the rearview and hit its lights and siren. CJ slammed on the gas, flew straight through two more signs, and was headed for a main road that carried traffic from one end of the county to the other. He flew out into traffic, skidding sideways as he made a sharp right. He nosed out a tow truck, causing it to hit the brakes, skip the sidewalk, and take out a bus stop.

The skid had thrown the van to the wrong side of the road. CJ accelerated anyway as oncoming traffic scattered off to the shoulder. CJ overcorrected, swerved back to the right lane and sideswiped a parked car. He then blew through a red light, his mind too scrambled to notice.

\*\*\*

The police unit slowed as it approached the main road. It stopped, and the officer on the passenger side got out to check the tow truck driver. He had a bloody lip but was okay. The lead officer radioed for backup as her partner jumped back into the car.

"This is unit forty-seven, suspect vehicle speeding north on Bailwick Road, headed toward Route Seven. Ten eighty, chase in progress, over."

\*\*\*

"Be careful with that doggie bag. I just had my truck detailed." Olivia wiped a smudge of dirt off the glossy, black tailgate.

"Yeah, yeah. Can we please listen to some music this time instead of your police radio?" Pat whined.

"No. Now get in before I make you ride in the back."

"You sound like me when I'm fussing at the boys."

An approaching siren was blaring from the far end of the mall. Olivia got into her truck and turned on the two-way radio.

*Suspect crossing Route Seven...Ten seventy-eight, request assistance, over.*

Pat stood outside the truck and listened as the siren got louder. Suddenly, a green van shot through an intersection in front of the mall. Seconds later, a police unit flew by.

"Pat, I need you to stay here!" Olivia turned on her dash strobe lights.

"Be careful!" Pat yelled out as Olivia sped off.

Olivia's last car chase dated back to her uniform days, but instinct was kicking in.

"This is unit ninety-eight, Detective Winston, joining pursuit, over," she said into her radio.

"Ten-four, Detective," the dispatcher responded.

Olivia caught up with the police unit and tried to get a look at the van that was about fifty yards ahead. The back doors were beat in, and the muffler swung low and scraped the asphalt.

Suddenly, the driver hit the brakes and made a hard left onto Government Road, a rural stretch that ran deep into the undeveloped part of the county. The lead unit and Olivia followed but lost sight of the van as the road started to wind and narrow. The unit then braked hard, making its rear shimmy and forcing Olivia to hit her brakes. She held the steering wheel tight just as her F-150 kissed the back end of the lead.

The van had clipped an oncoming car, forcing it to veer into the unit's path. The driver was shaken up but managed to steer her car off to the shoulder. The lead unit picked up speed again with Olivia on its tail, but they couldn't see the van for the next half mile. An approaching car flashed its headlights several times, and its driver waved his hand out the window. The lead unit and Olivia both slowed.

The excited driver yelled, "A van turned down the dirt road on the right! I think the engine's on fire!"

The lead unit took off with Olivia close behind, both following a trail of black smoke down the dirt road. Straight ahead was the van, run into the grass with the driver-side door open and steady smoke rising from underneath the hood. The unit stopped within five yards of the van's rear, and the officers exited with weapons drawn. Both took cover behind the car doors. The lead's driver looked back at Olivia as she got out of her truck and flashed her badge before drawing her pistol. She took cover behind her own driver-side door.

"Let me see your hands!" both uniforms yelled at the van. They continued yelling as the officer on the passenger side approached the van with his weapon aimed at the back.

"Driver, turn off the engine and show me your hands!"

Just then, the sound of grinding metal howled out from the front end of the van, and the engine stopped. But the smoke billowed, and flames leapt up from underneath the left front fender.

Olivia wanted to give cover on the passenger side, so she started moving toward the unit's passenger door.

*What was that?* She could see movement in the distance out of the corner of her eye. She turned to her right and spotted something in the high grass and bushes moving slow across the ground. She stooped behind the lead unit as the officer approaching the van looked in the rear windows and moved to the passenger side. He signaled the van was empty.

The lead officer radioed in the fire, "Ten eighty-seven, vehicle fire at crash site, over."

"Hey, I saw something move." Olivia pointed over to her right.

All three ran toward the bushes and saw a dirt path covered in tire tracks with fresh footprints. They cautiously followed the path, one behind the other with weapons still drawn.

\*\*\*

CJ had stumbled and fallen into the high grass. He thought if he could just make it down the path, he would be home and Malley would know what to do. But he couldn't move because he had nothing left--no adrenaline, no high, no nothing. He just lay there, facedown heaving violently.

"Get up, man. Move," he finally said to himself.

He got up on all fours and started to crawl. He struggled to his feet and staggered sideways back onto the path.

\*\*\*

"There he is!" the officer in front shouted and took off running. He yelled, "Down on the ground! Don't move!"

But the van driver was ahead by half a football

field and just kept moving.

Olivia and the other officer were yards behind the first who was now in a full sprint.

Five strides back, the officer dove headfirst at the exact moment that the driver fell forward. The officer missed his target, somersaulted through the air, and landed in the grass.

Olivia came up fast and pinned the driver to the ground with her weight on his back and her forearm to the back of his head. He was nothing but skin and bones as she pulled his left and right arms back to cuff him.

The officer behind Olivia checked on her partner who was sprawled out on his back.

"You trying out for the Olympics or something?" she joked as she helped him to his feet.

The embarrassed look on his face told her he was okay.

*Rookie,* Olivia thought. She Mirandized the suspect and left him on the ground while the female officer radioed in.

"Ten fifteen, suspect in custody, over."

"Damn, that was wild!" the rookie said. "Hey, Detective, you all right?"

"Yeah, I'm good," Olivia said. She pulled the driver to his feet, but he collapsed right back to the ground. "Guys, looks like you're toting this one back."

More sirens approached, and Olivia headed back down the path to the burning van. Her phone then rang.

"You okay, partner?" Marcus asked.

"I'm okay. I thought you hated listening to the

scanner?"

"I do, but it's the first time my partner's jumped in the middle of a car chase. Have you heard the news about our burglary victim, Bertrand Lewis?"

Olivia stopped in her tracks. "What news?"

"The roadrunner you just caught is a suspect in an attack on Lewis. Lewis is in the emergency room right now."

Olivia turned around and headed back toward the suspect who was still on the ground. The two officers were standing around re-enacting the chase. She bent down and carefully checked the suspect's pockets for ID, finding only a twenty-dollar bill. She tried to rouse him by shaking his head.

"What's your name, what's your name?" she kept asking.

The suspect was semi-conscious and slurred, "Calvin…'CJ' Henry. Let Mal know…" He blacked out.

"Call an ambulance for this guy," Olivia told the officers. "He looks bad."

"Marcus, you still there?"

"Yeah, I'm here."

"I think we just solved our burglaries. I'll see you in about an hour."

Olivia dialed Pat. "Hey, you okay?"

"I'm fine," Pat said. "Just sitting here on the curb where you abandoned me like an old flip phone. Are you okay?"

"I'm good. Can you call Eric to pick you up?"

"Of course I can, Ollie. Be careful and call me later."

Olivia looked back at Calvin Henry. *One suspect in custody. One more reason to call Maureen.*

# CHAPTER NINE

"How was your trip?" Carol asked and looked up from her desk.

"Busy, but fruitful." Maureen went into her office, dropped her bags, and started unpacking her laptop.

"Carol, do you have this morning's paper?!"

"Sure do. It's on your desk!"

Maureen had been in Atlanta for the past two days meeting with local agents and Atlanta PD's Major Fraud Unit. Last night, she caught part of a story on the late news about an attack on a business owner in Goslyn and a car chase. It made her think about calling Olivia. She could've just called her aunt and uncle to see if they knew anything. But she really wanted to talk to the detective again. Besides, she did have some information from her Atlanta trip that she wanted to share.

She turned the pages of the paper, looking for anything about the attack or chase but found only a three-sentence summary in the metro section.

She logged into her laptop and pulled up her e-mails. A reminder was the first thing to pop up. *Return Gloria's call re: weekend at Auntie's.* Her inbox had plenty of new e-mails but nothing urgent.

She pulled up her notes from her Atlanta trip, did some editing, and printed them out.

"Carol, I need the hardcopy of the Lewis file, please!"

"Coming right up!" Carol came in and placed the file on Maureen's desk. "Don't forget to check your voice messages before your meeting at ten," she said on her way back to her desk.

Maureen briefly checked the websites of the local news channels--still not much on the Goslyn incident. She put her notes in the file and called her voicemail. The first half dozen messages were from her supervisor who had a bad case of insomnia and was infamous for leaving late night messages regarding upcoming projects.

Then she heard, *Hello, Special Agent Jeffries. This is Detective Winston. I thought I would catch you working late this evening. Just wanted to share some info. Give me a call when you get a chance.* Then she heard, *Press seven to erase this call. Press eight to return. Press nine to save.* She pressed nine and debated whether to return the call before or after her meeting. It was only eight thirty, and she could use the time to respond to some of the e-mails. Instead, she decided to go over her Atlanta notes again.

Atlanta PD had recently formed a task force to surveil several small gangs that were flashing wads of cash and driving high-end cars. The police suspected the gangs had carved out a larger part of the local drug market. But the amount of cash some of the members were rumored to have didn't match up with the amount of drugs currently being sold on the streets. The police thought the gangs had to have another stream of income.

The task force set up checkpoints throughout the city in gang neighborhoods and in gang-neutral territory. The plan was to check for valid licenses and registrations. The police would also use the stops to check for any outstanding warrants.

The first five stops hit jackpot. The police netted three members with expired licenses and two with parole violations. On an initial search through glove boxes and trunks, the police found handwritten lists of names, social security numbers and dates of birth.

Maureen and an agent from her Atlanta team sat in on the interrogations but gained little intel as each member pleaded the Fifth. Maureen and the Fraud Unit then spent hours combing through every piece of paper found in the suspects' vehicles. They found several tattered notebooks filled with identity information and eventually matched some names and social security numbers to taxpayers who had used Bertrand Lewis' tax services back in Goslyn.

On a pat-down search of a member, an arresting officer also found a list of abbreviations or codes. 'Clvrmn' and 'WRon95' obviously meant something. Each was written at the top of a long list of dates and dollar amounts ranging from one hundred to five hundred dollars. The question now was who was supplying the gangs with the taxpayers' personal data.

The Atlanta team would continue working with the local police, and the checkpoints would stay in place. Maureen would return to Richmond and run through her findings with her IT department.

Notes updated and e-mails answered, Maureen still had plenty of time before her conference call. "Why are you afraid to call her?" she said aloud.

"Afraid to call who?" Carol asked as she walked in with a cup of tea and a raisin bagel.

Maureen was startled and pretended to organize

papers on her desk. "Just thinking out loud. Is that for me?"

"You know Friday means free breakfast around here." Carol handed her the treats and turned to leave. She lingered in the doorway for a few seconds and gave a curious look.

Maureen purposely ignored her and stirred her tea.

"It's after nine. I think she's in."

"Who's in?"

"Please, woman!" Carol said as she walked back to her desk. "I'll block some time on your schedule right after the meeting," she said over her shoulder, "but it's up to you to use it, Special Agent Jeffries!"

Maureen thought, *I've been working with that woman way too long*.

*** 

The meeting dragged on, and Maureen struggled to stay focus. Her supervisor didn't help by yawning every five minutes.

Maureen briefed everyone on her Atlanta trip and passed information on to IT. While listening to updates on other cases, her mind wandered, and she missed what her supervisor was saying about the assault and car chase in Gosyln.

"Maureen, you've been working with Goslyn PD. Have you heard anything?"

Maureen was caught off guard but recovered quickly. "No, but I have a call with them after the meeting. I'll let you know." *I guess I will be calling Olivia this morning.*

The meeting ended an hour later, and she went

back to her office and stared at her laptop. She fiddled around on a few websites and tried to work up the nerve to make the call. "I feel like the school nerd asking the head cheerleader out."

When she had mustered up the courage to call, her direct line rang.

"Good morning, Special Agent Jeffries," Detective Winston said.

"Detective!" Maureen couldn't hide the surprise in her voice when she answered.

"Yes, Ms. Taylor said you were returning my call."

"She did?" Maureen saw Carol peek into her office and give a thumbs-up. Maureen balled up a Post-it and threw it at her. "Uh…yes, I wanted to fill you in on my trip to Atlanta. But I heard you had some excitement yesterday."

"We did. Bertrand Lewis is in the hospital after an attack by a burglary suspect. He's in ICU suffering from a heart attack and a concussion."

"How's he doing? Have you been able to talk to him?"

"He's expected to pull through, but he's in no condition to talk yet. We have the suspect in custody, and he's in the hospital too--meth withdrawal. We plan to question him later today."

"And the car chase? Was that the suspect?"

"Yeah. The idiot could've killed somebody. I spent most of the evening filling out report forms and talking to my lieutenant and the media rep."

"You were in the chase?!" Maureen again couldn't hide the emotion in her voice.

"I'm fine. Don't worry about it--just some

scratches and dents in my truck. We think the suspect is a Calvin Henry who goes by the nickname 'CJ.' We matched his prints to some found at the three offices. I'm surprised this guy wasn't already in the system, given his drug habit."

Maureen could hear Olivia take a breath after she finished. She just held the receiver as if she was mesmerized by the sound on the other end.

"Hello? You still there?" Olivia asked.

"Yeah. Just taking notes," Maureen fibbed. "Anything else?" She could hear Olivia turning pages and clicking her mouse.

"We think CJ had some help with the burglaries. We may be able to confirm that soon. We also may have a good Internet lead that could help your guys. There was some noise in a hacker chat room about Goslyn and identity info. I can fax a copy of the printout to you."

"I should buy you lunch for doing all the heavy lifting here, Detective," Maureen said.

The phone got quiet.

"Detective?"

"I love Chinese," Olivia blurted out. "I'll eat while you tell me about your trip to Atlanta."

*I walked right in to that one.* Maureen was trying to think fast. Her schedule was full through lunch that day, and she really wanted to see Olivia in a more relaxed, less formal setting. *The weekend.*

"How about lunch tomorrow, Saturday, if that's okay? I have some relatives in Goslyn I'll be visiting." Maureen held her breath.

"You have relatives in Goslyn?" Olivia asked with a childlike interest.

"I do. I can tell you all about them at lunch." Maureen was feeling confident.

"Okay. How about Chinese at the mall on Bailwick at one o'clock?"

"I know where it is, and I'll see you tomorrow, Detective."

"Whew!" Maureen, feeling exhausted and relieved at the same time, worried that she sounded desperate. "You're a grown woman," she chided herself. "Act like one."

She got up and headed for a tea refill. But Carol was standing in the doorway, grinning.

"You obviously don't have enough work to do," Maureen said.

"I have plenty to do. I just know how to multitask."

"Yeah, yeah. Back to work, slacker."

***

Olivia couldn't believe how nervous she felt. She was sweating. She looked across her desk at her partner and said, "Not one word from you."

But Marcus couldn't help himself. "Lunch at the mall, Ms. Winston? My, my, whatever will you wear?"

That made Olivia laugh. "Hey, there's nothing wrong with discussing a case over a friendly lunch. Can we get back to work?"

"Sure, Miss Winston, just a friendly lunch," Marcus teased. He opened the Lewis file and ran down the latest details.

"Bertrand Lewis was assaulted yesterday evening at one of his three tax offices. Based on fingerprints found at the crime scene, we think the assault was committed by a Calvin 'CJ' Henry who's currently three floors below Mr. Lewis at VCU Medical Center." Marcus adjusted his glasses and continued, "We also think Mr. Henry was involved in all three burglaries based on matching prints. No criminal history pops up on him, and no driver's license. And the crime scene unit is still trying to come up with a license or registration number for the suspect's van--or what's left of it from the fire."

"Okay, now for the unanswered stuff," Olivia said. "Why did Calvin Henry attack Bertrand Lewis? Who is Malley? Was he involved in the burglaries and or attack? And where can we find him?" Olivia ran a quick check in the system on CJ's surname--Henry--for relatives and associates and found nothing close to Malley's name. She picked up her mug and headed for the break room. "I need more tea," she said.

Marcus' cell phone beeped seconds later. "Detective Rowland speaking…Yeah, we'll be there in half an hour." Marcus put on his leather blazer and quick-stepped to the break room.

"Hey, partner, our guy is awake."

"It's about time. Let's go."

# CHAPTER TEN

Malcolm 'Malley' Henry, Jr., stood outside the 7-Eleven nervously scratching the gray stubble on his chin and looking at the Bud Light poster taped to the store's window. Drinking had taken a toll on him, making his light-skinned complexion seem hard and worn. He had been trying since last night to reach his brother Ronnie, and he didn't have a clue what to do about his brother CJ. He needed to get back to the trailer and get rid of the stuff CJ had stolen from those offices. He could burn it all deep in the woods out back. He didn't want any part of it anyway, and Ronnie had already taken what he wanted and paid CJ for it.

*But what if CJ told the cops about the trailer?* He leaned his tired, six-two frame against the convenience store wall. "Damn," he said. "I need a drink." But taking a drink would've been like walking off a cliff. Malley had tried AA at least four times in the past two years, always intending to get his world back on track. The new business was supposed to kick-start everything. Then he could help CJ get clean.

Still, Malley couldn't shake the feeling that he had messed up again.

*You dumb ass.* "Nobody in their right mind would borrow money from a drunk," he scolded himself.

Malley thought he could bring back the days long gone when he rode shotgun with his dad and watched him make loans to politicians, businessmen, and crapshooters.

And why couldn't it work? There were plenty of men like Bertrand Lewis--men who looked important but had addictions--addictions that required loans they couldn't get at the local bank. And there would always be some guy caught skimming a little from the boss' till and needing some quick cash to keep it all quiet. This could work, if he could just stay sober.

He dialed the number again on his cell phone. "Ronnie!"

"Mal, I heard about it, and I got nothing to say!" his younger brother yelled. "I told you it would go bad if you let CJ run wild."

"I know, Ronnie, but they got him in lockup," Malley pleaded, "and that Lewis man could be in bad shape. It's been on the news and in the paper."

"Listen, Mal, I did my part like I said I would. I fronted you the hundred twenty and set up the drop. I got nothing to do with what happened after that."

"Don't get stupid on me!" Malley shouted into the phone. "You know damn well you bought some of that stolen shit off CJ the last time you came through here! So don't haul ass now!"

Malley's temper was flaring, and his head was starting to pound. All he could think about was a cold beer and another cold one. He looked at the poster again.

Malley had learned from his dad that not every man pays his debts, and Bertrand Lewis was that kind of man. He should've loaned him a smaller amount and gotten him hooked. Desperate gamblers were easy to get hooked on bad loans. But Malley wanted to make an impression. He wanted people to think his money was large and to think he could handle the business.

When he ran in to an old acquaintance from his sober days--Bobby Lewis--and listened to Bobby's money problems, he thought he had found a good mark. Besides, he never thought Bobby or his cousin had the guts to cross him, not after he and CJ showed up that night to tell the cousin where he could pick up the money.

But he was wrong. Malley could still hear in his head the announcer in the background calling the next race when Bobby Lewis called him from the OTB. Bobby had some weak story about his cousin missing the repayment date because of a family emergency. The next week, it was some other lie about waiting for a check to clear a company account. By the third week, Malley thought about threatening both Bobby and his cousin. He wasn't above using violence, especially when he drank and felt self-pity. But his dad had warned him to never let money guide his emotions. So Malley wrote it off and swallowed his pride hard. That was part of doing business sometimes. And he didn't want to do anything that could land him in jail--a place he had managed to avoid despite several close calls after nights of hard drinking.

"Mal, I'm not comin' back up there," Ronnie said. "You need to get back to the trailer and clean up that mess, and I'm not just talking about what CJ stole. You know CJ's friends cooked that meth shit in there too." Ronnie sighed and said, "I can get you some money quick, but it's on you when it comes to CJ."

Malley didn't know what to do. He loved both of his younger brothers. Ronnie could always get by on his own. But he felt a need to look out for CJ ever since their mom died. For years, he kept his baby brother out of trouble, kept him close to home, and got him good labor jobs under the table. Yet the more Malley struggled with alcohol, the less his baby brother would listen to him. CJ crossed the line the day he tried meth on a dare from some stupid friends. Over the past year, he had spun out of control.

Looking back, Malley knew he was wrong for telling CJ about the amount he had loaned to Bertrand Lewis, and that Lewis never paid him back. But he was drunk and angry. Part of him did want CJ to do something stupid.

"Fine." Malley tried to calm down. "I'll see if I can get back to the house and over to the trailer. I don't think the police knew CJ was going back there when they grabbed him. I haven't seen his picture on TV or in the paper yet."

"Okay. I can wire some money to Leslie. How much you need?" Ronnie asked.

"Enough to make her happy. I'll stay with her for awhile, but we'll have to move to a new place just to be safe. I can't go back to my job, not with this happening."

Malley's girlfriend, Leslie, had seen him through some rough times. He seriously thought this could be the last time.

*** 

"This place is too big. I always get lost in here." Marcus turned a corner and just missed bumping into a gurney. "Why didn't the EMTs take this guy to the Goslyn ER?"

"I guess this one was closer," Olivia said.

"What room is it again?"

"Just look for the uniform posted outside the door."

Marcus turned another corner and spotted the officer straight ahead.

"Good morning," Marcus said to the young man who looked bored stiff.

"Morning, Sir." The officer yawned and nodded at Olivia as she followed Marcus into the room.

Two steps in, the man they saw was husk, old, and tired. The hospital had cleaned him up, but it couldn't wash away the damage CJ had done to himself. Meth showed no mercy on him. For several seconds, the detectives looked at him. Then they moved closer.

"Mr. Henry, I'm Detective Rowland. This is my partner, Detective Winston."

"I feel like crap, man. When can I go home?" CJ asked in a raspy voice.

"Tell me where it is and maybe we can work something out," Marcus said, knowing that they were still trying to track down an address on their suspect. "Hey, man," Marcus repeated, "where's home?"

CJ sat up in the bed and focused his sight on Olivia, as if trying to recognize her. He looked at Marcus and tried to raise his right hand, but it was cuffed to the bed. "How'd I get here?"

"You tell us," Marcus said. "What the hell were

you running from yesterday, man?" Marcus pulled a chair up to the bed and sat down.

"My van was breaking down. I was heading…going to see a friend."

"Really? What's your friend's name?"

Olivia stood on the other side of the bed and leaned against the wall. She enjoyed watching her partner interrogate.

CJ bit his lip and stared at his cuffed hand. Marcus and Olivia could tell he was struggling, either with the truth or details of another lie.

"Just some dude I know," he finally said. "I must have blacked out or something when I was driving. That's why I crashed."

"That was a serious blackout, man. It lasted a good five miles. Were you coming from your friend's place at Patterson and Glenside, you know, near that tax refund place?" Marcus was trying to back the suspect into a corner. CSI had already lifted CJ's prints from the petty cash box found smashed open next to Bertrand Lewis and from the steel pipe he had used to terrorize the old man. But Detective Rowland wanted a confession.

"Nah, man. He was just over that way seeing some girl. I was picking him up, but my van kept stalling." CJ lowered his head and seemed to be avoiding eye contact with the detectives.

"Is that right?" Marcus asked, pulling CJ's attention back to him. "I need you to write down your friend's name and phone number. Here, man." Marcus took out a pad and pen from an inside pocket and tossed it on CJ's lap close to his cuffed hand.

CJ picked up the pad with his other hand and just looked at it.

"People call him 'Skip', 'Skip' something. I don't know his last name. He moves around, you know...to different girlfriends and...different relatives...you know." CJ was rambling, and Marcus knew he was being fed more lies.

"CJ, my friend, I got some news for you." Marcus moved to the edge of his seat and said, "I know somebody who saw you go into the tax refund office near Patterson and Glenside early yesterday evening," he paused and stared at CJ, "and they tell me that they saw you leave through the back alley." Marcus leaned back in his chair and waited.

The blood drained from CJ's face, and sweat beads ran across his forehead. Marcus pulled the room's trash can into position in case CJ needed to throw up.

"Listen, officer," CJ said. "I don't know anybody over there and ..." CJ hesitated, and his hands started to tremble. "I was looking for a place to park my van because it kept stalling."

"Calvin, listen to me. It is Calvin Henry, right?" Marcus asked.

CJ nodded and said, "Yeah, man. Calvin Henry."

"Calvin, I got more news for you. I also know somebody who saw you talking to an older man who works at that office. You know who I'm talking about, Calvin? You know the one--kinda short, white hair, heavy-set, real nice old man everybody in the neighborhood likes?" Marcus was betting CJ had a conscience.

CJ blinked nervously. "Man, I didn't hit…Shit. Maybe I…No. I didn't talk to anybody over there."

Both Marcus and Olivia could tell the suspect's mind was racing. He was biting his lip again. Olivia signaled to her partner and pointed up at the ceiling.

Marcus said slowly and deliberately, "Calvin, the news gets real bad now. That same old man--the one somebody saw you with--that old man, at this very moment, is three floors above you in the intensive care unit. And you put him there. I know it. My partner knows it. And you know it."

CJ stared ahead. Marcus and Olivia could almost hear the wheels spin.

Marcus got up, leaned in close, and whispered," How much did Bertrand owe you?"

CJ broke down. He started crying and couldn't catch his breath.

"Please, mama, forgive me!" he blurted out between sobs. "All he had to do was give me the money. That's all he had to do. Please, mama, forgive me." He kept sobbing.

Marcus remembered the report of the large deposit to Bertrand Lewis' account ten month ago. He bent over and whispered, "Hundred twenty thousand, right?"

CJ nodded his head. "Yeah, but…but I didn't hurt him bad, man. I swear. He fell on the floor." CJ threw his head back on the pillow, closed his eyes, and tried to catch his breath again.

Marcus wanted more before the suspect's guilt wore off. He knew they didn't have any physical evidence against Malley. CSI didn't find any other prints at the break-ins, and no one saw a second person with CJ after the assault. But the money was a strong motive for Malley to send a clear message to Bertrand to pay up or get beat down.

The detective whispered, "CJ, you're in this one deep, but I can help you if you help us. Where's Malley?"

CJ opened his eyes and looked first at Marcus then at Olivia. He took several breaths and said, "I want a lawyer, man."

"All right, my friend." Marcus stepped back from the bed. "I wish you luck 'cause you're gonna need some."

CJ rolled over and buried himself underneath the covers.

***

"Good work, partner," Olivia said as she pushed the elevator button.

"We still don't have our person of interest--Mr. Malley." Marcus sounded disappointed.

"We've got CJ who connects directly to the burglaries. That's more than we had a month ago." Olivia always looked for the upside.

They stopped by ICU and got an update on Bertrand. He was stable, but the doctor still wouldn't allow any visitors.

They made their way back to the hospital's parking deck.

"Which way is the Federal Building?" Olivia asked.

"About five blocks that way," Marcus said as he pointed off to his left. "Thinking about dropping in on your date, Miss Winston?"

"Mind your own business and get in the truck."

\*\*\*

Olivia rummaged through her bedroom closet looking for something appropriate to wear. Black jeans, blue jeans, and shorts were all the casual stuff she owned. Pat was on the other end of Olivia's cell phone, which lay on the bed in speakerphone mode.

Olivia bent over the phone. "Blues jeans and my green Hanes T-shirt. That'll work. But what about the shoes? Sneakers or loafers?"

"Don't you have anything less tomboy and more grown-up for weekends?" Pat said.

"I save my grown-up stuff for work."

"That means I need to take you shopping. I think a nice pair of pressed khakis with a light colored blouse and your light brown loafers would look good. I know you have khakis because I bought them for you last summer."

Olivia shuffled through her closet and drawers looking for khakis. To her surprise, she found a pink polo shirt. She raised her voice, "Where did this come from?!"

"What is it?" Pat asked.

"I found a nice pink shirt in the bottom drawer." She laid it on the bed and kept digging. "There they are, beige khakis." She laid them next to the polo shirt. "Looks good."

"It should, I bought you that pink polo too. Are we done yet? I'm hungry."

"Stop being cranky. You're just sitting around watching movies. What else does an old, married woman like you do on a Friday night anyway?"

"I'm trying to enjoy a movie all by myself, and I'm hanging up on you. Don't forget to call me

91

tomorrow."

"All right. I'll let you know how it went."

\*\*\*

Maureen hadn't bothered to unpack from her Atlanta trip. Her closet and drawers were overflowing with winter and spring clothes, and she didn't have the patience to try shoving anything back to where it belonged. "I really need to donate some of this stuff."

"Or have a yard sale," her sister, Gloria, said as she wrestled on the bed with her son. "Just iron some tight blue jeans and a nice blouse with a little cleavage."

"Get your mind out of the gutter. I don't want to send the wrong message." Maureen walked across the hall to her other bedroom and opened a set of drawers. She pulled out a pair of black jeans and a white T-shirt and brought them in for Gloria to see. "I want to keep it simple. What do you think?"

"That's not simple," Gloria said, "that's boring." Maureen's nephew pointed at her and giggled. Gloria added, "See? Even Elijah thinks so."

Maureen went back and returned with a pair of dark blue khakis and a yellow v-neck blouse. She held it up for Gloria.

"The blouse is much better, but go back to the black jeans," Gloria said.

"All right, the yellow v-neck with my black jeans," Maureen announced as she came back into the room, "and my black loafers. Done."

"I don't remember spending this much time picking out clothes for a date," Gloria said.

"Because you've had date nights with the same man for the last seven years. You do remember Wallace, your husband?"

Gloria looked at her watch. "Gotta go. The baseball game should be almost over, and I need to pick him up from the high school."

"How's Coach handling the two losses so far?" Maureen asked about her brother-in-law.

"Like he's down three games in the World Series. We've got seven more games to go this season." Gloria picked up Elijah and headed down the hall and out the front door with Maureen behind her.

"All right, sis, we'll see you tomorrow morning at Auntie's," Gloria said as she buckled up.

Maureen watched as they pulled off and saw Elijah wave from his safety seat.

*The life of a two-year-old. If only dating were that easy.*

# CHAPTER ELEVEN

At a quarter to one, Maureen turned into the mall parking lot. She kicked herself for not wearing the white T-shirt after all. She thought yellow screamed desperate.

She had arrived at her aunt's house earlier that morning and helped Uncle Frank clear out the garden section of the backyard before he rushed off to the barbershop to catch up on the latest gossip. Aunt Lena had been up since sunrise and had already fixed breakfast--buttered grits, buttered toast, and strong black coffee. Gloria had tried her best to keep up with Elijah as he chased after feral rabbits that dashed through the yard. Both were exhausted by the time Aunt Lena had Elijah's favorite lunch ready--ravioli smothered in ketchup.

Maureen parked in front of the restaurant and sat for five minutes. She was nervous and couldn't stop fiddling with her watchband. "Here we go," she said as she got out and walked toward the front doors.

Only a handful of patrons were at the buffet with a couple at the bar. As Maureen waited to be seated, she saw Olivia come from the rear of the restaurant and sit at a booth table. Her eyes were fixed on the detective. Pink shirt, beige khakis, and a walk that aroused Maureen.

Maureen felt frozen. "Seating for one, ma'am?" she heard a voice ask.

Maureen snapped to attention and looked at the waiter. "No thanks. I see my date--my party--over there."

From her seat in the booth, Olivia tried not to stare as Maureen approached. But she couldn't help it. *Yellow looks good on her,* Olivia thought.

Olivia had been up with the roosters, as her Grandma Rita liked to say. She had wanted to get as much garden work done on her own before the gray-haired taskmaster had a chance to find work for her. After gardening, she took a long shower and debated over and over whether the lunch was a good idea. She convinced herself that it was important to the Lewis case. She had arrived early at the restaurant and had gone to the rear restroom a couple of times to check herself in the mirror. She was starting to think her pink polo was too casual.

"Good to see you again, Maureen--Special Agent Jeffries," she said when Maureen reached the table.

"Good to see you too," Maureen said and extended her hand.

They shook hands, and Maureen slid into the booth.

"Is this table okay?" Olivia asked. "We can move if you like."

"It's fine, and you can call me Maureen if you don't mind me calling you Olivia?"

"Sure." Olivia took a deep breath that she hoped Maureen didn't notice.

The waiter came over with the usual fried noodle chips and took their drink orders before heading to the bar.

"Come here much?" Maureen asked Olivia as she opened the menu.

"Every chance I get." Olivia chuckled at

herself.

"What do you recommend?"

Olivia pretended to read the menu. "The steamed chicken with mixed vegetables and brown sauce is pretty good."

"Okay. I'll try it with a wonton soup."

The waiter returned with two ice teas and took their orders.

"So how was Atlanta? Maureen?" Olivia noticed a faint smile flicker across Maureen's lips, and her shoulders seemed to relax.

"The trip was good," Maureen said. "We found some of the Lewis client data when we searched some gang members. We're working on finding out how they got it."

The waiter interrupted with the soup before vanishing to another table.

Olivia sipped her tea and asked, "Any news from your cyber guys?"

"Not yet. But they're working on the info you faxed me and the codes I got in Atlanta. Please thank your friend for doing that web search."

Olivia nibbled on the noodle chips and watched Maureen poke at the dumplings in her bowl. How was she going to jump-start a personal conversation?

The waiter was back in minutes with their lunch and a tea refill for Olivia.

"I've got some good news on my burglaries," Olivia said. "We got a confession from our suspect."

"You are good. Maybe you should come to Atlanta with me on my next trip."

Olivia looked up, startled, and caught Maureen just avoiding her eyes. Was that a personal invitation? Or was she misreading the Agent? Olivia killed the awkward moment by getting back to business. "My partner, Marcus, did the heavy lifting on that one," she said. "And we're still looking for at least one other person."

"How long have you been partners?" Maureen asked.

"Almost seven years. He's great at interrogating, and he's got a good sense of humor too."

"My partner's been on maternity leave with his wife," Maureen said. "They're already planning for their next kid." Maureen sipped her tea and added, "You have any kids?"

"No. How about you?"

"No." Maureen said.

Olivia recalled an earlier conversation. "But you do have relatives here in Goslyn?" she asked.

"Yes, my aunt and uncle, Lena and Frank Williams. They live by that old water tower near your police department. That's where I grew up when my parents owned a house over there." Maureen sipped again. "Do you want kids?"

"I thought about it when I was younger." Olivia stiffened and hesitated. "But it would've been kind of…awkward. I would've needed a donor since I'm gay." There, it was out.

"You know, I'm a sucker for a single woman in a flannel shirt," Maureen said.

"How about one in a pink polo?" Olivia popped up her collar.

They both laughed with relief.

"We must be showing our age, Maureen," Olivia said. "I know plenty of twenty-year-olds who wouldn't have hesitated to ask *and* tell."

Life in Goslyn dominated rest of the conversation as Olivia and Maureen got acquainted. They were amazed that they knew so many of the same people, including Mr. Brooks. They even discovered they had attended a junior 4-H summer camp at the same time. The thought of crossing paths as kids gave Maureen the courage to tell Olivia about the first time she saw her.

"I don't want to freak you out," Maureen said, "but I used to see you just about every morning before school."

"Really?" Olivia raised a curious brow. "How's that?"

"My school bus passed you every day when you walked to Lincoln High. I think my bus driver set her watch by what time she spotted you crossing the street. I recognized you when your lieutenant introduced us in your squad room."

"Maureen, this is crazy! I've heard of six degrees of separation. But this is like coming full circle. I'm gonna be ticked off if you tell me we're cousins!"

Maureen almost knocked over her drink as she laughed. "I don't think we're cousins. We could've had the same pediatrician though."

For two hours, they traded tales about their college days, how they got to their current positions, and what they planned to do later in their careers. The waiter politely interrupted and asked if he could have the booth for a waiting family of five.

"I didn't realize we had been here that long," Olivia said to Maureen. "You have any plans for rest of the day?"

"Nothing special. I'll have a late dinner with my aunt and uncle unless they decide to go to a card game tonight. Until then, I'm free as a bird. What about you, Olivia?"

*Olivia.* That, Olivia thought, sounded much better than *detective.* "I don't have anything planned. Would you like to walk the mall when we leave here?"

"You lead. I'll follow."

\*\*\*

A walk through the mall had turned in to a slow two-hour stroll in and out of every store including a stop at a cookie and ice cream parlor. Maureen and Olivia were now seated on a bench outside the mall's bookstore. Olivia licked on a double chocolate cone as Maureen pinched off pieces of a large chocolate chip cookie.

"After I started working at entry level, I moved out of my dad's house and rented an apartment in Richmond," Maureen said. "That's where I met Denise, in Richmond, at a tax seminar. She was teaching business courses at Virginia Union at that time." Maureen stopped for a moment, wiped the crumbs from her hands, and took a sip from her bottled water. "We would see each other occasionally at community events organized by the Agency. At one event, I noticed she had a LGBT pamphlet sticking out of a notebook. So I struck up a conversation, and we started seeing each other for lunch or dinner."

Olivia finished off her ice cream and gestured to Maureen for a napkin. "Was it serious?" she asked as she wiped chocolate sprinkles from her mouth.

"It became serious. We dated for two years, and she moved into my apartment. But a year later, things started to change." Maureen got up and tossed her napkin and rest of her cookie into a nearby trash can. She sat back down and was in deep thought for a moment.

Olivia stayed quiet.

"Denise came from a very close, Catholic family," Maureen continued, "and she really wanted them to accept me as family too. But some of them, her dad mainly, were never comfortable with her being gay, let alone her living with another woman. On top of that, her older sisters just couldn't wrap their minds around a black woman being gay." Maureen shook her head and fiddled with the plastic bottle top. "But we knew our relationship was just as important as hers was with them. So we stayed together and tried to show them it wasn't the end of the world." Maureen stopped again and ran her fingers through her hair.

Olivia was hanging on every word. It brought back feelings she once had for Kendra--those feelings of caring deeply for someone and wanting the world to respect it.

Maureen went on. "It lasted another year. We even planned a ceremony in the same month I was to start as a special agent. But her dad fell ill for awhile, and her mom wanted Denise to help take care of him. She started spending most nights at their place, which meant we had less time together. And when we were together, she avoided having any real conversations with me. It was always just silly small talk. One day, I asked her if she still loved me." Maureen paused a final time and pretended to brush crumbs from her lap. The trip down memory lane was thorny. "She started crying and wouldn't stop. I didn't need any words after that to tell me it was over between us, and I honestly believe she felt guilty about being gay."

Maureen looked at Olivia and knew Olivia could see the sadness in her eyes.

"Sorry, I don't know why I brought all of that up," she said. "Hope I didn't make you depressed."

"Not at all, Maureen. Now I feel bad for telling you about Kendra. She seems like a jerk compared to Denise. Where's Denise now?"

"She teaches at a college down in Norfolk. I've heard she has a partner and a house full of cats." Maureen showed a thin smile.

Another half hour passed as they soaked in the early evening sun and watched the mall parking lot clear.

"I think we've talked about everything except politics and sex," Olivia said out of the blue.

Maureen blushed and was speechless.

"Sorry, Maureen. I don't know where that came from."

"Don't worry about it. You just reminded me of Carol, my receptionist. She's far more graphic though. Let's make another date so we can talk about politics. Then…perhaps a third date for sex? I mean, to talk about it."

Olivia jumped on both offers. "Same time on Saturdays and you pick the place for the next lunch."

"Deal. We'll do Italian in Richmond. I love spaghetti marinara."

They strolled back to their vehicles, chatted some more about their cases, and said their good-byes.

Olivia extended her right hand for a handshake.

Maureen, however, extended her left, slid her fingers across Olivia's palm, and wrapped her hand around Olivia's. She held on intentionally long and said, "Can't wait to see you again, Olivia."

Olivia felt good in all the right places as she watched Maureen slowly walk to her car and leave. "That," she said to herself as she climbed into her truck, "was way better than planting sweet potatoes."

# CHAPTER TWELVE

"How'd it go?" Gloria asked as she sat on the edge of the tub, holding her cell phone.

"It was perfect," Maureen said.

"Perfect? Nobody has a perfect first date. She must have gotten food stuck in her front teeth, knocked over a glass, or something." Gloria splashed water on Elijah who was in the tub surrounded by bubbles. Elijah splashed her back, soaking the bathroom floor and just missing the cell phone. "Hold on a second, Maureen." Gloria took Elijah out of the tub, dried his feet, and wrapped a towel around him. "Okay, you little rug rat, run and tell your daddy to dry you off."

The toddler trotted and giggled his way down the hall to his parents' bedroom.

Gloria picked up the phone again. "All right, what was I saying?"

"Never mind what you were saying," Maureen said. "Just listen. She grew up just a few miles from us, and she knows Mr. Brooks. Isn't that wild?"

"Yeah, wild. So what's she like?"

"She's funny. She's smart. She's easy to talk to. She's--"

Gloria snored into the phone.

"Gloria!" Maureen yelled.

"Oops. I must have dozed off waiting for the good part. Is she good-looking?"

"Yes, she's very attractive."

"Finally, we're getting somewhere. You thinking about hookin' up with her?"

"Gloria, why is sex always on your mind?

You're like a horny teenage boy!"

"Because Wallace and I are too busy to have any. You'll find out one day when you have your own rug rats." Gloria pulled a towel out of the closet and dropped it on the puddle covering the bathroom floor. "Now stop acting like a nun and tell me what you really think about her."

"I really like her…a lot. But--"

"But you don't want to rush into anything. Blah, blah, blah." Gloria headed for the kitchen and a bag of chips on top of the fridge.

"Will you be quiet? That's not what I was going to say. I was going to say I want to see how our next date goes."

"Good, a second date. Where're you going?"

"We're having lunch here in the city, and I was thinking about taking her to the new Black History museum."

"Sounds nice, but can I make a suggestion?" Gloria asked before munching on a chip.

"As long as it doesn't involve sex."

Gloria laughed. "Okay, okay." She laughed again. "You should take a walk around the old canal. I hear the city re-opened it."

"That's a good idea. I haven't been there in years."

Gloria knew Maureen hadn't been there since she and Denise had broken up. It was a waterway dating back to the Civil War, and the city had renovated it by installing a walkway running along the James River and ending at a space set up for concerts.

"See, I do think of other stuff besides sex,"

Gloria said.

"And you know it was one of my favorite places to take Denise."

"That's the whole point, Einstein! You said you really like her. Don't you share your favorite things with people you like?"

"When did you start talking like Oprah?" Maureen said.

Gloria laughed even more and handed the bag of chips to Elijah who was now standing right in front of her wearing nothing but a pair of Mickey Mouse socks. "I've got to go," she said to Maureen. "Wallace still hasn't figured out how to get this boy ready for bed."

\*\*\*

Maureen turned on her CD player and slid in an old Sarah Vaughan jazz disc that belonged to her late mom. It was too early for bed, especially for a Saturday night.

"Time for housekeeping," she said and headed for her bedroom to finally sort out her closet and drawers. But one look at the sweaters piled high changed her mind. She ended up in the third bedroom where she kept a shelf full of paperback books. She grabbed her favorite, headed back to the living room, and got comfortable in the recliner. An old *Miss Marple* mystery was always good. Yet she was barely in to the first sentence when she started to think about Olivia.

*I wonder if she likes roses?*

\*\*\*

Jesse heard the phone ring and dove for it before his brother could get to it. "Hello?"

"Hey, buddy, how was the soccer game?" Olivia asked her godson.

"I scored a goal, Aunt Ollie!" Jesse said and kicked his soccer ball against the back of the living room couch.

"Me too, Aunt Ollie!" Jaylon shouted and snatched the phone from Jesse. "And we beat them two times in a row!"

"Congratulations! When do you play again?"

"Next Saturday," Jaylon said. "Can you come this time? I wanna show you my trick shot."

"Sorry, buddy. I've got something planned that day."

"You got another date with your new girlfriend?"

"What! Who told you I had a girlfriend?"

"Mommy did. And guess what? I got a girlfriend too."

Jesse snatched the phone back. "Yeah, and she plays soccer better than he does!"

"Shut up, bighead!" Jaylon snapped back.

"You shut up, blockhead!"

"No name calling!" Olivia said.

"Sorry Aunt Ollie. Can we meet your new girlfriend?"

"Can we?" Jaylon asked as he pressed his head against his brother's to speak into the receiver. "Is she a policewoman like you?"

"All right. All right. She's just a new friend. I'll let you meet her soon. And yes, she's a policewoman. Now give the phone to your mom."

The nine-year-olds stampeded through the house, each trying to trip the other as they headed for the laundry room.

"That's enough, you two!" Pat said and stopped them in their tracks before they could knock over a clean load neatly folded. "Give me that phone and go get those dirty socks from underneath your beds."

The two rumbled off like a small tornado. Pat watched as they disappeared and wondered if she ever had that much energy.

She put the phone to her ear. "Please tell me you want to adopt them starting tonight," was the first thing out of her mouth.

"No way, no how," Olivia said.

"Coward. Fill me in about this hot date." Pat closed and turned on the dryer.

"It was great, and we already planned our next two dates."

"Woo hoo! Somebody's feeling lucky. Do I need to give you the safe sex talk, young lady?"

Olivia's voice went high and girly, "No thanks, mom. I think I'm up to speed there!"

"Tell me about her. Is she better than you expected?"

"Yes! I really liked talking to her, and it was so funny finding out she grew up here. She told me she used to see me walking to Lincoln High."

"You mean she's been scoping you out for the last twenty years? Talk about a woman with a mission!" Pat switched the phone to her other ear. "And patience!"

"Who hid in the bushes and scoped out Eric every day at his bus stop?"

"I was just protecting my interests," Pat said as she tossed her husband's boxers into the washer.

Olivia giggled at her friend. "Do you think I should send her some flowers to say 'Thank You' for the date?"

"It depends."

"On what?"

"On how hot she is."

"Pat, will you be serious for a minute."

"I am serious. Is she attractive?"

"Yes, very. Should I do flowers?"

"Flowers are outdated to me. How about a snazzy digital 'Thank You' card? I can find one for you."

"No, that's too…impersonal. I think I'll do the flowers--maybe something yellow."

"You're so old-fashioned," Pat said just before she heard the wrestling match down the hall. "It's time to play referee again. One of these days, I'm going to drop those two off at your door and never pick them up. Sweet dreams about your new girlfriend."

"Good night, Pat."

\*\*\*

Olivia turned on her radio and hummed along with Smokey and the Miracles. She then logged into her laptop at her kitchen table. The computer chimed the second after she opened her e-mails. It was Mama Winston asking for more pictures and for details about her date.

"I swear that woman is as bad as Pat," Olivia said to herself.

She replied back that she wasn't giving up any information until her mom convinced Grandma Rita to get rid of her old box TV. Olivia knew that would never happen, so she was safe--at least for another week.

Another e-mail popped up with attached photos. It was Marcus showing off another shelf full of shiny tool he had ordered off Amazon.com. Olivia responded that she would tattle to his wife unless he came with her to her next workout at the gym.

Her mind then went back to Maureen and how good it felt talking with her. "What's a perfect yellow flower?" she said as she looked at a Richmond florist's website. She found it after a quick browse. "Can't go wrong with lilies."

# CHAPTER THIRTEEN

Olivia looked at a row of minibuses lined up in front of the Frederick Douglass Day Care Center. "Who had the brilliant idea to put an OTB across the street from kids?" she asked.

"Probably somebody we voted for in the last election," Marcus said as he dunked a granola bar into his coffee. "You sure this is the right location?"

"Yeah, it's the only OTB in the county, and Lewis' wife said he was here last week." Olivia checked the clock on her truck's dashboard as they waited at a red light. It was only nine thirty, and Monday had already gotten off to a fast start.

First, Mrs. Bobby Lewis called 9-1-1 early that morning to report her husband missing. She hadn't seen him since his cousin, Bertrand Lewis, was attacked, and she feared he might have been kidnapped. Then Bobby himself called 9-1-1 claiming his life was in danger and that he needed to talk to somebody immediately about the tax office burglaries. The operator's supervisor contacted Olivia's department once she realized Mr. Lewis was drunk and had tried to make the same call an hour earlier.

Despite the morning excitement, Olivia did manage to order flowers that the florist would deliver to Maureen before lunch.

"What's he driving?" Marcus asked.

"His wife says he's in a gray Chevy SUV." Olivia turned into the OTB parking lot.

Marcus scanned the vehicles. "There, over by the light pole."

Olivia pulled up beside a SUV with its windows covered from the inside with torn sheets and greasy newspaper. "Don't tell me this guy's been living in this thing since last Thursday?"

"Fear makes people do dumb stuff, so heads up," Marcus warned.

"I got your back."

Olivia got out of the truck and stood at the SUV's rear driver side. Marcus walked around to the passenger side and placed his hand on his sidearm as he peeked through a tear in one of the sheets. He signaled to Olivia when he saw a body curled up in the back.

Olivia knocked on the window. "Mr. Lewis! Goslyn PD!" She banged on the door. No answer, no movement. "You think he's--"

"Nah, just passed out," Marcus said. "I saw at least four empty wine bottles. Hit your siren."

Olivia reached into her truck and flipped a switch a couple of times.

They heard a thump from inside the vehicle.

"Goslyn PD, Mr. Lewis!" Olivia yelled and knocked on the window again.

The rear hatch door popped open and a scruffy, ashy-faced man poked his head over the rear bumper. "Ouch! Crap!" he complained and rubbed his knee that he had wacked against the car jack. "All right. You found me. Please…no more knocking," he groaned. He slowly swung his thin legs out the back, sat on the bumper, and cradled his head in his hands.

"Good morning, Mr. Lewis. I'm Detective Winston, and that's Detective Rowland!" Olivia was deliberately loud. She wanted his full attention, and the stench of musty socks and cigarettes coming from inside the SUV annoyed her.

"Morning," Bobby whispered. He managed to lift his head and look at Marcus. "You wouldn't happen to have some aspirin, would you?"

"Sorry, man, I'm all out. But I'm sure we can find some down at the station."

Olivia opened the rear passenger door of her truck. "Hop in, Mr. Lewis. We'll treat you to some free coffee."

Bobby wasn't hopping into anything. "Ma'am, you don't want me in the back of that truck right now." He put his hand on his large belly and belched loudly.

Olivia saw his blood shot eyes and quickly shut the truck door. "You're right." *I just had the carpets cleaned.* She moved closer to him and placed her hand on his shoulder. "Mr. Lewis, we're very sorry about your cousin. But you need to pull yourself together and tell us what you know about the attack."

"We can talk in there." Marcus pointed to a small diner next door to the OTB. A waitress was outside sweeping the sidewalk.

"Come on, Mr. Lewis. You can freshen up in the bathroom," Olivia said.

Bobby wiped his face with his shirtsleeve and slowly stood. He wobbled a little but caught his balance as he reached up to pull the hatch door back down. He led the two detectives into the diner and practically ran to the bathroom the second he smelled bacon and eggs.

"I think he's about to revisit last night's dinner," Olivia said as another waitress led them to a table then disappeared behind the counter.

"You would've pouted for days if he had messed up your backseat. You treat that truck like it's your child."

"I treat it the same way you treat your tools. Buy me a cup of tea."

Marcus got the waitress' attention when she reappeared and placed orders for tea and two cups of coffee.

Just then, Bobby came out of the bathroom looking only slightly better. He moved like he was trying not to make any noise.

"My head's killing me," he said. "The toilet flush sounded like a train coming through the wall."

The waitress placed a coffee in front of him and one in front of Marcus. She gave Olivia a cup of steaming water and a tea bag.

"Mr. Lewis, again, we're sorry about the situation," Olivia said. "But we need you to tell us everything you know." She dunked her tea bag into the water and added some raw sugar packs.

Bobby looked down at his cup. "You know Bert loves coffee and…if he doesn't make it through this…" Bobby choked up as if he was about to cry.

"We know this is hard," Marcus said. "But the more we know, the sooner we can find out who else is involved. Do you know anything about the man we arrested--Calvin Henry?"

Bobby slowly shook his head. "No. The first time I ever saw him was the night before Bert got the money. He showed up with Malley."

"You know Malley?" Olivia asked.

"We're sort of acquainted. We met a long time ago when I used to represent some commercial builders. He did some off-the-books construction work for one of my clients and sometimes hit me up for free legal advice whenever I came down to the site." Bobby wiped his face again with his sleeve. "It's my fault for telling Bert we could get a loan this way. I knew it could be risky, but I never thought Malley would take it this far."

"Do you know where we can find him?"

"I don't. He was pretty guarded when it came to his personal life. He never even told me his full name. I happened to run into him last year outside a 7-Eleven in the city. He surprised me when he told me he was just out of rehab. I told him I was having some money problems." Bobby stopped and took a gulp of coffee. He opened one of the free snacks on the table and nibbled on a saltine before he continued. "That's when he said he could do a loan for me."

"Any idea where he got the money?" Marcus asked.

"I don't know. I just know Bert had the money in his hands the day after we met with Malley and that wacked-out guy you arrested. He didn't tell me where or how he picked it up."

"Do you know anybody related to Malley or associated with him?"

"No. Like I said, he didn't get too personal." Bobby took another gulp of coffee.

Olivia kept dunking her tea bag as she looked at Bobby Lewis. She thought about her students and the hundreds of times she had told them how a good education could take them far. Yet here was Mr. Lewis, a well-educated man who somehow got derailed and was sleeping outside a betting parlor.

Marcus asked Bobby for a physical description of Malley then handed him a card. "Okay, Mr. Lewis. If you think of anything that could help, please call us." He and Olivia stood up to leave.

"Detectives, do you think I'm in danger? Do you think Malley will come after me?"

"We honestly don't know," Olivia said. "We'll have a unit patrol your neighborhood for a few days just in case. In the meantime, go home to your wife. And Mr. Lewis," Olivia hesitated and looked him in the eye, "I don't mean to preach, but your cousin really needs you. That means he needs you to stay sober and away from the place next door."

Bobby seemed embarrassed as he looked down at his coffee again. "I appreciate that, Detective."

Olivia and Marcus went back to the truck and sat for a few minutes. They both felt deflated and doubtful that Bobby Lewis would stay clear of the OTB. But Marcus had a quick remedy to change the mood.

"Miss Winston, what fashion statement did you make on your lunch date?" he asked.

"Like you really care what I wore," Olivia said.

"I do care. I have to report back to Phyllis."

"To Phyllis? Why is everybody so interested in my love life!"

"Because that's what married people do. We talk about our single friends. Phyllis says you look good in red. But I told her that's the wrong color for a first date. It sends the wrong message and--" Marcus saw the dumfounded look on Olivia's face. "What?" I know a thing or two about dating and color-coordinating."

Olivia just laughed as she started the truck. "Remind me to call you before I get dressed in the mornings."

*** 

Maureen scribbled a note in the Lewis file and spoke into the phone, "Any luck talking to that jeweler?"

"No luck there," Special Agent Abrams said. "He asked for a lawyer the minute he saw us. We think the gangs used him to fence some jewelry. We still don't know if he's involved in the identity thefts. So Atlanta PD had to cut him loose after he made bail on the suspended license charge."

"Okay, Abrams. Keep me posted." Maureen hung up and got back to Carol who was hovering over her shoulder.

"Show me what you sent her," Carol said.

"Those." Maureen pointed to her computer screen.

"Ooo, nice. You know pink is the color of romance."

"You think I should've been more subtle?"

"Heck no! The brightest peacock wins the prize."

"What in the world does that mean?"

"That's an old saying from my Jamaican grandmother, long before you were born. Did she get them yet?"

"I got an auto e-mail saying they were delivered twenty minutes ago. I hope she likes them," Maureen said as she clicked on her inbox."

"Of course she will. You want some of this?" Carol tapped on the take-out containers that she had stacked on Maureen's desk. The smell of jerk chicken and stewed cabbage filled the office.

"No thanks. This'll hold me until dinner." Maureen opened a taco salad dripping with extra tomatoes.

Carol was about to chide her for eating like a rabbit when she heard Jackie, the part-time receptionist, talking to someone out front. Maureen's cell phone rang, and she knew exactly who was on the other end.

"Hello, Olivia," she said.

"Hello to you too. Pink is my new favorite color."

"So you like them?" Maureen winked at Carol who gave one of her silly thumbs-up before leaving with her lunch.

"I love them!" Olivia said. "Thank you. I hope you like lilies."

"Lilies?" Maureen turned when she heard a light knock on the door. Jackie was standing in the doorway with a yellow bouquet. "Oh, Olivia, they are beautiful. Yellow is definitely my new favorite color."

"How's your day going?" Olivia asked.

"It's getting better every minute," Maureen said as she took the flowers and held them close to her chest. "How about you? I hope you're not too busy."

"The usual routine stuff. I had a good time on Saturday."

"So did I. I really enjoyed our time." Maureen rubbed a petal on one of the lilies. "You have any plans for this evening?" she asked.

"Finish off some of my grandma's leftovers and a movie on the DVD player. And you?"

"Just my usual run then I'll curl up with a good mystery."

"What about dinner?"

Maureen didn't want to mention her awful cooking skills. She looked at her lunch and said, "I'll probably just have a salad."

"Oh, okay. Well…enjoy your salad tonight. I'll see you on Saturday?"

"Yes, at a little place called *Il Bistro*. It's on Ninth Street, two blocks from the city's main library."

"I'll see you there," Olivia said. "Have a good week, Maureen."

"You have a good one too, and thank you for the lilies."

Maureen waited for Olivia to hang up first. Then it struck her. "Was she inviting me to dinner? Damn, I totally missed that." Or maybe it was just Maureen's imagination. She didn't want things to move too fast, though part of her didn't mind if they did. She craved romance and wanted to experience it at every opportunity. Would the second date be an opportunity?

She looked at the lilies and rubbed a petal again between her fingers. *Just maybe I am the brightest peacock.*

# CHAPTER FOURTEEN

Chief Anderson quickly shut his office door on the heels of the two County Board Supervisors. He was so angry, he couldn't speak. He took a slow, deep breath followed by a blood pressure pill and a drink of water. He had gotten news of the car chase from his Deputy Chief via e-mail while attending an out of town conference. He was reading the official report for a third time over lunch when the Supervisors showed up demanding a meeting.

"For Christ's sake!" he said, crushing the Styrofoam cup in his hand before throwing it into the trash. "A tow driver with a busted lip, citizens run off the road, and a business owner sent to intensive care. What the hell happened?!"

Lieutenant Beal, who the chief had ordered to wait outside during the meeting, stood at attention. "Sir, the suspect was high and out of his mind. The patrol unit and Detective Winston contained the situation the best they could."

"Contained?! You call this contained?!" Chief Anderson jabbed his finger down on the report papers spread out on his desk. "My phone's been ringing off the hook with calls from residents who think this county is out of control, and the Board is in a panic!" The chief fished through the papers and picked up Olivia's statement. "And what the hell was *she* doing there?!"

"Detective Winston was in the area, sir. She followed standard procedure as a backup on the call."

Chief Anderson dropped the statement down on his desk. "Lieutenant, that is not an acceptable answer." He sat down and motioned for the lieutenant to do the same. "I will not have any member of this department acting recklessly and putting civilians at risk."

"Sir, it was the suspect who was acting recklessly and putting civilians at risk."

Chief Anderson slammed his fist on the desk and picked up Olivia's statement again. "If you can't control your detectives then I will!"

He knew by the raised eyebrows on Lieutenant Beal's face that he was overreacting. He tried to dial back his aggression. "I'm not questioning your leadership skills, Lieutenant. But I don't like the way this case is going. It's sloppy, and I want it cleaned up."

"With all due respect, sir, no one under my command is out of control," the lieutenant said. "If they were, I would be the first to put them in check." She brushed her dreadlocks back and straightened her button-down collar. "It will get cleaned up, sir. Is that all?"

"For now." The chief waited until the lieutenant was at the door before he asked his final question--a question based on rumors swirling through the Department.

"Lieutenant, are you aware of a personal relationship between Detective Winston and that IRS agent?"

Lieutenant Beal turned on a dime. "Personal?"

The chief answered the lieutenant's stare with his own and didn't offer a clue as to why he had asked.

"No, sir. I'm not aware."

"Keep me briefed as usual," the chief said.

***

"God damn," Lieutenant Beal mumbled as she sprinted down the stairs and into the squad room. She needed something to calm her nerves so she wouldn't run outside and light up.

Before making a detour to the break room, she shouted to Olivia and Marcus. "Detectives, meeting in one minute!"

In the break room, she poured from the orange-bottomed pot then walked into her heavily-scented office where she was relying on flameless aroma candles and meditation as well as coffee to help quash her nicotine craving.

"All right, gang, have a seat," she said as she shut her office door and plopped down in her chair. She took a long drink from a double-sized mug and raised it. "It's decaf."

"Good idea, ma'am," Marcus said.

"I know. I don't need another bad habit." Beal sighed and caught a coffee drop dribbling down her chin. "I just received a butt-kicking from the chief. Apparently, several business owners near that tax office assault are terrified they'll be the next victims."

"Ma'am, the Lewis assault was not random," Olivia said. "The victim owed money to the perp. So it's not like there's a drug addict running around attacking people. We have the guy in custody."

"I know that, Detective. Try explaining that to those Supervisors whose constituents are worried about their own safety and about losing customers. And don't forget about the three break-ins and the car chase that nearly went from one end of the county to the other. This one case has generated more media coverage than all your other cases combined." Lieutenant Beal took another sip. "Look, I know you're giving me your best as usual. But you know the drill--when the chief starts to catch flack from the community, it rolls downhill to us."

"Okay," Marcus said. "We know we're in the spotlight on this one, and we're working every angle. But our victim's in no condition to talk, his cousin didn't know much, and the perp has lawyered-up."

Lieutenant Beal looked at Olivia.

"So far, that's all we've got," Olivia said.

The lieutenant picked up a pencil and held it like a cigarette. "I need more than that, and I need it soon." Her computer chimed, alerting her to a new e-mail. "Great! The chief's already scheduled my next butt-kicking."

Beal dismissed Marcus but told Olivia to stay. She gnawed on the pencil and paced in front of the aroma candles. She gave a long look at Olivia. "The chief's taken an interest in what you do outside the office. You want to tell me why?" she asked.

"Excuse me? I don't follow you, ma'am."

"He asked me if you have a personal relationship with Special Agent Jeffries."

"What? Why?"

Lieutenant Beal sighed. She knew Olivia's long tense history with the chief and the chief's son. "Please, don't answer my question with a question. Is there something I need to know?"

"No, ma'am. We had lunch to talk about our cases. It's nothing I thought I needed to write up and post in the break room."

"Listen, you and I both know the chief's had you under his microscope for years. Somehow you put a dent in his ego, and the man just can't let it go."

"Lieutenant, that's ancient history," Olivia said, "and Clifford is still a good friend and--"

"Olivia, don't dig up the past for me. As long as you do your job, I've got your back. But I don't like surprises. Understand?"

"Yes, ma'am."

"Good. Get this case wrapped up, and try to get through the week without causing any more damage."

Olivia went back to her desk, and Lieutenant Beal, with pencil in mouth, headed back to the orange-bottomed pot for her fourth cup of decaf.

# CHAPTER FIFTEEN

Olivia stood up in the cucumber patch and brushed the garden dirt from her gloves. "Need any help unloading those crates, Mr. Brooks?" she asked.

Mr. Brooks stacked the eggs onto a stand next to Grandma Rita's back door. They made the best omelets in town according to Mama Winston.

"No thanks," Mr. Brooks said. "The load's light this morning. The girls laid only half their usual."

"Maybe they're finally tired of that mean, old rooster bossing them around. He must be a hundred years old by now."

"Could be. The girls have put up with him for a long time." Mr. Brooks was one of the few residents who still had a chicken coop in his backyard. His neighbors appreciated that little bit of country-living.

Olivia went back to planting cucumbers seeds while the garden volunteers debated who made the best deviled eggs. Mr. Brooks went to the tool shed, got his shovel, and started digging holes to plant potatoes near where Olivia was working.

"Detective, I hear last Saturday was a good day for you," he said with a sly grin.

Olivia wiped the sweat from her brow. "Pardon me?"

"Last Saturday? Maureen?"

"Mr. Brooks, how do you manage to know what's going on with everybody?"

Mr. Brooks laughed as he kept digging. "Because I worked at the Grand Central Station of all gossip for half my life---the first Goslyn post office. And I get my hair cut at the second best source--the oldest barbershop in the county."

Olivia stood and put her hands on her hips. She didn't know if she should be irritated or tickled that everybody was so interested in who she was dating.

"If you must know, I had a wonderful Saturday with Maureen," she said. "That's all I'm telling."

"I hear the weather will be perfect this afternoon--perfect for another date."

"Yes it will, sir, and that's all I'm saying about that." Olivia went back to planting but her imagination conjured up an image of Mr. Brooks forming a spy network with Mama Winston and Pat as co-conspirators tracking her love life.

She wiped her brow again and checked the time on her cell phone. The morning was creeping by like a snail. "I should demand payment for all of this labor," she griped to herself. She went inside to give her grandma a piece of her mind.

"I want you to know I'm feeling underappreciated for my services." Olivia tried to keep a straight face.

Grandma Rita was sitting at the kitchen table peeling husk off corncobs and reading a soap opera magazine.

"Child, what are you talking about? You only been here an hour."

Olivia faked exhaustion and slouched down at the kitchen table. She picked up another magazine and started fanning with it.

"I'm talking about all the hard work I do in that garden. I deserve a break."

"A break?" Grandma Rita rolled her eyes. "Stop acting like I put you on a chain gang. You'll get a break when you're out with your new friend this afternoon."

Olivia grinned and sat up. She grabbed some of the cobs and started peeling.

"When do I get to meet this young lady?" Grandma asked.

Olivia wasn't quick to answer. So far, she had mentioned Maureen only once or twice to her grandma because she didn't want to get her own hopes up too high. Kendra was the last girlfriend that she had ever discussed with her family, and her grandma knew how that had ended.

"In due time," Olivia said. "It's only our second date."

"A second date must mean you did something right on the first date, right?" Grandma asked.

Olivia blushed. "I guess so."

"I know so. Now get out of here and finish planting those cumbers and come back and help me finish this corn."

Olivia faked exhaustion again. "If I didn't love you as much as I do, I would go on strike."

"If I didn't love you as much as I do, I would work you only half as much. Get to work before I get my broom!"

"Yes, ma'am. But I'm filing a complaint with the proper authorities."

"I am the proper authorities!" Grandma Rita said.

It made both of them laugh, and Olivia headed back to the garden and counted down the hours.

***

Maureen put her fork down and inhaled the pesto aroma that floated around the restaurant. She watched a waiter whisk by carrying a plate of lasagna layered so thick it resembled a slice of cake.

"I think pasta's addictive," she said.

Olivia nodded. "Uh-huh."

"Your chicken scampi looks good."

"It tastes good too," Olivia said. "I've already eaten half of it. How's your spaghetti marinara?"

"It's excellent, and the bread is really soft. Here, try some."

Maureen passed a plate to Olivia who dipped a bread strip into her scampi and took a big bite.

"That's something we have in common. We both like to dip," Maureen said.

Olivia nodded and swallowed. "And we both know how to find a good meal."

"Your Chinese restaurant is now on my list of favorite places to eat."

"How'd you find this place?" Olivia asked.

"My co-workers brought me here for lunch one day, and I've been hooked ever since." Maureen spun spaghetti onto her fork and savored the oregano. She watched as Olivia dipped another piece of bread.

"Is dipping a sign of a Democrat?" she asked.

"It's a sign of a liberal who thinks both parties behave like spoiled brats," Olivia said.

"You sound like my dad. He thinks we should vote everybody out of office and replace them with CPAs who can balance the budget."

"I like the way your dad thinks. What about you? Are you hitched to the liberal wagon?"

Maureen reached for a bread strip on the plate she had passed to Olivia. "I'm hitched to any wagon that takes me by an Italian restaurant." She laughed as she dipped the bread in her sauce. "And I'm pro-anything that supports my rights as a woman--especially a gay, black woman."

"Good, that's another thing we have in common. We're three for three," Olivia said. "You now officially qualify for a free copy of my grandma's cooking newsletter."

Maureen laughed again. "Sign me up. I'm a pro with a microwave."

Maureen realized the meal was almost over, but the conversation was too good to pause now. *Should I bring up religion? Cross my fingers. Here it goes.* "Does your grandmother drag you to church before Sunday dinner?"

Olivia showed a thin smile and took a drink of water. "You have a polite and indirect way of getting information. It must be the investigator in you," she said.

"I plead guilty, Olivia. I didn't want to be direct just in case it was a sensitive subject."

"It's okay, I don't mind." Olivia took another drink. "I prefer to spend my Sunday mornings where I feel welcome," she said. "Church…isn't one of those places."

Maureen nodded that she understood. "Any place in particular?" she asked.

"With my best friend Pat and her family. Her kids love it when I show up with Egg McMuffins and hash browns."

Maureen fiddled with her napkin for a moment. "I follow my dad's advice when it comes to church. He says he can worship anywhere including the back nine of his favorite golf course."

"I really like the way he thinks," Olivia said as she placed her napkin on her plate. "Everything was delicious."

"It was. You still want to walk around the canal?"

"I do. I haven't been down to the river since I was in high school."

*** 

Maureen sat next to Olivia on a bench and crossed her legs. "I know that tune. It's by Duke Ellington."

"Are you a jazz fan?" Olivia asked.

"My mom was. She used to play it really loud in the house on Saturday mornings. She called it her wakeup music."

Olivia started tapping her foot to the beat.

Maureen noticed and asked, "Do you like to dance, Olivia?"

"Only in my living room where nobody can see me. For a colored girl, I don't have a lick of rhythm. How about you?"

"I hate to brag, but I was the best tap dancer in my first grade dance class."

"Really? Care to show off a little?"

"Never! I was the best only because nobody else could remember their right foot from their left. Let's go farther down the canal."

They stood and walked slowly, passing several couples holding hands or pushing strollers filled with wide-eyed toddlers. They reached an opening where a row of people had cast lines into the river, hoping to catch that evening's dinner.

"That brings back memories," Olivia said.

"Fishing in the river?"

"My dad and his friends loved to bring me here. We would sit for hours waiting to get a bite. I liked playing with the worms more than I liked catching the fish."

"Are your parents still together?" Maureen asked.

"My dad died just a few years ago."

"I'm sorry, Olivia."

"Thank you. He left us plenty of memories and a wonderful home he built for my mama."

They reached the end of the canal walk and sat on a bench underneath a huge oak tree with branches reaching toward the river.

"I bet this old thing could tell some stories," Olivia said.

"I bet it could. Some folks left their mark." Maureen pointed to the names carved into the bark. "You ever carve hearts and kisses into a tree?" she asked.

"Nah, the closest I came was carving my favorite Algebra teacher's name into a piece of wood in shop class."

"Sounds like a serious crush."

"For about a week until she doubled my homework for talking in class. You had any serious crushes?"

"On my home economics teacher who baked chocolate chip cookies every Friday. My mom blamed her for my sweet tooth and my first cavity." Maureen laughed.

For awhile, they watched the river flow by and could still hear the jazz band in the distance covering more Duke. Olivia spotted one of her math students walking by with his girlfriend. She waved at him and told Maureen about the students she taught. Maureen kidded her about being a numbers nerd, and Olivia teased her back about her addiction to Italian food. Before they knew it, the Sun was setting, and the music had stopped.

"Are you ready to go?" Maureen asked.

"Not really, but it's getting late," Olivia said.

They walked back to the parking area where Maureen circled Olivia's F-150.

"I like your truck, Olivia. The shine is gorgeous."

"Thanks. I've been accused of treating it like my child."

"My brother-in-law's the same way with his Mustang." Maureen checked her watch. "I want to get a short run in this evening. Where would you like to meet next time?"

"Some place where we won't be overheard by a waiter. Remember, it's our third date, and the conversation could get R-rated."

Maureen smiled. "How could I forget. Do you have a place in mind?"

"The park in Goslyn, and I'll bring lunch," Olivia said.

Maureen didn't respond but gave a look that Olivia couldn't read.

"You don't like picnics?" Olivia asked.

"Sure. It's just that…Olivia, would you mind if we got together before Saturday?"

Olivia didn't know if that was a good or bad thing. "Before Saturday?"

"If you're available. I'm free any evening after six."

"That's fine. But…are you trying to get rid of me sooner than later?" Olivia hoped that didn't sound as serious as she meant it.

"Sorry. I was being polite and indirect again. How's this--I'm dying to see you again, and I would like to do it over dinner as soon as possible."

Olivia felt a slight rush. She also felt a silly grin on her face and couldn't control it. "That was direct!"

"Good. What day?" Maureen asked.

Olivia thought for a moment. "Wednesday works for me. I'll let my students out early, and I'll meet you for dinner."

"Okay. The city has a beautiful *night garden*. We can order a pizza and have it there while we talk in private. Remember, it's our third date."

Olivia liked Maureen's confidence which boosted her own. "Yes we can. And I like extra everything on my slices."

"One more thing we have in common," Maureen said as she took Olivia by the hand and

133

rubbed Olivia's fingers with her thumb. "I'll see you Wednesday. Good night."

"Good night." Olivia leaned against her truck, swooning as she watched Maureen walk away. She thought of Grandma Rita and laughed out loud. *That lady knows I must be doing something right.*

# CHAPTER SIXTEEN

The Chairwoman gaveled the regular Wednesday Board meeting to order as security closed the auditorium doors. It was a full house as residents crowded in to give their opinion on a proposed referendum to increase the county sales tax. The Board would use the money to build two elementary schools.

Chief Anderson sat in the front row in clear view of everyone. He wanted to appear more accessible in light of the Lewis assault and the car chase. Back at his office was a list of reporters expecting a return call about the incident and a memo from Risk Management calculating the total in property damages. The thought of both gave him a headache.

The Board's clerk read several announcements that didn't seem to interest anyone other than a government watchdog group that attended and recorded every meeting. A local news cameraman was still setting up a camera aimed at the audience.

The first significant order of business concerned a proposed change to the county's refuse service. Garbage collectors would only pick up trash that was in county issued containers that were placed no more than four feet from the curb or ally entranceway. There were some groans but no objections after the clerk announced the containers were free.

Then the meeting moved on to the sales tax which got everyone's attention including Chief Anderson. Prior to the meeting, a Board member had informed him that part of the increased tax revenues could be allocated toward the new emergency response center. However, some members wanted to direct the funds toward upgrading the county's IT department and implementing the long awaited cyber-based crimes division. Chief Anderson worried that his dream of Goslyn being a major law enforcement hub would be delayed if not scrapped altogether.

A line quickly formed at the front podium and flowed back to the main entrance. The first speaker set the tone for the evening.

"Always good to see you, Madame Chairwoman," a tall man in overalls said. He adjusted the microphone mount to his height. "My name is Harold Brooks, and I'm a longtime resident of Goslyn. As a senior citizen on a fixed income, I oppose any tax increase."

The crowd gave a healthy applause, and a woman in the watchdog group angled her camcorder to get a better view of Harold.

Harold said, "In fact, the school budget should have a surplus according to an audit the Board issued two years ago." He held up a booklet with the County Seal on the front. "So it doesn't make sense to me why the county would ask us to pay more in taxes to raise money it should already have."

Another round of applause followed, louder than the first.

Harold glanced at the timer on the podium that showed a minute remaining. "I also think the Board's got its priorities wrong. Instead of having a meeting about raising taxes, this meeting should be about the crime that's taking place in this community. I have friends on the force, and I respect what they do. But there was a time when we didn't need a neighborhood watch sign posted in every neighborhood. The Board should be concerned about *that* instead of trying to take more money out of our pockets."

The applause was louder a third time as Harold put the booklet in the front pocket of his overalls. The watchdog camcorder pointed toward the chief as he tried to appear professional and unmoved.

The next dozen speakers echoed Harold's comments, and the proposed referendum started to take a backseat to a discussion on community safety.

Chief Anderson felt like his department was on trial, and that he was in enemy territory. He held his composure and tried to ignore the blinking red light on the camcorder aimed at him again.

A Board member intervened before the next speaker approached the microphone.

"Madame Chairwoman," Supervisor Cleo Jacobs said, "in light of the concerns being expressed, I think we should give Chief Anderson the opportunity to speak."

The Chairwoman agreed, and Chief Anderson stood and adjusted his uniform. He told himself not to raise his voice or pound on the podium as he approached.

"Thank you, Madame Chairwoman. As Chief of the Goslyn Police Department, I would like to reassure everyone that my department is fully committed to servicing and protecting this community each and every day. However, challenges do exist, and the main challenge is keeping pace with the county's growth." The chief hated his response. He thought it sounded like a politician reading from a teleprompter. "Of course, Goslyn PD is doing everything possible to attract the best and the brightest police officers. The Board is providing the resources necessary to help accomplish that. But we've got stiff competition from Richmond and surrounding counties. Still, our presence will be felt in every neighborhood. And I, along with my staff, are open to any and all suggestions as to how we keep Goslyn as one of the best places to live in the Commonwealth." He mentally rolled his eyes. *God, I feel like an official ass-kisser.*

"Thank you, Chief Anderson," the Chairwoman said. "The floor is still open for the next speaker."

Chief Anderson sat and listened as the meeting got back on track. No one was in favor of the tax hike, and the Supervisors mumbled among themselves whether it was worth putting it as a referendum on the next voter ballot.

The chief could see the funding for his response center slipping away and there was nothing he could do about it. He was tired and stifled a yawn that he didn't want replayed over and over again on the late news.

The Chairwoman called a ten minute recess after the next speaker approached the podium wearing a 'Death Before Taxes' T-shirt and insisted on reciting parts of the State's Constitution.

Chief Anderson followed a crowd out a side door that led to the public restrooms and a soda machine. He was tempted to walk out the main exit and head off to a private gin rummy game hosted by friends from the Rotary Club. But given how things had gone so far, he thought a reporter would probably follow him.

He was right. Just as he turned toward the soda machine, someone called out his name.

"Chief Anderson! I have a quick question for you!" It was the woman from the watchdog group. With her camcorder.

The chief cringed. "Damn it." He turned with a smile and offered a handshake.

The woman had a strong grip coupled with a sharp question. "Chief Anderson, are you aware of the Board secretly talking to Homeland Security about using taxpayer funds to build an overpriced and unnecessary emergency response center?"

"Uh…excuse me?" The chief fumbled around in his pocket for change to put in the soda machine. He hated sodas but was stalling for time. "What do you mean by secret, ma'am?" He put quarters in the coin slot and randomly made a selection. The machine buzzed as he pressed the button again. Nothing came out.

"I'm referring to a memo we obtained under the Freedom of Information Act," the woman said as she pushed her sliding black rimmed glasses back up on her sun-tanned nose.

"A memo…uh…" The chief pressed every button until finally a bottle dropped. "I'm not aware of any memo from Homeland Security, ma'am." He picked up the ice-cold bottle and clenched it firmly with both hands.

The woman stepped closer until she nearly had him backed against the machine. "I can show you a copy right now." Camcorder in one hand, she held up an iPhone in her other.

Chief Anderson didn't look at the phone's screen. He looked for an escape route instead. His hands were wet from the cold bottle sweat, and he suddenly had to use the bathroom.

"Sorry, I don't have my reading glasses," he said. "Why don't you forward a copy to my office, and I'll have my staff contact you. Excuse me."

He maneuvered around the woman who didn't give any ground. He pushed open the men's room door and immediately threw the bottle into an old, tin wastebasket sitting underneath a paper towel dispenser. The bottle made a loud thud and shook the basket. "Nosey woman," he growled as he snatched a towel from the dispenser and dried his hands. As he turned and walked to a stall, another stall door opened and a familiar but unwelcome face appeared.

"Tough crowd tonight," Harold said as he went to the sink and washed his hands.

Chief Anderson was tempted to hurl a sarcastic response but held his tongue. He and Harold were no strangers. Olivia had introduced them at a community picnic when she and Clifford Anderson were still partners. The picnic was where the two men had their first cordial disagreement about county politics. They had a few more encounters at other events--each ending with the chief thinking

Harold was a relic of the old Goslyn when people were naïve enough to leave their doors unlocked or put a spare key under a flower pot.

"Tough crowds come with the job," Chief Anderson said and brushed his mustache. He was still flustered by the reporter but didn't want it to show. Instead of going into the stall, he turned to the sink and mirror and adjusted the badge pinned to his uniform jacket. "That's why they pay me the big bucks."

Harold dried his hands and opened the door. "I'll see you in there for the next round, Chief. Say 'hello' to your son for me."

Chief Anderson took the last comment as a cheap shot. He knew that Harold, thanks to Olivia, not only knew about his strained relationship with Clifford but also knew the sordid details behind Clifford leaving the force.

"Old buzzard," he groaned to himself. He used the rest room and checked his uniform in the mirror again. "All right, let's get this over with." He opened the door and looked around the corner. *Coast is clear.* The second he stepped back into the auditorium, however, the blinking red light on the woman's camcorder greeted him. He returned to his front row seat and breathed a sigh of relief when he saw a short line of speakers waiting at the podium. Maybe he would make it to the gin rummy game after all.

# CHAPTER SEVENTEEN

A lone mosquito poked at its reflection in the *night garden's* birdbath, and lights lining the gravel walkways attracted a small entourage of playful moths.

"Did your parents ever explain sex to you?" Olivia asked.

"My dad was too freaked out to talk about it until I was in my teens," Maureen said. "But when I was eight years old, my mom called it 'baking the dough.' I was so confused. I thought the Pillsbury Doughboy was having sex whenever my mom baked one of his cakes." Maureen offered Olivia the last pepperoni on her slice of pizza. "What about your parents?" she asked.

Olivia dipped the pepperoni into a cup of pizza sauce. "When I was ten, they first tried to explain it to me by calling it the 'birds and the bees.' And my mama had these crazy names for body parts. Breasts were called 'ta-tas' and my vagina was my 'ya-ya.' But I had too many questions, so they bought a book with pictures and read it to me. You want more of this salad?" Olivia held a bowl across the picnic table.

"Yeah, the tomatoes," Maureen said as she poked her fork in. "When was your first kiss?"

"When I was twelve," Olivia said, "and it was totally by accident. I tried to tackle Pat's brother one day when we were playing football in their backyard. We crashed face-first into each other."

"Your best friend's brother was your first experience at locking lips?"

"And it was gross! He started crying, and I ran home and brushed my teeth."

"I had mine in elementary school," Maureen said. "Her name was Candice Miller. She kissed me one day in the cafeteria after I tied her shoe for her."

"Was that when you knew you were gay?" Olivia asked as she finished her pizza.

"I worried about it when I was in high school. I knew for sure when I started college."

"What about your family? Did they ever say anything to you before you knew for sure?"

"Looking back, I think everybody suspected I was gay," Maureen said. "But they never said a word. I didn't officially come out until my first year with the Agency." Maureen wiped her mouth and hands and passed a few napkins to Olivia.

"I was a brash tomboy," Olivia said. "I knew I liked girls even before I knew what the word homosexual meant."

"Did your parents know?" Maureen asked.

They knew but never used the word homosexual. Instead, they sat me down after church one day and told me it was okay to be who I was, and that they loved me. So I've always been out without making a big announcement." Olivia closed the pizza box and gave rest of the salad to Maureen. "That was good. We should order one of those again."

"That was genuine Italian pizza," Maureen said. "Here, that's for you." Maureen handed Olivia a bottled water. "Fireflies before summer," she said and pointed to the glow bugs gliding over the lilac and honeysuckles.

"I didn't know this place existed. It's really nice out here."

"I know the groundskeeper who's on duty tonight," Maureen said as she took off her jacket and folded it across her lap. "It's kind of warm this evening."

Olivia looked at the red, silk blouse Maureen was wearing. It fit her nicely and showed a little cleavage where Maureen had undone two buttons. Olivia suddenly thought about Marcus giving her dressing tips.

"Olivia," Maureen asked, "what kind of relationship are you looking for?"

Olivia cleared her throat. For a moment, she was having a private fantasy about Maureen undoing more buttons on her blouse. "I guess the kind some people call old-fashioned--a monogamous and committed one."

"Me too. Have you ever been in a bad relationship?"

"How do you mean?" Olivia asked.

"I mean abusive or disrespectful?"

"No. I've dealt with enough suspects and victims who have, and I just couldn't tolerate it personally." Olivia took off her jacket and hung it over the picnic bench. "Are you asking for a particular reason?"

"I had a couple of college friends who were, and the effects lasted for years. It's something I couldn't tolerate either. May I ask a more personal question?"

Olivia saw Maureen's eyes quickly glance down. *She's checking me out*, Olivia thought. "Is it about my choice in shirts? Blame my grandma if you don't like blue oxfords."

"I like it. It looks good on you, especially with those slacks."

Olivia liked Maureen's answer. "I've got one in pink too," she said. "So what's your question?'

"What are you looking for sexually?"

Olivia felt here eyes widened.

"I'm sorry. Was that too direct?"

"Don't apologize. It's a good question. It's just that no one's ever asked me before. Not even Kendra." Olivia took a deep breath. "I like a natural woman--no artificial appendages or other devices, if you know what I mean."

Maureen laughed. "I know what you mean. I'm partial to lips and thighs myself. And you?"

"Breasts or ta-tas, as my mama would say."

They both laughed and watched more fireflies. The groundskeeper strolled by and stopped briefly to brag about the garden. He offered to throw away the pizza box and pointed to several night butterflies floating in the air. Olivia and Maureen watched him leave before they started again. Olivia went first.

"Have you heard the term 'mutual pleasure' in a sexual context?" she asked.

"I don't think so. What is it?"

"It's when both partners care about pleasing each other."

"I get it. It's the opposite of 'wham bam thank you ma'am'."

"Right. Are you okay with that?"

"I am. I think sex is what you do *with* your partner, not what you do *to* her."

"Well said. Can I ask a more personal one?"

Maureen smiled. "I think we're in deep enough that you can ask anything."

"Okay. When was the last time you had sex?"

"Does that exclude pleasing myself?" Maureen asked without missing a beat.

"Whoa! I didn't see that one coming!" Olivia took a long swig of water and wiped her forehead with a napkin. She tried to ignore a flashing image she had created in her head of Maureen masturbating. "Yeah…it excludes that."

Maureen seemed to stiffen up. "Not since I broke up with Denise. I got to first base with a couple of dates. But…I have to be in love to have sex with someone, and I haven't been in love in a long time."

"After Kendra, the most I ever did on dates was hold hands," Olivia said, "and give a coupon for a free eggroll…good only on Thursdays after five p.m."

Maureen laughed. "I like your sense of humor, Olivia, and I want one of those coupons."

"Do you want to be in love again?" Olivia asked. She could see Maureen's shoulders relax.

"I do. Very much."

The conversation paused as the crickets started their nightly chant. The chirping grew louder until interrupted by the groundskeeper turning on sprinklers that gently showered a collection of lemon lilies.

"My grandma would be jealous if she saw this place," Olivia said.

"It's awesome. Nice flowers too." Maureen nodded to the lemon lilies.

Olivia glanced at them. "Is yellow still your new favorite color?" she asked.

"Yes, and the lilies still look as fresh as the first day."

"My whole squad room took over my roses. Marcus even had the nerve to put them on his desk."

"Sounds like something Carol would do at my office," Maureen said as she extended her legs underneath the table. She accidentally kicked Olivia. "Oh, excuse me, Olivia."

Olivia noticed that Maureen had slipped off her shoes and was barefoot. "Good to see you're not ready to leave. I have one more question."

"I'm all ears."

How do you feel about taking an HIV test if I take one too?" Olivia felt a twinge of nerves after asking. Was she being presumptuous? It was only their third date.

Maureen extended her legs again and let her bare feet rest on top of Olivia's. "I'm okay with that. Knowing we're both okay could make 'mutual pleasure' even better."

Olivia saw a sparkle in Maureen's eyes that made Olivia hot all over. "You're right. It is kind of warm this evening," she said and bucked her water bottle.

The crickets chimed in again and continued non-stop. Olivia and Maureen listened for a moment and talked more about their prior loves. Olivia shared with Maureen how she felt the day Kendra announced that she wasn't ready for a commitment. Olivia still couldn't understand how someone who seemed to love her could keep her true feelings hidden. Maureen also had had a partner who didn't tell her that her feelings had changed.

"I had another wonderful time," Maureen said as she slid her loafers back on.

"Me too, and I added this garden to my favorites list."

"Want to do it again on Saturday?"

"Absolutely," Olivia said. "We can do a daytime picnic in Goslyn, and I'll ask my grandma to pack us a lunch. You'll add her to your favorites list once you taste what *that* woman can do with tomatoes."

*** 

Olivia wiped shower steam from the bathroom mirror and dried her back. She lotioned her arms and legs and massaged her breasts before putting on her favorite terry cloth robe--a gift from Pat who had swiped it from a hotel during a family vacation in Hawaii.

Olivia couldn't stop thinking about Maureen as she went to the living room and turned on the radio. The DJ was playing his regular *Quiet Storm* session and had just cued up a classic by Gladys Knight and the Pipps. Gladys sang *If I Were Your Woman* as Olivia went to her bedroom and lay across her bed with her robe wide open. She massaged her breasts again and looked at the closet door. That's where she kept the vibrator--second shelf, tucked underneath an old college tie-dyed blanket. She laughed at herself. "I've got to change the batteries in that thing."

She then ran her fingers over her clitoris and held her hand there. She closed her eyes as an unshakeable image of Maureen doing the same danced in her head. She wondered if Maureen had the same thoughts about her.

"God, what am I thinking?" She rolled onto her side and hugged her pillow. "It's only been three dates." It was also too soon to expect anything other than a good meal and good conversation that coming Saturday.

Still, Olivia liked Maureen's frank talk about sex. She also wanted what Maureen wanted--a faithful and committed partner. That was a lot to feel good about even if it was just a third date.

"What the hell, you only live once." Olivia got up and slid on a pair of sweats and a T-shirt. She was making a trip to the local Walgreens. As she put on her jacket, the DJ announced the next slow jam--*Sexual Healing* by Marvin Gaye. Olivia rolled her eyes. "Size double-A batteries, here I come."

# CHAPTER EIGHTEEN

Summer came and went, and a month into a crisp fall of that year, the case against Calvin "CJ" Henry had become just another file in the busy Commonwealth Attorney's Office. The Assistant CA assured Olivia and Marcus that the evidence of burglary and assault was solid. He argued at CJ's bail hearing that CJ was a threat to Bertrand Lewis and a potential flight risk. The judge agreed and sent CJ back to jail where he was still waiting for a follow-up meeting with his court-appointed lawyer.

Olivia and Marcus were just as busy dealing with their own workload. They just hoped CJ didn't get lost somewhere in the shuffle or wind up dead while in custody. The Sheriff's Department had already lost CJ once in a mix-up with work-release inmates. Then they found him and his cellmate half conscious after both had snorted meth smuggled in by another inmate's girlfriend. That was another charge against CJ after two days in the hospital.

Bertrand Lewis' heart attack had left him helpless. He attended daily physical therapy to regain strength in his arms and legs after being in the hospital through the summer. He couldn't remember much about the first time he had met Malley and CJ, but he did finger CJ as his attacker. And he recalled CJ yelling something about disrespecting Malley because he didn't get his money. But Bertrand, like his cousin Bobby, had no idea where Malley and CJ had gotten the hundred twenty thousand.

So far, running CJ's mug shot in the paper

hadn't generated the typical calls--nosey neighbors or ex-drug buddies willing to throw CJ under the bus if they thought it would get them some reward money.

The best possible lead was the charred and rusted VIN number tag CSI had finally pieced together from the van fire. A Leslie Collins was the registered owner of the van, and Olivia and Marcus went to the address of record where they discovered Ms. Collins had moved out with no forwarding address. They spoke with several of Collins' neighbors and showed CJ's mug shot. Still no hits, but neighbors often saw Collins with a tall, older man. Olivia ran Collins' name through the police database and found prior drug and check kiting convictions. She checked regularly with Collins' parole officer hoping to find Collins.

"You got plans for the weekend?" Olivia asked Marcus as she looked at her computer screen and dipped a spring roll in duck sauce.

"Paint the garage before the weather gets too cold and play with my new tool set." Marcus tossed a *Popular Mechanics* into his desk drawer and looked over the rim of his eyeglasses at Olivia. "I know what you'll be doing, Miss Winston."

"Yes, my Saturday is booked *solid*." Olivia grinned. She was having a good time getting to know Maureen. Their dates would last until the late evenings and now included some weeknights. Neither wanted to be the first to hang up when they talked on the phone.

After more intimate conversations at the *night garden*, they had had Sunday dinner with each other's families. Maureen had invited Olivia to Aunt Lena and Uncle Frank's where she met everyone, including Elijah who entertained her with his non-stop giggles. At dinner, Uncle Frank reminisced about projects he had worked on with Olivia's dad.

Olivia returned the invitation and treated Maureen to roasted turkey at Grandma Rita's. The menu included an energetic greeting by the twins and a friendly interrogation by Mama Winston and Pat. Maureen took it all in stride knowing they had been there for Olivia years ago when her heart was broken.

Olivia's desk phone interrupted her thoughts about Maureen. She gulped the last bite of her spring roll and lifted the handset. "Detective Winston," she managed to mumbled with a mouthful.

"Detective, this is Richie." Jim Richie, gray and seasoned, manned the Department's main desk. He had known Olivia as far back as her rookie year.

"Hey, Sergeant. What can I do for you?"

"I've got a woman on the line who says she needs to talk to somebody about a burglary suspect. She keeps talking about a mug shot and her daughter."

Olivia put the call on speakerphone. "Put her through, Sergeant."

"Hello, who is this?!" an agitated voice asked.

"Ma'am, this is Detective Winston. How can I help you?"

The woman yelled," I need to talk to somebody right now! I have had 'nough of this shit wit' my daughter and her boyfrien' and--"

"Ma'am, ma'am," Olivia interrupted, "calm down and tell me your name!"

"My name is Betty Collins, and I'm done tryin' to take care of her babies when I been workin' twelve hour shifts at the nursin' home!"

"Who's your daughter, ma'am?"

"Leslie Collins!" Betty yelled again.

Marcus typed the name into the system and pulled out the Lewis file.

"Where's your daughter right now?" Olivia asked.

"I don't know! Somewhere wit' that damn Malley. I told her a thousan' times he was gon' drag her ass right back down in the dirt. I got granbabies here she dropped off wit' no word to nobody. I told her if she don't do somethin' 'bout this shit by the end of last week I was gon' call 'bout that boy I saw in the news early this year!"

Olivia and Marcus could hear Ms. Collins huffing through the speakerphone. It sounded like she was trying to catch her breath.

"Ms. Collins, tell us what you know about Malley," Olivia said. "Do you know where he lives?"

"Lady, I don't know and don't care. I guess wherever that crazy dope head stay at when he ain't laid out drunk wit' Leslie."

"Dope head?"

"The boy in the paper! CJ! Malley's brother!"

Olivia and Marcus looked at each other. Marcus fished a pen from his pocket and began scribbling.

"Ms. Collins, we can help you if you help us," Olivia said. "Tell me how to reach your daughter Leslie."

There was silence on the line for a moment. "Lady, I need to know what to do 'bout these babies. I cain't 'fford to lose my job messin' 'round wit' this shit. Leslie said she was gon' call me and--"

Olivia interrupted again, "Do you have a phone number for her, any number?"

Olivia and Marcus could hear the grandmother shuffling through papers.

"I got her cell phone number but she keep it turned off 'til she call me." Betty gave Olivia the number.

"When did you last talk to her?"

"Two weeks ago when I told her she need to do somethin' 'bout this. She told me she was headin' this way. She and Malley was to bring some stuff here for the babies."

"Do you know where Malley stays when he's not with Leslie?" Olivia pressed.

"I told you I don't know. All I know is he and that boy would come and go as they please somewhere in the backwoods."

"We need to come see you this afternoon, ma'am," Olivia said as she looked at Marcus. "And we'll bring whatever you need for the babies."

"That include a babysitta?" Betty snapped.

"We'll figure something out, ma'am."

Olivia took down the woman's address and listened as the woman ran down a list of supplies-- toddler size pampers, socks and tees, apple juice, and plenty of milk and cold cereal.

Marcus ran Betty Collins' name through the system and found no priors or outstanding warrants. He wanted to make sure they weren't walking into any surprises.

They set up a time for early evening. In the meantime, Olivia called in a favor and asked a plainclothes unit to do some surveillance on Betty Collins' address starting that evening and through the weekend. She wanted a heads-up if Ms. Collins had any visitors.

"You got any ideas about a babysitter?" Marcus asked and peered over his glasses.

"Nope, and I don't know how to change a pamper either."

\*\*\*

"...I'm tryin' to find an inmate, a Calvin Henry," Leslie Collins said to the deputy on the other end of the line. She swatted yet another fly that had snuck in through the hole at the bottom of the motel door. "Can you tell me if you have him?" She batted at two more of the nasty pests with a rolled-up *Good Housekeeping* magazine she had found behind the bathroom commode.

Leslie was getting fed up with Malley. It was bad enough that she had moved out of her apartment. Now she was stuck in a cheap room two counties away from her kids and waiting to hear back about a rental application.

"Yeah, I'm still here," she said as she pulled her hair back into a ponytail. The gray strands outnumbered the blonde ones. "...You have him?...Yeah, that's him."

Leslie felt like yanking the phone out of the wall after she hung up. "Why the fuck am I keepin' track of that asshole?" she said about CJ. She knew the answer. She was doing it for Malley who lay sprawled out asleep on the bed after wolfing down a large pizza and a six-pack. She knew if she kept seeing him he would do something stupid that would put both of them back in rehab or in jail. Yet she loved him, and that kept her bound to him.

Leslie swung the magazine one more time and hit her target. She didn't know if she was satisfied or disgusted at the fly mess smeared on the nightstand.

***

Olivia sniffed her leather jacket and searched through her truck's center console. "Where's my hand sanitizer?"

"I told you to stop playing with the kid," Marcus said and giggled. "Little ones pee or poop when you tickle them."

The meeting with Betty Collins had lasted over two hours. Between feeding cereal to a four-year-old and trying to dress a two-year-old, Olivia and Marcus finally got Ms. Collins settled down. Social Services would provide temporary child care for the coming week, and Betty's niece would watch the kids for the next two days.

Betty knew little about Malley other than he had spent time in rehab with Leslie. She did recall his mentioning a family house that he got from his folks. She had never been there but thought Leslie had stayed there a few times.

She gave Olivia and Marcus a trash bag full of

papers that Leslie had left behind. The detectives would look for anything that could lead them to the couple.

"It's been another long Friday, partner," Olivia said and rubbed the sanitizer between her palms.

"And busy." Marcus slouched down in his seat. "I'll start going through that bag tonight while I wait for Phyllis to pick me up. The boys have my car again."

"I'll hang late with you," Olivia said and yawned. She glanced at the clock on her dashboard.

"Sure about that? I want you fresh for your date tomorrow, Miss Winston. Besides, I owe you one for letting me handle the Henry interrogation after you made the arrest."

"Handle it? It's what you do best." Olivia yawned again. "I'll try Leslie's phone number a couple of times."

They arrived back at the squad room and entered notes on the Lewis file. Marcus refused to let Olivia open the trash bag and shooed her off. He told her to go home, and he would call her if he found anything useful.

Olivia did try Leslie Collins' number, and it rolled straight to voice mail. She decided not to leave a message. If Leslie planned to see her kids again, Olivia didn't want to spook her off.

Olivia headed home and relished the thought of sleeping late the next morning. Garden duty had ended for the year. But she knew better than to think Grandma Rita or Mama Winston wouldn't call at the first sight of sunrise with something for her to do. The upside was spending the rest of tomorrow with Maureen.

# CHAPTER NINETEEN

Malley kept his eyes on the street. "Don't park in front. Pull around the back and knock on the kitchen window. You sure your mama's home?"

Leslie swung the car around. "It's Saturday. Lunchtime. Where else would she be?" She backed the Buick into her mom's yard and popped opened the rusty trunk. She left the keys in the ignition.

Malley put on his cap and jacket with the collar up. He unloaded the bags while Leslie walked quickly up the stairs to her mom's back door and tapped on the window. They had finally showed up with pampers and milk and a week's worth of dirty laundry.

Malley waited by the car just in case someone other than Betty looked out the window. Leslie signaled him over.

Betty opened the back door and stood guard in the doorway. She was short and wide and wore a bright floral housedress that clung tight around her thick biceps and hinged up past her knees. She looked ready for battle.

"You must be out yo mind!" she said loud enough to startle the neighbor's dog across the street. "You runnin' 'roun' hidin' from the police while I had to git the County to help take care of yo babies!"

"Mama, I know," Leslie said while trying to work her way around Betty. "I promise we'll pay you back."

Malley climbed the stairs and just stood there.

Betty looked at the bags. "How you git the

money this time?" she asked.

"Betty, I know we messed up, but I swear Leslie and I didn't steal from that man or hurt him. CJ had to be high, and it all went wrong."

Betty said nothing, and Leslie sat down on the porch and nervously tugged at her ponytail.

Malley put down the bags and pleaded, "Betty, all I need is just a few hours here to think, then I'll go to my place."

"And then what? You got plans for Leslie and the babies?"

"Mama, my apartment came through this morning in Richmond," Leslie said as she stood up. "Me and the boys can move in next week, and I found a job too."

Betty stepped aside and let her in. She blocked the door again when Malley picked up the bags.

"I swear, Betty, just a few hours," he pleaded again.

Betty finally allowed him in but scowled at the laundry bag he left on the porch.

*\*\**

Olivia held out the spoon and tucked one hand under it to catch any drippings. "Be honest, how is it this time?" Olivia, with Grandma Rita's help, had been honing her culinary skills so she could impress Maureen.

Maureen tried the marinara sauce once more. "Another dash of oregano," she said as she took parmesan bread out of Olivia's oven and stirred a pitcher of ice tea. Maureen confessed to being hopeless at cooking but an expert at ordering takeout and microwaving popcorn.

"Okay, one more taste test," Olivia said. This was her third try at making a sauce that didn't taste like ketchup. She held the spoon again as Maureen took a taste. She watched and felt a tingle behind her ears that ran down her back.

"Mmm! Pour it on the spaghetti and let's eat."

"The bread smells good. Where'd you get it?" Olivia asked as she sat across from Maureen.

"I stopped by a bakery in Richmond." Maureen broke off a piece and dipped it in her sauce. She reached across the table and offered to place it in Olivia's mouth.

Olivia got that tingling feeling again and, for a second, forgot to chew as she looked into those brown eyes smiling at her. She managed to say, "Keep doing that, Ms. Jeffries, and we'll never finish lunch." But those same brown eyes told her that Maureen was just getting started.

"Did you know some people say tomatoes are a 'feel good' food?" Maureen asked. She soaked a larger piece this time and took a bite before offering the rest to Olivia.

Olivia opened her mouth and took it in.

Maureen used her thumb and forefinger to wipe Olivia's lips and slowly wiped her own with the same fingers. "Feeling good, Miss Winston?" she asked.

Olivia blushed as a heat wave moved down her back and across her thighs.

Maureen laughed and reached out to hold Olivia's hand.

"If tomatoes make you flirt like this, I'm starting my own garden next spring," Olivia said.

"It's easy flirting with you." Maureen entwined her fingers with Olivia's.

Olivia squeezed Maureen's hand and looked into her eyes. She couldn't resist flirting back. "I think I've heard one or two things about tomatoes too," she said.

"Really? Tell me."

"I've heard that just one bite of a tomato makes you want to kiss the woman sitting across from you." Olivia waited for approval. Until now, she and Maureen had shared only light kisses on the cheek and brief hugs at the end of their dates. Their sexual attraction was strong but restrained. Neither wanted to move too fast or create any expectations.

"I've heard the same," Maureen said.

*Approved.* Olivia, seizing the moment, released Maureen's hand and stood. She stepped closer until she was looking down at the gorgeous, brown woman. She bent and brushed her lips over Maureen's slightly open mouth and pressed gently until she felt Maureen's mouth open wider. She opened wider too and felt Maureen's hand on the back of her head. The kiss was deep.

Olivia pulled away slowly and saw a familiar sparkle in Maureen's eyes.

Maureen rose out of her seat and wrapped her arms around Olivia. She then whispered in Olivia's ear, "My turn." She ran her hands down Olivia's back and up to her shoulders.

Olivia pressed closer. Nothing compared to feeling Maureen's breasts touching hers. The soft beat between her legs was telling her so.

Maureen kissed Olivia on her ear and cheek

and brushed the tip of her tongue across Olivia's brow. She continued down to Olivia's nose and lips where she used her tongue to open Olivia's mouth and slide inside.

Olivia heard herself moan as her tongue rubbed against Maureen's. She could feel Maureen's firm thighs pressing against her and realized she might come right there.

Maureen slowly removed her tongue and brushed her lips against Olivia's. She whispered again, "We need more tomatoes."

Olivia laughed. One quick kiss was followed by another. "Our spaghetti's getting cold," she said.

Maureen licked her lips. "I'm still hot. Let's do this again for dessert."

\*\*\*

Malley was nursing a cup of coffee at the kitchen sink and could hear Leslie on the bedroom phone talking to her cousin who was babysitting Leslie's kids. Leslie was still too paranoid to use her cell phone. They had been at Betty's for four hours--long enough to use most of the hot water taking showers and running the washing machine.

Malley heard the floorboards creak and knew it was Betty approaching. She arrived at the archway between the kitchen and living room and stood with her hands on her hips.

"I need to git some rest then go to work. When you leavin'?" Betty asked as she looked at Malley and waited for an answer.

Malley looked at the cheap, faded clock on the wall. It was a minute before five. He downed his coffee and snatched his jacket from the back of the kitchen chair. "I'll take Leslie to see the babies on my way home."

Malley hadn't been back to the trailer since CJ was arrested. He had been to the house several times by taking a back road and walking up through the woods. The house set back on a wooded lot separate from the trailer, and neither was visible from the main road.

The senior Malcolm Henry had built their home with his bare hands a year before Malley was born. It was a classic three-bedroom log cabin with a stone fireplace and a ceiling that boasted large, wooden support beams. And a vegetable garden took up the entire backyard. Nobody would have guessed that Lucille Henry, a former schoolteacher from Danville, had home-schooled her three boys there. She had kept her sons in line.

She and Malcolm, Sr., had also kept their boys close at hand--so close that the family never set foot in Mr. Brooks' 'Grand Central Station' post office and had stayed off the local rumor mill radar.

The Henrys had good reason to be reclusive. They were an interracial couple in the Commonwealth and hoped Goslyn was a safe place to settle and start a family. Malcolm, Sr., after a brief stint as an Army engineer, had worked days as a farm hand and nights as a moonshine runner until he could afford the private wooded lots. He used any extra money to make low interest loans to county officials who regularly "misplaced" taxpayer dollars and to businessmen who blew their profits in card games before they made it home to their wives. The loans gave some guarantee that any locals, troubled by a white man living with a black woman, wouldn't harass him and Lucille.

They still had a good life after Malcolm, Sr.'s, death twenty years ago. Ronnie and Calvin were in their early twenties and Malley in his mid-thirties. Malley, taught by his dad how to build a house from the ground up, used his skills to help support the family.

Lucille Henry maintained a decent life for her sons, and all three continued to live at home. But she wanted CJ, her youngest, to be more independent. So she bought a trailer for him to live in on the other lot. After her death five years ago, CJ slowly lost his way despite help from Malley. Ronnie dabbled in get-rich-quick schemes and went off on his own. Malley, as the oldest, felt like he had failed his parents by not keeping his brothers together. He used beer to drown the guilt--guilt that grew deeper each time he had to manhandle CJ after catching him rummaging through the house for money to buy drugs. Life at the Henry home was nothing like it used to be.

Malley put on his jacket and picked up the bag of pampers. Leslie quickly packed her things and kissed her mom on the cheek. She opened the back door but turned before stepping out.

"It'll be okay, mama," she said. "I promise."

Malley forced himself to look Betty in the eye. He had no idea how things would turn out. He was sure of only two things--that he would do anything to stay out of jail and that he desperately wanted another drink.

"Take care, Betty," he said. He followed Leslie

and closed the door behind him.

***

"Think you have an ice cream addiction?" Maureen asked as she and Olivia left the grocery store.

"For any kind that's got chocolate in it," Olivia said.

Lunch had ended with more flirting and kissing and had left Maureen craving for something sweet. She easily talked Olivia into making a junk food run. Hershey Kisses and a half-gallon of royal fudge would be dessert as she and Olivia planned to spend rest of the day watching a classic movie channel.

"What's your favorite movie of all time?" Maureen asked on the way back to her car.

"The original *Heat of the Night* with Sidney Poitier," Olivia said.

"Good one. I also like him in *Buck and the Preacher.*"

"So do I, but don't ever mention that to my grandma. She thinks *Guess Who's Coming to Dinner* is the best movie he ever made. "What's your favorite movie?" Olivia asked.

"*Inherit the Wind* with Spencer Tracy."

"I don't think I've seen that one."

"We can watch the DVD at my place next week," Maureen said.

Olivia's phone rang just as she tore open the Hershey bag. "Hey, partner. Don't tell me you're in the squad room on a Saturday?"

"Painting the garage was supposed to be a family affair until everybody bailed on me," Marcus said. "I came in to finish going through that stuff we got from Betty Collins. I got a message from the front desk that your plainclothes friends spotted a man and a woman pulling out of the alley behind Betty's house. They think it was Malley and Leslie. The man dropped the woman off at a 7-Eleven."

"I owe them big," Olivia said. She glanced over at Maureen and knew their plans were about to change.

"They couldn't get a clear look at the tags and lost him somewhere off of Bailwick," Marcus said. "I think I know where he's headed though."

Olivia could hear Marcus flipping pages.

"I found pieces of torn up letters from the County Tax Assessor's Office. They look like past due notices for taxes owed by a Lucille Henry--two lots located on Government Road. Had you chased CJ another fifty yards into those woods, you would've been on Malley's front doorstep."

"You mean the dirt road where he crashed the van?" Olivia noticed Maureen was on the street that led directly to the county's police department. "Hold on a second, Marcus." She looked at Maureen, "You can drop me off, and I'll get a ride home."

"No way. I wanna play too. You guys have a freezer for the royal fudge?"

167

# CHAPTER TWENTY

Willie watched as Tony lit his pipe and filled his lungs with smoke. Tony held his breath for a second and exhaled as he leaned back against the ATV parked in the high, thick grass.

"Damn, that's good," Tony said. "I feel like I'm ridin' a train." His hands were shaking, and he cocked one ear to the tree line."You hear that, man?"

"Stop trippin'," Willie said. "You know you hear crazy shit when you get high. Help me bag this stuff and don't take none of it. I need to get some other stuff from the trailer and wake up Pete."

Willie and Tony regularly cooked up small meth batches in the trailer by using items they stole from the local Walmart. It was enough to make some quick cash selling it Friday and Saturday nights at a local club.

The trailer stank of heavy chemicals and rotten trash. One hot spark or a dropped match on the tax files that were scattered on the floor would blow up or burn down the place in minutes.

It was CJ's trailer but after Willie and Tony had introduced CJ to meth with a free hit, it was easy for them to take over the double-wide. The more meth CJ wanted, the more desperate he became to find a way to pay for it. Half out of his mind one day as he fought withdrawal, he'd gone to Malley begging for money. Malley, drunk and angry, ranted about Bertrand Lewis stiffing him on the one hundred twenty thousand. That's when CJ made Bertrand a target.

Willie and Tony were lookouts on the three break-ins as CJ tossed files and laptops out the back door of each office and into a van he had stolen from Leslie. After breaking into the third office, Willie and Tony took a handful of papers with names, social security numbers, and dates of birth then disappeared for awhile.

CJ, however, didn't know what to do even after his brother, Ronnie, had coached him on how to get credit cards and fraudulent tax refunds. CJ just wanted cash. So Ronnie gave him a couple thousand for the files and the master client list.

While Willie and Tony were hiding out, CJ and more of his drug buddies found another meth dealer in the city and smoked their way through the entire two grand within a week. When the drugs were gone and CJ had come down from his high, he wanted to do it all over again. But he was broke and knew better than to ask Malley. So he went back to the well--Bertrand Lewis--with the intent of getting money regardless of how he had to do it. He found Bertrand, and the encounter put CJ behind bars and Bertrand in a hospital bed.

Willie and Tony waited several weeks after CJ was arrested before they returned to the trailer. So far, it was business as usual. They even let one of their club customers, Pete, use it to sleep off his highs as long as he kept being a customer. Nobody cared that Malley didn't want them on the property. Willie and Tony had no respect for a man too drunk to stop people from taking advantage of his baby brother. But they feared him enough not to step foot into the Henry home.

"Pete! Wake up, man! Time to go!" Willie kicked the bare mattress on the trailer's bedroom floor. A long body wrapped underneath a dirty blanket slowly moved. "Pete, time to go!"

The body moaned and sat up. "What time is it?"

"Half past late! Get up and go home!"

Pete pulled the blanket off his head and staggered to his feet. Hair tangled and matted on one side and eyes barely open, he crept to the front of the trailer and down the steps. "Which way, man?" he asked Willie who was right behind him.

"The way you go all the time. Walk to the house and take the path on the other side of the bushes. Move, man! We gotta get ready for the club tonight."

Pete pulled his hoodie over his head and wandered off as fast as a man with a hangover could move.

Tony was doing donuts with the ATV in the high grass behind the trailer. He hooped and hollered like a cowboy at a rodeo.

Willie shouted out the back door, "Tony! Tony!" Willie cared more about the duffle bag strapped to the back of the ATV than about Tony flying off and breaking his neck. He wasted a good five minutes shouting.

Tony kept going until he couldn't steer straight. He finally stopped, jumped off, and fell on his face.

Willie ran over and checked the bag. "Man, you gotta stop acting crazy before we go do business."

Tony, pale and emaciated, got up and tugged at

his shirt pocket. "I…I need to go…" He dug out his meth pipe and headed toward the trailer.

"Hey, man, we need to go to my house and get ready for the club. Tony!" Willie was wasting his breath.

Tony went through the back door and dropped right in the spot where Pete had been minutes before. Pipe in one hand and a lighter in the other, he smoked another hit and lay out on the bare mattress.

Willie knew he wouldn't be leaving any time soon unless he left Tony behind. But he couldn't do that because Tony watched for cops at the front of the club while he sold his meth in the back. Tony had done this plenty of times--"taste tested" the product before selling it. He would stay on that filthy mattress at least another hour and do one more test.

Willie checked the duffle bag and went inside the trailer where he turned on a mini propane burner that he used to cook his batches. He lit a joint on the burner and took quick puffs as he kicked around half-empty bottles of nail polish and Drano that littered the trailer floor--both key ingredients to making his meth. The chemicals spilled out and flowed across the crooked wooden panels.

\*\*\*

Malley unlocked the back door of his home and mumbled to himself, "Welcome back." He looked around and was glad the place still looked decent despite all the chaos. He had Leslie to thank for that. She loved the place as much as he did and always cleaned up after him. He had left her at a 7-

Eleven a few blocks from her cousin's place so she could walk rest of the way. He thought if the cops were following him, they would stick with him and leave her alone. She and her kids could stay with their cousin until the new apartment was ready. In the meantime, Malley planned to clean out the trailer, dump everything in a barrel, and burn it. If only he knew what to do about CJ.

He checked the fridge--frozen pizza and flat soda. He opened the pantry--Ramen Noodles and Campbell's chicken soup. Malley knew he should eat something to get drinking off his mind. That last six-pack yesterday at the motel was another mistake he tried to forget, and the coffee at Betty's didn't help much to keep him awake. He decided to lie down. *Damn, I'm tired.* He closed his eyes and was out like a light.

***

Olivia looked over Marcus' shoulder. "See if you can find it on Google," she said.

Marcus typed in the information from one of the torn tax notices and pulled up directions to the Henry property. As he zoomed in on the satellite images, a lead plainclothes officer looked over Marcus' other shoulder and turned to a whiteboard to draw a rough outline of the lots. Two other officers where there and would assist with bringing Malley in for questioning.

"That's a big piece of property and well overgrown," the lead officer said.

The images showed two lots, the second uphill from the first and both surrounded by thick woods and divided by low bushes. A one-story house sat on the first lot, and a double-wide trailer sat on the second. The main dirt road was a hundred yards long and split in-two at the front of each lot. The trailer lay another twenty yards back from its property line.

"Here's what we'll do." The lead officer sketched out a plan. He and the other officers would be in one vehicle followed by Olivia and Marcus in another. Maureen would follow in third position. Two officers would approach the front door of the house. The lead officer, with the detectives, would cover the sides and back. Maureen would stay with the vehicles and provide additional coverage. If Malley was there, the officers would take him into custody. If not, everyone would approach the trailer the same way as they had approached the house.

The officers headed out first in an unmarked van. Marcus went to the equipment room for three Kevlar vests while Maureen called her supervisor to give her a quick rundown. Olivia checked and re-holstered her sidearm and typed notes into the Lewis file. She looked up and caught Maureen looking right back at her.

*Please let this go right tonight,* Olivia thought.

Maureen flipped her phone shut and walked over to Olivia's desk. "I didn't know dating you would be this exciting," she said.

"Neither did I. Be careful out there. I've got another tomato recipe I want to try out on you." Olivia stood and gave Maureen a quick kiss.

Marcus returned and handed each a vest and Maureen a two-way radio. "Time to roll, ladies."

\*\*\*

173

Twenty minutes later, the three vehicles gathered in the parking lot at a gas station less than a mile from the Henry place. Everyone reviewed the layout of the property one more time and a more recent description of Malley that Betty Collins had given: a light-skinned, black male about six feet tall, mid to late fifties, a hundred eighty to two hundred pounds with short, black hair. They loaded up again and headed down Government Road.

*** 

Pete hadn't made it far. His hangover was killing him, and he craved a hit. He had missed the footpath and was leaning on the trunk of a car parked on the far side of the Henry house. He needed to rest for a moment and clear his head. He sat on the rear bumper and nodded off.

***

"Crap!" Willie had stepped in a greasy pizza box on the floor and dropped his joint into a moldy pile of hamburger wrappers.

Tony was on the bedroom mattress and struggling to get his lighter to work. "C'mon, baby, burn. Hey, Willie!" he yelled down the hall. "I need a light!" Tony staggered to his feet. "My damn lighter won't work, man! Give me a light!" He walked to the front of the trailer, flipping the lighter switch again and again. He gave up and tossed it to the floor.

Willie was on his knees picking through the wrappers. "Man, I ain't got time for your…Tony, look out!"

The lighter had sparked on impact and landed in a puddle of nail polish. Willie jumped up and ran toward the flame, intending to stomp it out. But his foot slipped on the tax files, and his left arm hit and flipped over the burner. The burner singed the papers and the trash on contact and further fueled the polish.

***

The police van pulled onto the dirt road, and the two cars followed. Everyone kept an eye on the high grass.

Olivia was especially caution as she remembered chasing down CJ. She said over the radio, "Maureen, check out the path to your right. Looks like four-wheeler tracks. Could be a back way to the property. "

Maureen slowed for a second and scanned the area.

As the van reached the split in the road and turned, it suddenly sped up. Over the radio the detectives and Maureen heard, *We got movement at far side of the house.* The van's side door flew open and out jumped two of the officers who took off running with weapons drawn.

"Police! Down on your knees!" both officers yelled at a man in a hoodie.

Pete fell off the bumper and quickly hopped to his feet. He hurled himself into the woods and tumbled downhill without regard for life or limb. The two officers leapt in and slid right behind him.

Olivia and Marcus quickly got out and gave cover on the house as the lead officer approached the front door.

He banged and shouted, "Gosling PD!" He banged again. "Open the door!"

175

Olivia stood on the front porch while Marcus moved to the near side of the house and headed toward the back.

Maureen gave cover by the driver's side of the van. She scanned the area to her left where Marcus was cautiously moving. She then looked behind her then back toward the woods where the two officers had run. As she looked to her right, she saw chimney smoke coming from the trailer. *Somebody's home,* she thought. She then saw smoke coming out the front door and a flame flash up from the backside of the roof.

***

"Stomp it!" Willie choked out.

Smoke billowed up the broken chimney flue as Willie and Tony tried to stop the fire. Papers were burning hot and fast. Flames had quickly ignited old nail polish bottles and spread up a wall and out the kitchen window. Trash bags started to melt, and Drano bottles popped and spat more chemicals out onto the floor.

Willie took off his jacket and swung wildly at the flames while Tony picked up burning trash with his bare hands and threw it out the front door. They both froze when they heard a roaring gust of air. The spreading flames had ignited a gas can used to fill up the ATV, and part of the back deck was now on fire.

***

"Fire on the hill!" Maureen yelled.

Everyone turned and looked. Olivia moved off the porch, and Marcus ran to the front of the house.

Maureen started uphill to the trailer with Olivia

on her heels. A shot rang out from the woods behind them. It was where the two officers had chased the suspect. Marcus and the lead officer ran in the direction of the gunshot.

***

Malley stumbled out of bed from a deep sleep. He thought he heard footsteps run across the porch, and he rushed to the living room. He looked out the front window and saw flames coming from the trailer. "Those damn fools!" He opened the front door but quickly slammed it shut after seeing the van out front. *Cops?* He looked out the window again and saw a woman running toward the trailer. "Who the hell is that?" He wasn't going to stick around to find out.

He rushed back to the bedroom, grabbed his phone off the bed, and ran back to the living room for his jacket and hat. He wouldn't chance taking the car.

*Out the back and up to Bailwick.*

He squatted down by the kitchen door and quietly opened it. After one quick look, he dashed out and through the overgrown garden.

***

"Chuck, Mike, where you at?" the lead officer yelled over his radio. He and Marcus tripped and stumbled over dead branches.

The radio crackled back, "Boss, this is Chuck! I busted my damn ankle. My gun went off. Mike's chasing the guy down to the old railroad tracks."

"Where you at, Chuck?"

"In a drop-off about thirty feet over to the right."

177

***

Maureen ran to the back of the trailer where fire engulfed the entire deck.

Olivia followed her but turned around when she heard a scream.

Willie had jumped out the front door, running for his life as flames burned through his shirt.

Olivia ran after the man and clipped him from behind. "Roll, damn it, roll!" She ripped off her jacket and used it to smother the flames.

Willie cried out in pain and shook before going still.

Olivia pulled her radio of her belt and called in, "This is unit ninety-eight! Need EMS now! Fire at location!"

At the back of the trailer, the fire and heat pushed Maureen away as she looked for a way in. She turned to the field behind her when she heard a motor crank and spotted a man speeding through the high grass on an ATV. She struggled to give chase then turned back and ran toward the front of the trailer. She thought the rider was heading for the path that led to the dirt road. If she could get to her car, she could cut him off.

When she reached the side of the trailer, the back suddenly collapsed, the propane burner exploded, and it shot straight up through the dangling roof. It banked off the chimney and flew like a wild flare over Maureen's head.

"Maureen!" Olivia shouted as she ran to the side. The two women nearly collided. They grabbed and held each other by the arms for a split second.

"Got a runner!" Maureen said and pointed to

178

the high grass. She sprinted down to her car. As she jumped into her Impala, she heard the ATV's loud motor in the distance. She slammed her car into reverse and punched the gas.

***

Tony's scorched hands were throbbing, and he struggled to hold onto the handlebars. Every bump in the path sent sharp pains through his palms and up his forearms. If he could make it to the dirt road, he could ride another mile down Government Road then ditch the ATV in the woods and head to his house on foot.

"What the…!" He spotted a car speeding at him--in reverse.

Maureen saw the man over her shoulder and knew she had to stop him. Her car and her foot speed were no match against his ATV if he crossed over into another part of the woods. She punched the gas harder and jerked the wheel to the right, aiming the back end of her car for the end of the path.

Tony made a quick sharp turn away, and the ATV leaned low to one side. He overcorrected, and the four-wheeler bucked like a bronco and tossed him high into the air. He came down like a rock on the car's rear window, bounced off, and rolled across the road and into the grass. He stopped spread-eagled and facedown.

The Impala's window caved when Maureen hit her brakes. She jumped out with her weapon aimed at the man's back. "Show me your hands!" she yelled and kicked his foot. She heard him moan and saw one of his hands move. It was blistered and red.

As she holstered her gun, he suddenly rolled over and threw a wild kick that hit Maureen on her hip and drove her back against her car. He got up and stumbled a few steps before Maureen tackled him from behind and pinned him to the ground with her knee. Olivia ran down the road and helped Maureen cuff him.

"Gun shot!" Maureen blurted out and pointed back to the house.

"Yeah, I radioed Marcus," Olivia said. "Everybody's okay, but we got the wrong guy. Who's this?"

Maureen rolled the man over. "He doesn't match the description."

Maureen and Olivia stood him up and put him in the backseat just as fire and EMS arrived followed by two police units.

The trailer was gone except for the front walls and the concrete steps.

Olivia heard Marcus over the radio, "Olivia, we're coming back your way."

Olivia radioed back, "We got one in custody and backup on the house. Going in now."

At the house, two officers covered the rear as another kicked in the front door. He entered the property followed by his partner and Olivia.

"Goslyn PD!" he shouted. "Show yourself!"

"Clear on this side!" the other officer yelled as he checked the bathroom.

Olivia checked the first and second bedrooms. She went to the third and saw a disheveled bed. She felt the sheets. "Still warm," she said to the officer covering her back. She checked the closet where she found a pair of men's work boots and a construction helmet. "Clear!" she yelled.

Everyone gathered on the front porch and came down from the adrenaline rush. They watched as firefighters hosed down the collapsed trailer and smoldering debris.

Willie was conscious and tried to sit up as EMS lifted him onto a gurney.

Marcus and the three officers returned through the woods with Pete in custody after pulling him out of an old boxcar. Pete babbled on about running because he was scared, that he didn't know anybody who lived on the property, and that he was taking a short cut to get to a convenience store. He provided a battered photo ID that he kept shoved down in his sock. Olivia asked him if he worked in construction. Pete claimed he was a janitor at a furniture store, and he rattled off a phone number she could call to verify.

"Call in a search team," Olivia told the lead officer. "I think our guy's on foot and close by." She walked back into the Henry home with Marcus and Maureen behind her.

Marcus sighed as he looked around the house. "This is not how I planned to spend my Saturday evening," he said.

"Neither did we," Olivia said and looked at Maureen. "There goes a night of royal fudge and chocolate Kisses."

# CHAPTER TWENTY-ONE

The squad room was buzzing with chatter by the time Olivia and Marcus had returned from the Henry property. Word had spread about the fire, and everyone--from the night patrol units to the front desk attendant--wanted to know what had happened. The arresting officers took their injured partner to a nearby outpatient medical center after they had dropped Pete off at central booking. Pete would stay in lockup until the police had followed up on his ID and contacted his employer. Both Willie and Tony were in the county's ER and facing a charge of manufacturing a controlled substance. Given all the empty containers at the scene, the Fire Crew Chief was amazed that the flames hadn't spread to the surrounding woods. A few tax files did survive--the ones Tony had thrown out the front door. However, the Fire Marshall wasn't letting anyone near the site until a HAZMAT team gave the okay.

A K-9 unit was still searching the dense woods around the property. At last check, the dog had tracked the bedroom scent to a gas station and to a bus stop. The trail went cold from there.

Nothing in the Henry house directly connected to the Lewis burglaries. But Marcus found a possible Atlanta connection. Searching through the kitchen cabinets, he ran across money wire receipts that listed Leslie Collins as the recipient and a "W.R. South" in Atlanta as the sender. He showed them to Olivia and Maureen who both recalled a similar name that appeared in the chat room printout. Maureen contacted her Atlanta team and asked them to pay a visit to the local Western Union office from where the sender had wired the money.

Olivia had searched an old teacher's desk where she found family photos. Most were of three boys in their early to late teens. The name Calvin James "CJ" appeared on the back of one. A second had the name Malcolm "Malley" Jr., and a third read Wm. Ronald "Ronnie." The resemblance between Malley and Ronnie was striking.

Olivia and Marcus completed a search of the home minutes before a local news crew showed up looking for a breaking story.

As the squad room settled down, Marcus was tempted to doze off.

"Is this day over yet?" he asked as he rubbed his eyes.

"No, and I'm hungry," Olivia said as she stared at her computer screen. "Have we updated everything?"

"I think so." Marcus looked around the squad room. "Where's Maureen?"

"In the lobby calling her insurance agent. She's trying to get a loaner car for her Impala." Olivia stretched and rested her head on her desk.

Marcus laughed. "I didn't know your girlfriend was a stunt driver, Olivia."

Olivia looked up and grinned. "She scared the crap out of that guy."

Tony had gone on a tirade when EMS tried to treat his hands at the scene. He threatened to sue Maureen for attempted murder and accused her of planting the meth on the back of the ATV.

Maureen entered the squad room just as Olivia and Marcus gave a simultaneous yawn.

"I'm sleepy too," she said, "and I'm starving."

"That makes two of you." Marcus pointed to Olivia.

"Any luck?" Olivia asked.

"Yeah, my agent can meet me tomorrow afternoon. He said I could leave the car here in the Department's garage, and he'll set up a rental for me in Richmond on Monday." Maureen slouched down at an empty desk. "That means we need a ride back to your place, Olivia."

Olivia looked at Marcus. "Pretty please? I hate trying to sign out a car at this hour."

Marcus stood and yawned again. "Okay, but no pit-stops for spring rolls and duck sauce."

"I need to stop by the garage first to get a bag out of my trunk," Maureen said.

"All right, ladies. Let's roll."

\*\*\*

Olivia went straight for her couch the second she opened her apartment door. Maureen crashed in an overstuffed chair. They could fall asleep right where they sat. Maureen checked her watch. It was almost twelve thirty. She gave a loud groan that caught Olivia's attention.

"I feel the same way," Olivia said. Her clothes smelled of smoke, and she was thinking of steamed chicken with mixed vegetables. She started to take off her shoes but remembered she had to drive Maureen back to Richmond. She looked over at her and saw Maureen's eyes closed and her head resting back on the chair. She couldn't stop staring.

184

*Those soft lips and that beautiful brown skin.* Olivia enjoyed the view and called softly, "Maureen?" She heard a faint snore in response. She decided to take a shower and then make the trip to Richmond. She tossed a blanket over Maureen and went to her bedroom.

***

A half hour later, Maureen was still asleep and had taken off her shoes and pulled the blanket up tight around her shoulders.

Olivia was in the kitchen re-heating some marinara sauce and parmesan bread. She opened the fridge to get the pitcher of tea. When she closed it, there stood Maureen.

"Hey, gorgeous, did you dream about me?"

Maureen gave a sleepy smile. "Yeah. And about some loudmouth that I ran over with my car."

"Are you ready to go home?" Olivia asked reluctantly.

"Would you mind if I slept on your couch? I don't think either one of us should be driving this late." Maureen leaned against the fridge and sighed.

*YES.* "Sure. No problem," Olivia said with a high pitch followed by a slight giggle. "Do you need something to sleep in?"

"I have some stuff in my bag that I put in your truck."

Olivia grabbed her keys off the kitchen table and rushed for the door. "Watch the sauce. I'll be right back." She was gone before Maureen could say a word.

***

Maureen rang out the dishcloth and wiped off

185

the kitchen table. "Dinner at one thirty in the morning--that was a first," she said.

"I once ate sardines and peanut butter for breakfast while studying for a stats exam." Olivia rinsed the last dish and placed it on the drying rack.

Maureen handed Olivia their empty glasses and looked at her from behind from head to toe as Olivia stood facing the sink.

Olivia wore one of her many Lincoln High T-shirts, a pair of fleece shorts, and a pair of Nike crew socks that her godsons gave her every year for Christmas.

Maureen too had showered before dinner and wore a pair of boxers, sweat socks, and a Washington Wizards Tee. She felt as comfortable in Olivia's apartment as she did in her own home.

"What time do you have to meet the insurance guy?" Olivia asked.

"He said it would be around two o'clock." Maureen walked into the living room, picked up the blanket from the chair, and placed it on the couch. She dug through her bag. "I'll be right back. I need to brush my teeth."

Olivia turned off the kitchen light and checked the front door lock. She grabbed sheets from the hall closet and spread them on the couch along with a pillow. When she heard the bathroom door open, she sat on the arm of the chair opposite the couch.

"You didn't have to do that," Maureen said as she looked at her sleeping spot for the night. She walked over and kissed Olivia on the forehead and lips. She then sat on the couch and looked straight at Olivia with a smile. She could feel an energy pulsating between them.

Olivia rattled off, "I need to brush too and go to bed. You need anything?"

"No. I'm good, Olivia. Good night."

Maureen watched Olivia leave the room before she stretched out on the couch. She knew exactly what those brown eyes were asking. Was it too soon for them to make love? They had talked plenty about their sexual attraction for each other, and Maureen had experienced her share of wet dreams about Olivia in the past months. For both of them, sex was an emotional investment, an investment Maureen felt ready to make personally. Yet it could change things between them professionally. In the end, they still had cases to solve. And the job came first.

*Stop thinking and just tell her,* Maureen told herself.

Olivia made a beeline back to the living room when Maureen called her name.

"Yeah?"

"You feel like talking?" Maureen asked as she stood in front of the couch. She took Olivia by the hand, and they sat. "Something's been on my mind since we kissed at lunch." She held on to Olivia's hand and brushed her thumb across Olivia's fingers. "I'm falling in love with you." She felt her shoulders tense up as she looked into Olivia's eyes.

As if on cue, Olivia kissed her. She pressed harder, and Maureen's mouth opened to her tongue. Maureen responded in kind, and the kiss was long and wet.

Olivia then whispered, "I'm falling in love with

you too." She kissed Maureen's hand and said, "And now what?"

"I know what comes next, but what happens Monday morning?"

Olivia ran her hands through Maureen's hair and held both her hands. "The same thing that happened tonight. We keep catching bad guys, even if you have to drive like James Bond to do it."

Maureen laughed.

"But seriously, Maureen, I expect you to be the professional you've been since the day I met you. I could never ask you to change the way you work a case just for me, and I couldn't do it for you."

"You're right," Maureen said. "It has to be that way."

"Let's make a promise. If one of us is bothered by what the other is doing on her case, we say so. Promise?"

"Promise. Now kiss me again!"

"Hold that thought."

Olivia stood, pulled Maureen up with her, and turned on the CD player. She wrapped her arms around Maureen and kissed her again.

Anita Baker's voice came through the speakers. "Caught Up In The Rapture" was one of Maureen's favorite songs.

"You are so good," Maureen said.

"It's easy with you." Olivia held her tighter. "Bedroom?"

"Bedroom," Maureen answered back.

Olivia led the way as Anita kept singing.

Olivia pulled back the covers and sat at the foot of the queen size bed. She guided Maureen in close between her legs, ran her hands up the back inside of Maureen's shorts, and gently squeezed her firm cheeks. They both moved onto the bed.

Maureen straddled Olivia and slowly pushed up the Lincoln High T-shirt while leaving kisses on Olivia's brow, nose, and lips where she gently sucked until her hands reached their goal. Olivia's nipples were erect and ready. Off came the T-shirt. Maureen planted the next kiss perfectly between Olivia's breasts and stroked one of Olivia's nipples with her tongue. Olivia's moan told Maureen it felt good, and that she wanted more. Maureen stroked the other nipple. She then lay on top of Olivia.

"My turn," Olivia said as she rolled Maureen onto her back. Inch by inch, she pushed up Maureen's T-shirt, leaving a trail of kisses--first, on Maureen's navel then across her stomach, stopping only to let her tongue play with Maureen's tight abs. Next, she kissed Maureen between her breasts and on a hard nipple that she gently sucked. Maureen arched her back and spread her legs. Olivia responded by licking the other nipple. Up and over Maureen's head went the Wizards Tee. And between her legs went Olivia's thigh.

Olivia continued with more kisses--first, on Maureen's neck, then cheek, and ear. She said, "Tell me how this feels." Her firm thigh muscle pressed slowly up against Maureen.

The answer was clear. "Take off my shorts," Maureen said.

Olivia didn't hesitate. She sat up and ran her hands over Maureen's breasts and down to her waist where she pulled at Maureen's shorts.

Maureen raised her hips as the shorts and panties slipped from underneath her, down her legs, and past her ankles. She watched Olivia until Olivia stood at the foot of the bed looking down at her. She could see Olivia's eyes roaming up and down her body, and they seemed to glow when they landed on the wet jet-black curls clinging to her thighs.

Maureen moved toward Olivia. "Need any help?" she asked. Olivia nodded and Maureen ran her fingers around the waistband of Olivia's shorts and pulled until the fleece and panties dropped to Olivia's ankles. She traced a line with her finger from Olivia's navel down to the short dark curls and to the tip of Olivia's wet warm folds. She heard Olivia inhale…and exhale before pulling Olivia down onto the bed and on top of her. As she glided her hands down Olivia's back, she rolled her over and took top position. She whispered, "Can I look at you too?"

Olivia nodded again, and Maureen sat up on her knees and moved past Olivia's hips. She gently pressed her hands against the inside of Olivia's thighs.

Olivia raised her knees and opened her legs wide to let Maureen in.

Maureen gazed at Olivia's swollen clitoris and ran her hands down Olivia's thighs to her soft spot and through the moist curls. The feeling aroused her even more. "Thank you," she said as she lay back on top of Olivia. She wanted to show just how much she wanted Olivia now.

She retraced the familiar path with one finger-- from Olivia's navel, over Olivia's mound and down to her clitoris, stimulating the outer lips and slowly stimulating the inner ones. She gently touched the round swollen spot with her thumb and felt it throbbing.

Olivia opened her legs wider. "Harder," she said.

Maureen rubbed back and forth with her thumb and could hear Olivia's breathing grow faster.

Olivia closed her eyes and grabbed at the sheets as if trying to hold on. Her mouth opened as her hips lifted off the bed. Her body vibrated as Maureen continued to stroke her. She stiffened for a long moment and blurted out, "Perfect!" Her breathing slowed, and her eyes fluttered open as she lowered her hips back onto the bed.

"Perfect?" Maureen asked.

Olivia managed to laugh. "You wanna try it?"

Maureen rolled over, and Olivia went down to her new favorite place--Maureen's navel. She kissed Maureen there and massaged her mound. The kisses moved up as the massaging moved down where Olivia ran her fingers through Maureen's wet folds.

Maureen moaned when Olivia's fingers touched her clitoris, and her breaths grew short and quick. She felt Olivia's wet curls pressing against her side as Olivia moved up and kissed her on the mouth. She started to come as Olivia made steady strokes, and a warmth flowed through her from head to toe. At her peak, she spread her legs and wrapped them around Olivia. She came down more than satisfied.

"Are you feeling good, Miss Jeffries?" Olivia

asked.

"All over, Miss Winston," Maureen said when she caught her breath. "Give me a second, and I'll be ready for the next round."

Olivia laughed again. "I'm already thinking about round three."

"I like your confidence." Maureen rolled onto her side and faced Olivia. "And I could spend ever night like this."

Olivia grinned. "So could I."

Maureen rolled Olivia onto her back, and with a kiss on Olivia's collarbone, she was ready for round two.

# CHAPTER TWENTY-TWO

The cell phone vibrated against the metal lamp and jarred Olivia awake. She reached for it on the nightstand with her eyes half open. "Hello?" she mumbled and accidentally hit the speakerphone button.

"Thank goodness you answered!" Mama Winston said. "Tell me you're okay!"

"Morning, Mama." Olivia thumbed off the speakerphone and rubbed the sleep from her eyes. "What time is it?"

"Don't change the subject! Are you okay?"

Olivia looked down at Maureen who was firmly planted on top of her. She was better than okay. She was in love again. "Why? What's wrong?"

"You tell me. Have you seen the news? Were you at that trailer fire last night?"

Olivia didn't want to think about last night except for Maureen being wrapped around her the entire time. But she didn't want to lie to her mom either.

"I was there," she said, "and I'm fine--not a scratch." At that moment, Maureen got up and headed for the bathroom. Olivia watched until the long, brown legs disappeared behind the bathroom door.

"What happened?" Mama Winston asked. "The news said the place was some kind of drug lab, and the police are looking for a man who lived on the property."

Olivia hated the local news sometimes,

especially when her mom wanted a rundown on the latest Goslyn crime.

"Mama, you know I can't get into details. I'll tell you what I can, at dinner."

Olivia heard the toilet flush followed by running water. She rubbed her eyes again in anticipation of the view to come and wasn't disappointed. The bathroom door opened and Maureen stood naked, drying her hands on a towel. Olivia watched her as she briefly stretched in front of the bathroom mirror and combed her fingers through her hair. She came back to bed and lay in the same position with the covers pulled over both of them.

For a moment, Olivia forgot she was on the phone until she heard her mom's clock chime in the background.

"Am I interrupting something?" Mama Winston asked.

"Oh...sorry, Mama. Do you need me to bring anything for supper?"

"No, we're good. Say good morning to Maureen for me."

"What!"

"Ollie, I have excellent hearing, and I wasn't born yesterday. Is she coming to dinner?"

Olivia didn't know what to say. She was a grown woman but still embarrassed at having a naked woman on top of her while she talked on the phone with her mom.

"I don't think so, but I'll ask," she said.

"All right. I love you."

"Love you too, Mama." Olivia hung up and

groaned as she looked at the time on her phone. "Six a.m. That woman never sleeps in."

"She's funny," Maureen said.

Olivia groaned again. "I'm still exhausted."

"Me too. Can you set your phone alarm for noon? I don't want to miss my insurance guy."

"Okay." Olivia keyed in the time and slid the phone back on the nightstand. "By the way, you were wonderful last night," she said.

"Thanks. You get an A-plus too." Maureen kissed Olivia on her chest. "Should I come to dinner tonight?"

Olivia chuckled. "Only if you want to be interrogated by a professional."

\*\*\*

Malley tucked the Greyhound bus ticket into his back pocket and sipped on bitter coffee from the station's vending machine. He had walked and taken bus rides all night between the county and city before making his way to Leslie's cousin's house at one in the morning. He crashed there on the couch from exhaustion. Leslie gave him money that Ronnie had wired to her, and her cousin brought him to the Greyhound station for a trip to Atlanta. He had no choice but to leave Goslyn after hearing the morning news.

According to Channel Six, there was an overnight fire at a trailer on Government Road. One suspect was in custody and two were in the hospital being treated for burns. Authorities found evidence of meth being produced in the trailer and were looking for a fourth suspect who was wanted for questioning in an assault and three burglaries.

Authorities had yet to release the fourth suspect's name or description but were expected to do so in the next twenty-four hours.

Malley called Ronnie after he had hopped on the first bus, and the two had argued. Malley tried to explain what had happened and that he couldn't go back home or stay in Goslyn anymore. Ronnie went off on a rant about Malley and CJ messing up everything for him. He told Malley that he wouldn't play babysitter to his big brother who couldn't stay sober. And he wasn't going to help his slow-wit baby brother who would probably spend the next ten years in prison.

Malley, in a hail of profanity, reminded Ronnie again that his hands were just as dirty. Ronnie gave in and agreed to call in favors from friends who could set Malley up with a place to stay when he got to Atlanta.

Malley was now trying to blend in with a morning crowd at the bus station. His nerves were on edge as he looked for a corner to huddle in before his boarding time. He feared falling asleep and waking up in handcuffs.

\*\*\*

Olivia swore she smelled cinnamon as she hugged her pillow and snuggled deeper under the covers. She rolled over and felt around the bed. No Maureen. She jumped up and grabbed her cell phone. "No alarm?"

She searched for her shorts and T-shirt on the floor, but they were gone. Maureen's clothes were gone too. She wrapped the bed cover around her and followed her nose.

"This is easier than I thought," Maureen said to herself and loaded the toaster again with more cinnamon bread. She checked the pot of grits on the stove and stirred in a spoonful of butter. She was going to cook at least one decent meal for Olivia.

She had gotten up an hour ahead of the alarm and canceled it, not wanting to wake Olivia who was sound asleep. As she had looked at her girlfriend sleeping, she thought to herself, *Life does go on after Denise.*

She had showered, thrown on a pair of jeans and a sweater, and tidied up the bedroom. It had been so long since she had shared a bed with anyone, she was no longer sure of proper etiquette.

"Hey, sleeping beauty, you hungry?" she asked as Olivia entered wrapped in a comforter.

"I am." Olivia was all smiles. She walked over to the stove and gave Maureen a big hug from behind.

"I hope you like everything. I raided your fridge."

Olivia kissed Maureen on the back of her neck. "I'm sure it's all good." She planted another kiss.

"Easy, sexy." Maureen reached around and patted Olivia on the behind. "Don't forget I've got an appointment."

"I'll be back in a jiffy," Olivia said and headed for the shower. She detoured to the bedroom when she heard her phone. One look at the number on the display and she knew what to expect.

"Pat, I'm not telling you anything!" she said.

"C'mon. How was it? And don't give me the

PG version."

"Pat, you and my mama have no shame!"

"And your point?" Pat asked.

Mama Winston had spread the Sunday news about her wakeup call to Olivia. By that evening, Olivia would be too embarrassed to show her face at Grandma Rita's for dinner.

"If I had a point it wouldn't matter because you wouldn't listen anyway." Olivia hunted through her dresser drawer for a pair of jeans and a sweatshirt.

"You're right," Pat said. "So give me the good parts and feel free to use sound effects."

Olivia couldn't resist laughing. She loved the way her best friend showed how much she cared. Pat was still the playful person she was when they were kids.

"No good parts or sound effects," Olivia said but paused for a second. "But you were right. Sometimes a first love can't be your only love. Now I'm hanging up."

"Don't you dare! I'll hack into your e-mail and delete your address book."

Olivia heard Maureen rattling in the kitchen. "Oh, yeah? When was the last time you were audited?"

\*\*\*

Olivia entered the squad room after dropping Maureen off at the Department's garage. It was a good time to sort out the next steps in her case as she settled in at her desk.

The first step was to put the public on notice about Malcolm Henry, Jr. She hesitated, however, when it came to his girlfriend, Leslie Collins. The police spotted Leslie with Malley, CJ was driving her van, and her name was on the Western Union receipts. It all implicated her. Yet Olivia couldn't get the two young Collins kids out of her head. *They deserve to have a mom regardless,* she thought.

Still, Olivia knew her personal feelings couldn't stop her from doing her job. In the end, it was about doing the right thing.

As she typed and sent an e-mail to the Department's media rep regarding Malley, she had an idea about Leslie. She searched for a phone number in the Lewis file and dialed. The phone rang twice then a third time. Maybe it would roll to voice mail again.

***

Austin Collins was so busy shooting zombies that he dropped the phone into his popcorn bowl. He fished it out after the third ring. "Hello?" he said.

"Hey, this is Ollie. Is Malley there?"

"Nah, he left this morning. What's your name again?" The young boy had enough sense to ask but was too distracted by the video game to care.

"Ollie. I need to talk to Malley about Ronnie."

"You know Ronnie?!" Austin yelled into the phone. "He's cool, man. He gave me this cool game."

"Yeah, I heard he did. You know where Malley went?"

"Nah, my sister, Dee, took him somewhere this morning. You wanna talk to my cousin Leslie? She's outside hanging up clothes."

"Tell her it's Ronnie's friend."

Austin yelled, "Leslie, phone! Somebody for Ronnie!"

"Boy, stop yellin,' " Leslie said when she came through the back door. She answered the phone, "Who is this?"

"Leslie, this is Detective Winston. You need to talk to me right now." Olivia sounded emphatic.

Leslie pulled at her gray strands. "Shit. I cain't deal with this no more!"

"I know he was there, Leslie. Think long and hard about your kids before you tell me a lie."

"Listen, I love my kids, and I cain't go back to jail." Leslie scrambled around her cousin's kitchen looking for a cigarette. "I don't know what CJ did. But I know Malley didn't hurt nobody." She tried lighting the cigarette over the stove pilot but couldn't steady her hand. She gave up, grabbed a beer from the fridge, and paced the floor.

"Leslie, don't put your kids through this. It'll be a long time before you see them again if you go down with CJ and Malley. And you know your mom can't take care of them by herself."

For a moment, neither spoke. Then the detective continued.

"*You* helped Malley stay one step ahead of us. CJ was driving y*our* van. *You* are the money contact between Malley and his brother Ronnie. You left a trail, Leslie, and I followed it right to you. Where is he?"

Leslie started to cry and walked out the back door. She sat underneath the sheets that hung from the clotheslines and flapped in the cool fall air. As her kids ran around the backyard, their screams and laughter only made her cry more.

"He took the bus to Atlanta this mornin'--the eight o'clock bus," she said through sobs.

"You did the right thing, Leslie."

***

Olivia knew she couldn't have more sympathy for Leslie than she did for Bertrand Lewis. He was the victim, after all, despite his poor judgment. She felt callous anyway. She logged off her computer and wanted to go home.

Maureen came into the squad room waving a set of car keys. "My agent is awesome," she said. "My loaner car is a brand new Impala."

Olivia looked at her with a frown.

"What's wrong?" Maureen asked.

"Malley's headed for Atlanta."

"So we know where to look. That's good news, right?"

"But I feel like an ass. I just threatened his girlfriend with losing her kids if she didn't cooperate." Olivia slouched back in her chair and sighed.

Maureen sat in a chair next to Olivia's desk. "How old are the kids?"

"Four and two. I met them at their grandmother's house. I even fed one of them, and the other one peed on me. Sometimes, this job sucks."

"Olivia, she should know better," Maureen said. "She's responsible for her kids, not you." Maureen stood behind Olivia and massaged her shoulders.

"I know, but--"

201

"No buts, Olivia. You've been doing this job a long time, and you know some people make bad choices. It's good you still have your compassion." Maureen gently patted Olivia's shoulders.

"I guess so," Olivia said, but she still couldn't get the two toddlers out of her head. "Maureen, you ever wonder what kind of parent you would've been?" she asked.

"Sometimes, when I'm babysitting Elijah. At this point, I think I'd need to clone myself just to keep up with a little one. What about you?"

"When I'm hanging out with the twins. They're so much like their mom when she was a kid-- curious about everything. I love to make them laugh, but they're more than a handful."

"I know what you mean. I don't know how Gloria and Wallace are getting through Elijah's 'terrible-twos.' I run for cover when he throws a tantrum."

Olivia sighed again. "All right. Enough of my pity party." Olivia kissed Maureen on the hand. "What's the deal with your car?"

"My agent brought me a rental, and the glass repair shop will fix my window on site here tomorrow."

"How'd you get so lucky?"

"You know Goslyn, Olivia. It seems no matter how much this place grows, you can still find somebody who knows somebody. My agent's on a bowling team with the Department's head mechanic and the glass shop owner." Maureen pulled up a chair and sat. "What's the next move on your case?" she asked.

"To show Malley's driver's license photo to the Greyhound employees and see if a ticket was purchased in his name." Olivia logged back into her computer. During the search of the Henry property, she found Malley's vehicle registration in the car there, and she obtained his photo from DMV. "Then I need to confirm that he got on the right bus and its arrival time in Atlanta." She looked at the time on her computer screen. "He's got about a six hour head-start by now. I could use your help in getting his photo to Atlanta PD in the next couple of hours."

"I know who to call," Maureen said as she got up and sat on a desk across from Olivia. "But I've got an idea. Why not have Atlanta hold off on executing the warrant and tail Malley instead? He may run straight to his brother."

Olivia was uneasy with the plan, and the frown on her face showed it. She stood and briefly paced behind her chair.

"That's risky," she said as she sat next to Maureen. "I can't let a suspect roam around another city in another State if I've got the papers to lock him up. We're talking about a man connected to three break-ins and who might've used his brother to beat down another man. And there's the meth trailer we found in throwing distance of his front door." Olivia returned to her desk but got a sense that Maureen, who was biting her bottom lip, wasn't convinced. "Are we on the same page?" Olivia asked.

"I'm on board," Maureen said. "Just a little anxious about my case going nowhere. What else can I do to help?"

"Give me a minute. I need to call Marcus and fill him in. He hates it when I play solo cop."

"That's right!" a voice boomed from the entranceway. "And don't bother calling!" Marcus trudged in. "I'm here."

"What happened to you?!" Olivia asked.

"My children happened to me!" Neon yellow paint streaked through Marcus' hair and covered his overalls, and his left sneaker had no shoelace. "This is what happens when you ask two teenagers and a six-year-old to help paint a garage. And it's *still* not finished!" Marcus flopped down at his desk. "This time, I bailed on them."

"One day you're going to look back and laugh at days like this," Maureen said.

"That's what my wife keeps telling me. I still don't believe her. What fun am I missing?"

Olivia quickly updated Marcus. They were facing a tight time frame. Malley would be stepping off a bus in Atlanta by that evening. They split up a To-do list and went to work. Marcus called Lieutenant Beal and immediately apologized for interrupting her Sunday afternoon. He knew she would have to call in a favor with the Commonwealth Attorney to get the ball rolling. So he made a note to chip in a little more for her Christmas gift--a new set of aroma candles and a personal supply of decaf.

Maureen called her contacts in the Atlanta DA's Office and faxed Malley's photo. They were on standby for the Virginia warrant and extradition papers.

Olivia, after confirming that the bus to Atlanta was scheduled to arrive at ten thirty, headed to the local Greyhound station. She crossed her fingers that this would be the final chase to get Malley. She also hoped that Mama Winston wouldn't ring her up at six a.m. the next morning expecting another news report.

# CHAPTER TWENTY-THREE

The entire house smelled of cinnamon as Grandma Rita took the candied yams out of her oven and placed them on a cooling rack. Mama Winston had set the pot roast and mashed potatoes on the dining room table and was buttering the handmade biscuits.

Olivia tried to busy herself with rearranging copies of her grandma's *Soap Digest* in the living room. She checked her cell phone again, hoping it would ring at any minute.

She closed her eyes for a moment and thought back over the day and last night with Maureen. She couldn't believe the last twenty-four hours--a meth trailer burned to the ground, three more arrests, and a girlfriend who was as tough as she was smart. And making love with her girlfriend who had grown up just minutes away. Olivia felt like she'd been dropped into a movie with a script she couldn't have imagined.

She and Maureen didn't talk much after they'd left the squad room for the evening. Maureen had picked up her things from Olivia's place and left to have dinner with her aunt and uncle. She told Olivia that she wanted to spend some time with them before the weekend ended. She would then drive back to Richmond. Olivia thought Maureen seemed distracted but didn't think much of it. She knew they had experienced more in one day than most officers would experience in a career.

"Okay, it's time to eat," Grandma Rita announced. "Ollie, tell Harold everything's ready."

"Yes, ma'am." Olivia went to her grandma's den. "Dinner's ready, Mr. Brooks. Who's winning?"

"The Wizards are up by two baskets." Mr. Brooks turned off the radio and followed Olivia to the dining room.

Everyone took their places at the table, and Mama Winston said a prayer for her Haitian students. Olivia, knowing her family, readied herself for the hundreds of questions that everyone was dying to ask about her case--and about Maureen.

***

Olivia turned on her radio to stay awake and grabbed two pillows from her couch and lay down on her living room floor. It was a quarter to nine, and she was still waiting to hear from her lieutenant. Marcus had texted her saying he would stay at the squad room for another hour then go home.

Her phone rang just as the radio DJ finished the weather report and cued up an Anita Baker ballad. She, of course, recognized the calling number.

"Hey, gorgeous, are you home yet?"

"I'm leaving now," Maureen said. "I just wanted to call…for an update."

"We're still waiting. The wheels of justice turn slow on weekends." Olivia could tell there was more. "You okay?" she asked.

Maureen sighed. "I'm just irritated with this case--my case. Every week the news slams my agency about these crooks ripping off taxpayers. And no matter how many we catch, another one pops up like some damn mole. We're always playing catch up with these guys, and I'm sick of it!"

Olivia waited a moment before speaking. She then said, "Feel better now?"

Maureen sighed again. "Not really."

"Maureen, remember what you said to me about Leslie Collins? You said it was good I still had compassion."

"I remember."

"You care about what you do, Maureen. If you didn't, this case wouldn't bother you so much." Olivia realized she sounded like her mom. "Did I just sound like a school teacher?"

Maureen gave another sigh. "I can tell you were raised by a very good one."

"I'll tell her you said so."

"Thanks for not letting me have my way about tailing Malley. It was a bad idea."

"I knew you wouldn't respect me in the morning if I did."

"There's something else, Olivia."

Olivia sat up at the tone in Maureen's voice. She swallowed hard and listened.

"I've been thinking about us," Maureen said, "...us making love last night. Olivia, I haven't been in a real relationship in a long time. So I don't know if I'm moving too fast--"

Olivia had to interrupt to get her heart out of her throat. "Are you having regrets? Just tell me if you are." She leaned against the couch to stop a sinking feeling she hadn't experienced since her breakup with Kendra years ago.

"No, Olivia, I'm not having any regrets,"

Maureen said. "I know how I feel about you. I just never thought I'd be in love again so quickly. And...I don't want it to end when your case is over."

Olivia put her hand on her chest and felt her heart pounding. She lay back on the pillows and smiled for a moment as her sense of humor kicked in. "Are you saying I should've made you more marinara sauce before you let me see your ta-tas?"

Maureen laughed. "Not exactly, but it's close. I just want you to know about us."

"I'm serious about us too, but I understand if you want to slow things down to catch your breath."

"I don't want to slow down, Olivia. I just want to know if we're moving at the same pace and in the same direction."

"I'm right beside you all the way. I would tell you if I wasn't. Okay?"

"Okay."

Olivia exhaled just as she heard Maureen do the same. Her call waiting beeped. "Hold on, Maureen."

"Tell me you got good news, partner."

"It's done," Marcus said. "The papers are being sent to Atlanta as we speak, and I'm outta here."

"See you in the morning." Olivia clicked back over to Maureen. "We got it!"

"Finally. I guess we'll be in Atlanta together?"

"I totally forgot about that. This case has got me sleep-deprived." It hadn't crossed Olivia's mind until now that their lieutenant would send her and Marcus to extradite Malley back to Goslyn after the IRS questioned him about his brother Ronnie.

"We've got some time before his bus arrives," Olivia said. "Anything else on your mind?"

"Only you. But I really should go home before I'm too sleepy to drive."

"I've heard that line before."

They both giggled like teenagers.

"I promise we'll have another sleepover," Maureen said. "Good night, Olivia."

"Good night, Maureen." Olivia put her cell phone next to the pillows. It was going to be another long night.

# CHAPTER TWENTY-FOUR

Ronnie Henry stood on the apartment balcony in the brisk Atlanta fall air. He hated Malley right now. He had no idea where to hide his brother after two friends had backed out. They had heard Ronnie complain about his relatives in Virginia and didn't want any part of the drama. Ronnie knew Malley was dragging him deep into a nightmare with no clear way out.

He went back inside to the bedroom and checked his Rolex on the dresser. He got back into bed, kissed Keith Claiborne on the shoulder, and gently tugged at Keith's long braids.

"Hey, handsome, wake up."

Keith rolled over and wrapped his boyfriend in a bear hug. "Oh, you're cold!"

Ronnie kissed him and teased his goatee. "I was outside thinking."

Keith was one of the reasons why Ronnie loved being in Atlanta. They had met at a downtown café where Ronnie and a friend were seated outside and testing out a stolen laptop. The friend was using a Wi-Fi signal to hack into the customer account list of a bookstore nearby. Keith had pulled up in an expensive convertible and hopped right out in front of them. He knew he had caught Ronnie's eye, and he winked at Ronnie as he walked into the café. Ronnie had tried to be discreet when it came to his attraction to men but had indulged himself enough to get a reputation among locals on the nightclub scene.

Before pulling off, Keith had handed Ronnie a

business card and told him to call if he wanted to go for a ride. Ronnie accepted the offer, and two years later, they were still seeing each other. Ronnie reluctantly told Keith exactly how he made his money. But Keith didn't pass judgment. His work as a car thief didn't put him on any higher moral ground.

Ronnie leaned back against the headboard. "Take a quick shower, and I'll fix you a sandwich."

He watched Keith get out of bed wearing a pair of black briefs and rubbing his brown bare chest as he headed to the bathroom. Seeing Keith like that usually made Ronnie want to stay in bed with him for hours. But his mind was racing around too many things right now. Should he put Malley up at a local motel? Should he pay his condo manager to let Malley stay in one of the vacant units? What about the apartment complex next door?

Ronnie knew he didn't want Malley staying with him. They'd tear each other apart. No way was he going to put up with Malley looking down his nose at him because of how he made his money--the same money Malley had no problem asking for when he needed help. And Ronnie wasn't in the mood to deal with his big brother's backhanded, queer comments. He had suffered enough of those insults after their mom had died. But he had to do something.

*** 

An unmarked SUV waited across the street from the Greyhound station's main entrance. Malley's photo was taped to the vehicle's dashboard.

"Gonzalez, stop dropping your damn crumbs in the backseat!" Sergeant Billups, head of the Fugitive Task Force, ordered as he looked in the rearview mirror. The sergeant was cranky about missing the Hawks' ten o'clock tipoff against the Lakers.

"Sorry, Sarge. Just trying out a new energy bar." Officer Gonzalez licked the chocolate wafers and wiped her mouth with the back of her hand. "These are good. Want one?"

"No! Next time, eat before we leave the office!"

"Yes, sir."

Officer Miller nudged Gonzalez in the side. "You're as bad as my wife eating cookies in bed."

The sergeant's radio beeped, and he heard, "Sarge, this is Mullins, over."

"Go ahead, Mullins."

"The Virginia bus arrives in half an hour, and the target's on board, over."

"All right. You stay inside with the station's security guard. Smitty, Atkins, you both there?"

The radio beeped back, "This is Smitty, Sarge. We hear you, over."

"Split up and hang close around the arrival area."

A second security guard stood outside and would give the signal when the bus was in sight. The original plan was to grab the target as soon as he got off the bus. But the station was crowded inside and out, and the risk of someone getting hurt was high. The Task Force would instead watch the target exit the bus and hoped he would quickly

213

separate from the other passengers and leave the station on foot. If it looked like the target was headed for a vehicle, the officers would be forced to stop him immediately.

***

Malley yawned and got a whiff of his own bad breath. He was finally awake after sleeping through a layover in Charlotte, and he started to replay in his head the instructions he got from Ronnie. When his bus pulled into the station, he was to call a cell number that Ronnie had given him and let it ring three times then hang up. When he got off the bus, he was to stay close to other passengers and cross the intersection to the corner brick building that was on the same side of the street as the station. He was to keep walking pass the building for two long blocks until he reached an overpass. At the overpass, he was to wait no more than thirty seconds. If no one was following him, a black convertible with the top down would approach from behind, and the driver would give the name "KC." That was his ride to Ronnie's. If the car didn't approach in thirty seconds, there was a problem, and it was every man for himself.

As the bus reached the interstate exit, Malley started to think about a drink. He hadn't touched a beer since that last six-pack in Goslyn, and he was feeling the effects. His hands were clammy, and his stomach burned. He wondered if a 7-Eleven was close by.

*Keep your head on straight,* he told himself.

***

The station security guard gave the hand signal

214

to the SUV at ten twenty-five.

Sergeant Billups called out over the radio, "Look alive, team. It's show time."

The officers in the arrival area tried to move closer to where the bus would unload, but the area was jammed with passengers and their bags. They tried to position themselves to get a visual on the target when he got off the bus. It was getting harder as the crowd grew.

"Sarge, this is Smitty," the sergeant heard over his radio. "We're gonna need eyes on both ends of the bus."

"All right. Gonzalez and Miller will get out on foot."

The two officers, in their unmarked jackets, made a beeline for the front and rear side of the corner brick building opposite the station's arrival area.

*\*\*\**

Keith nervously picked at his goatee and drummed his fingers against the steering wheel of his convertible. He pulled his cell phone out and dialed. "Did he call?"

"Yeah, he called," Ronnie said. "Give 'em about twenty minutes to come your way."

"Okay. I'm ready." Keith hung up and checked his car's gas gauge again. He was parked in an alley just before the overpass and had agreed to pick Malley up. He knew all the back streets and could quickly get back to Ronnie's place.

*\*\*\**

Ronnie looked back over his shoulder at the station and flipped up the collar on his jacket. He had given up on trying to scope out any undercover cops and headed back to his car. The station crowd was too big, and he was too impatient. He was still an amateur at that part of the game anyway despite all the coaching he got from Keith.

***

Malley's stomach cramped, and the bus felt the size of a phone booth. He pulled his duffle bag from the overhead compartment and sat back down. A dozen or more people were in front of him waiting for the driver to open the door. He felt faint and thought about using the bathroom in the rear of the bus. But passengers near the back were up and blocking his way. *Hold on 'til you get off this damn thing.* He looked out the window and saw an obstacle course of people and luggage. He decided to wait until everyone else was off then he would go to the rear.

***

Sergeant Billups did a double-take as a man walked toward the SUV. He looked at the photo on the dashboard again. *Is that him?* He stared at the younger man who approached and passed right in front of him. He called over his radio, "Smitty, did the target get off the bus?!"

"Not yet. The driver just opened the doors, over."

The sergeant checked the photo again and the issue date of the license. The photo was only six years old. "That can't be the target." He got out and walked to the corner where he could see the man get into a dark colored Audi parked half a block away. He was close enough to read the front plate.

216

He called out over his radio, "Listen up, team. Either the target did a Houdini, or he's got family here. I got eyes on a man out front who looks like our guy."

"What's the plan, Sarge?" Smitty radioed back.

"Stay with the bus and stand by."

Back in the SUV, the sergeant ran the plates. They came back registered to a car dealership--one well known to Atlanta PD.

"All right, team, we're baggin' two for one tonight," Sarge radioed. "We'll stick with the bus. I'll have somebody come take a look at this other guy."

*\*\**

The line finally moved, and Malley made his way back to the bathroom. He splashed his face with cold water and relieved himself. It didn't stop his stomach from reminding him that he needed a cold one. He turned up his jacket collar, pulled his baseball cap down tight on his head, and looked in the mirror. "Okay. Cross the street and two blocks down."

A few people were ahead of him as he made his way to the front of the bus. A crowd waited at the foot of the door to get their luggage from the bus' undercarriage. He looked out the bus windows again and saw a sea of people. Another bus was parked in front, and two more were double-parked on the other side and unloading more passengers.

*\*\**

An unmarked cruiser followed another past the Audi. Both circled back and parked a block behind the car. The lead cruiser radioed Sergeant Billups,

"This is unit eight-twelve. Vehicle in sight. How you wanna do this?"

"Stand by," the sergeant said.

The cruisers waited and watched the Audi and its driver. The lead cruiser then heard the sergeant.

"Unit eight-twelve, I'm going in. The second you see me crossing the street, you roll up and take him down. Use all caution, he could be related to our target."

***

Ronnie's mind was racing again, and he couldn't stop venting out loud. "God damn it! Can't believe I'm at the fuckin' bus station!"

He looked briefly at a man crossing the street but was too angry to pick up on the signs that the man was a cop--signs like the man adjusting his sleeve to hide a radio mic and tugging at the hem of his jacket to hide his sidearm.

Ronnie turned the car radio to a random station and pulled out the disposable phone he had used to call Malley. He played with the dial buttons, but the phone reminded him why he was there. He was tempted to break it in half and throw it out the window. He smacked it against the car's gearshift instead and shoved it into the glove box. A split second later, he heard a voice that made his heart stop.

"Driver, let me see your hands!"
***

Malley lifted the duffle bag on his right shoulder to help hide his face. He stepped off the bus and immediately bumped into one passenger and another. Before he knew it, he was moving toward the station instead of toward the street. The musty body heat from the crowd made him feel worse, and he didn't think he could stand up much longer.

\*\*\*

Officer Smitty hopped onto a pile of suitcases and called out over his radio, "I think I see him, Sarge. Black duffle bag and black baseball cap. I got too many bodies between us."

\*\*\*

Sergeant Billups stood inside the front doors of the station and spoke into his hidden mic, "Gonzalez, Miller, get off the corners and get across the street."

The officers had to maneuver between the double-parked buses and the passengers who had just unloaded.

\*\*\*

Malley dropped his duffle bag, stooped down, and leaned against a trash can. He took off his cap and struggled out of his jacket as people shuffled around him. Disoriented by the crowd, he couldn't tell which direction to go to get to the intersection. His mind said, W*alk back to the bus and cross the street.*

\*\*\*

Sergeant Billups scanned the many faces as he looked around the station. "Talk to me, people! Anybody got a visual on the target? The damn place ain't that big!"

Officer Atkins radioed back, "I got nothing but pissed off passengers yelling about a handbag. Crap! Somebody threw a punch!"

*\*\**

The commotion snapped Malley to attention and to his feet. He tucked his hat and jacket under his arm and picked up his bag. He tried to make his way back to the bus as the crowd moved in three directions--some pushing toward the commotion, some heading into the station, others fleeing into the street. Malley fell in with the street crowd. He moved quickly toward the buses, stepped behind one, and came out on the other side of the two double-parked ones. He crossed the street and headed to the front of the brick building. Still swayed by the momentum of the fleeing crowd, he tried to walk inconspicuously. He turned in front of the building and started the two-block march.

*\*\**

The officer cuffed Ronnie and padded him down. "You got any weapons on you? Anything that could stick me?"

"No, sir. What's this about, sir?" Ronnie asked.

The officer didn't answer. He pulled Ronnie's wallet out of his back pocket and opened it. "This your driver's license?"

"Yes, sir."

"This your car?"

"No, sir, it's a loaner from a dealership."

The officer's partner fiddled with the broken phone she found in the glove box. Another officer was checking the trunk while a third stood in front of the Audi with her hand on her sidearm.

"Who loaned it to you?" the officer asked.

*Fuck, don't tell me Keith gave me a hot car.* "I guess the guy who owns the dealership, sir. I got it while they work on my car." Ronnie was scrambling for something that would make sense if they checked his story. He did leave his car at the dealership owned by one of Keith's associates. It wasn't for repairs though. It was to have a stolen high-end sound system installed.

The officer escorted Ronnie back to his cruiser. "Watch your head." He stuffed him into the backseat and buckled him in.

"Officer, why am I being arrested?"

Still no response. The officer spoke into his hand radio, "This is unit eight-twelve requesting a tow truck."

\*\*\*

Malley looked up at the overpass to reassure himself as he counted out loud, "Fifteen… twenty…twenty-five…thirty." He watched as a car approached. It wasn't the black convertible, and he counted again. Another car approached at a high speed and stopped on a dime. The top was down, and Malley looked at the driver.

A young man with braids twisted into a ponytail sat behind the wheel. "I'm KC! You ready to go?"

Malley didn't hesitate. He tossed everything in the back and squeezed himself into the front.

Keith raised the top, pumped the gas, and sped off into the night.

\*\*\*

Sergeant Billups threw his jacket on the hood of the SUV. "We blew this one," he said to his crew as they assembled outside the station. By the time they and security had restored order, the sergeant

221

knew the target had slipped passed them.

"I guess you still owe Agent Jeffries a favor, huh, Sarge?" Gonzalez asked as she unwrapped a candy bar.

The sergeant snatched the chocolate wafers, bit a chunk, and grumbled, "Maybe not. I got a feeling we caught one that'll make her day."

***

The officer scanned Ronnie's fingerprints into the PD database and instructed him to stand behind the tape on the floor. She snapped a front and side photo. The mug shot would be available to the media in a matter of hours, and the charge was possession of a stolen vehicle. Ronnie closed his eyes for a moment and hoped this really was just a nightmare--one that would end when he opened his eyes again. But the cold steel cuffs on his wrists told him it was real and that he was in deeper than before.

# CHAPTER TWENTY-FIVE

*"It tickles when you do that," Maureen said and rolled onto her back.*

*Olivia unzipped Maureen's pants and kissed her just below her navel. "How low can I go?" she asked.*

*"Until I say stop. Down. Down. Oh...right...there."*

Maureen's eyes popped open. "Whoa, that was a good one." She rubbed her pubis and smiled. Her dreams about Olivia were getting better and better.

She rolled over and looked at the clock. Another four hours of sleep was available before she had to get up and get ready for another Monday morning. But she was awake and wanted to know what had happened in Atlanta last night. She hadn't heard from Olivia before she went to bed, and no word came from the Fugitive Task Force.

She got up and checked her cell phone. No missed calls. She headed for the living room and turned on the TV. The late-late news was re-capping yesterday's events, and the movie channel was showing an old western. She kept clicking the remote until she settled on a home shopping channel. An MP3 player with a matching watch was the latest hot item. "Carol would like that." In just over a month, it would be Christmas, and she needed to make her shopping list. She had no idea what to buy Olivia. They hadn't even discussed Thanksgiving, which was next week.

Her phone rang as she changed the channel again.

"Hey, beautiful," she answered.

"You're up?" Olivia said. "I expected to get your voicemail at this hour."

"I woke up and couldn't fall back to sleep. What's going on?" Maureen went to the kitchen to heat water for a cup of tea.

"Bad news and good news from my lieutenant. Malley slipped by the Atlanta guys."

"Sorry, Olivia. You know they'll keep looking for him, right?"

"I know, and it may not take long to find him. Guess who they *snatched up* last night?"

"Snatched up? Who?" Maureen suddenly remembered the chat room conversation. "They found Ronald?!"

"Parked right outside the bus station. They're holding him on an auto theft charge. The car he was in had a VIN number belonging to another car in Illinois."

"You mean while my team's been burning both ends chasing this guy around the Internet, the locals caught him in a stolen car? Life is too damn funny."

"Funny and good," Olivia said.

Maureen sat at the kitchen table and stared at the tea bag in her cup. "So you won't be coming to Atlanta with me?" She knew she sounded disappointed.

"Depends on how soon you can get Ronald to tell you where to find his brother."

"I'll do my best, and I'll see you this evening when I pick up my car."

"Okay. Now go back to bed. You're going to need your energy."

The kitchen clock read two thirty, and Maureen wished she could fast-forward the entire work day.

*\*\**

Keith was still awake and staring at the empty soda cans on the living room table. "That damn car, I thought it was clean," he kept repeating to himself. He knew he should have checked out the bus station himself. His boyfriend was now sitting in lockup.

After Keith had picked up Malley, they'd gone to Ronnie's condo and waited. But Ronnie never came back and never called. Keith didn't find out until after midnight--from a close friend whose girlfriend worked in central booking--that the cops had arrested Ronnie. Atlanta PD was also looking for Malley on a fugitive warrant, and the Feds were rumored to be involved.

Keith knew he and Malley couldn't stay at the condo. The cops would soon show up with a search warrant and take the place apart. So he packed up Ronnie's laptops and as much personal stuff as he could find and brought it and Malley to his apartment. His gut told him that it was a bad move, but it was the best he could do.

Malley was asleep on the couch and hadn't moved or made a sound all night. At one point, Keith thought he had stopped breathing; one loud snore said otherwise.

"Man, this is bad," Keith said aloud.

Malley moved and sat up. He wiped his eyes and asked, "Mind if I use your bathroom?"

"Down the hall on the left."

Malley didn't seem sure of his legs. He stood using the couch armrest to keep his balance and walked slowly down the hall, dragging his duffle bag behind him.

Keith wondered if Ronnie had told his brother about him. Ronnie did talk about the grief he took from Malley when he told him he was gay. It was one of the reasons he'd left Goslyn. How ironic that Keith would be the one helping Malley to hide from the cops.

Malley returned to the couch ten minutes later.

"Look, man," Keith said, "I'm not sure what to do about Ronnie. I don't even know if he'll get bail, and I hear Virginia put a warrant out for you." Keith rubbed his forehead in frustration. He was stressed and exhausted. "You can stay here until we figure something out." He didn't wait for a response. He went to his bedroom and crawled into bed.

Malley didn't have any answers either. He was a wanted man who was hundreds of miles away from home and sleeping on somebody else's couch. He was also hungry and craved a drink. Badly. He had some money in his pocket but couldn't go wandering off by himself.

He got up and checked the fridge. "This guys a soda freak." Mountain Dew lined the door shelves and vegetable bin. Malley shoved around takeout containers and found some cold cuts and cheese in a sandwich bag. He then spotted a familiar and welcome sight--two cold Coronas.

He didn't bother trying to talk himself out of opening the first bottle, and the fact that he was in someone else's home wasn't enough to stop him. He downed the beer like a glass of water, and, as an afterthought, rolled together the slices of meat and cheese. It disappeared as quickly as the first Corona.

He took the second bottle back to the living room and collapsed on the couch. As he reflected on the last two days, it slowly dawned on him just how much he had lost--his family home that was now a crime scene, two brothers who were in jail, and a girlfriend who had risked everything for him. Drinking another beer seemed like the best thing to do at the moment.

"Here's to nothing." He toasted the empty room and took a gulp. He looked around at the place and saw nothing that reminded him of home. *Who is this Keith guy? I wonder if he's dating Ronnie. Damn, ain't that something? Rescued by my brother's boyfriend.*

He finished off the bottle and added it to the cans on the table in front of him. He started to think about Ronnie not getting bail. Even if he did, Keith couldn't risk showing up to post it. The cops could be looking for him too, and they would pressure Ronnie to tell them where to look for his brother.

The more Malley thought about everything, the clearer it became that he had to get out of Atlanta. Fast.

# CHAPTER TWENTY-SIX

Chief Anderson flung the morning paper into his office trash can and dropped two Alka-Seltzers into a plastic cup. He glanced up from his desk at Lieutenant Beal who he had summoned to his office but hadn't invited to sit down.

The trailer fire had made the front page, and the chief's Monday had started with a six a.m. call from Channel Six News. A weekend hunting trip with a Board Supervisor had prevented him from personally getting a handle on things before the media started to swarm. Nor did a brief news conference by the Deputy Chief do much to stop the wave of e-mails and phone calls flooding the chief's office.

"This case is beyond sloppy. It's a goddamn mess!" the chief said. "Who the hell told that IRS agent she could ride along on the arrest!" He gulped from the cup and winced as the seltzer fizzled in his throat. "I want Detectives Winston and Rowland on desk duty until further notice, and neither one is to have any contact with the IRS. Am I clear?"

"Clear, sir," Lieutenant Beal said as she stood at attention.

"You need to notify Special Agent Jeffries that she should direct any case related matters to *you* and not to your detectives. I also want the name of the young man who claimed the agent ran him over. He'll probably blab to some reporter and sue the damn Department!"

"Sir, it's not as bad as it looks. They found a meth trailer--"

Chief Anderson held his hand up. "Lieutenant, I'm not in the mood for excuses. This case has dragged on for months and caused the most property damage this department has seen in years. I've had enough!" He slapped his hand down on the desk and turned toward his computer. "You'll get an e-mail with additional instructions," he said.

Lieutenant Beal had also had enough. Of Chief Anderson. She knew his blow ups were more about Olivia than about the professional conduct of her detectives. She nodded and left his office without another word.

She passed through the squad room where she saw both Olivia and Marcus on the phones. She knew it was time to make a phone call herself--a call to a friend in Internal Affairs who could dig up an old file for her. She first delivered the chief's orders to two of her best detectives who stared back at her as if she had two heads.

*** 

Maureen turned the volume up on the conference phone as her co-workers dove into a box of mixed donuts. The chocolate éclairs were disappearing fast.

"Maureen, do you know if Ronald Henry has a bail hearing scheduled?" her supervisor asked from the other end of the line.

"Carol checked this morning, and the Atlanta DA's office said the hearing is set for Wednesday. The DA plans to ask the Court to deny bail. She thinks Henry is a flight risk based on his brother already being a fugitive."

"Are we second in line at getting our hands on

this guy?"

"Right now, we may be third." Maureen opened the Lewis file and browsed her notes. "Atlanta PD and the FBI think he's involved in a car cloning operation. The stolen car the police caught him in is registered to a dealership known for selling luxury cars with fake DMV papers and VIN numbers copied from other cars. Also, the owner of the dealership has been on the FBI's radar for a chop shop that ships parts and cars out of the country. So we've got plenty of company when it comes to prosecuting Mr. Henry."

"Regardless, I still want a crack at him. We haven't done all this work for nothing. Maureen, we'll conference again next week." The supervisor disconnected from the call. She was a day into her two-week Thanksgiving vacation.

Maureen grabbed the last éclair and headed back to her office.

"You know you're making everybody fat around here," she said to Carol as she passed her desk. "I'll have to run an extra mile tonight."

"I'm only giving people what they want. I can't help it if they don't have any will power." Carol followed Maureen into her office. "Check your e-mail for your flight and hotel reservations, and here's a new file." Carol placed the folder on Maureen's desk.

"What time is my flight tomorrow?"

"Eight fifteen with a return next Tuesday. Your insurance agent called. He said your car will be ready this afternoon." Carol turned to leave and took her usual pose in the doorway.

"What?" Maureen asked.

"Nothing, it's just good to see you're safe after a crazy weekend…and happy."

"Stop it before you make me blush," Maureen said and smiled. "By the way, I already picked out your Christmas present, so don't go shopping for anything that plays music."

"Ahh, that was nice of you. I'll bring more donuts next week."

***

The Sun dipped behind the horizon as Maureen ran another lap around the park. She was trying to run off the urge to punch something. Lieutenant Beal's call explaining why she was now the point of contact instead of Olivia was subtle. But Maureen could read between the lines. Olivia had ticked off somebody.

As she circled the park one more time, Maureen spotted Olivia getting out of her truck. Maureen stopped and sat on the ground underneath a tree as Olivia approached.

"What are you doing here, Olivia?" she asked.

"I'm taking a customer service survey for your insurance company. They want to know if you're satisfied with the new window." Olivia sat and took out a handkerchief and wiped sweat from Maureen's forehead.

Maureen grabbed her hand and held it. "Olivia, this is serious. You could get reprimanded or worse."

"Maureen, I'm not a child. I can take care of my career, and I'm not going to be told who I can talk to or see."

Maureen released Olivia's hand and used her head bandana to wipe the sweat from her face. "This is the wrong time to act like a brash rookie trying to buck the system," she said. "We can see each other after your case is over."

"You're missing my point, Maureen," Olivia said as she stood up. "This stupid order came from my chief who acts like a bully and can't stand the fact that I have a better relationship with his son than he does."

"It doesn't matter, Olivia. I'm not going to let you do anything to your career that you'll regret later." Maureen stood and tucked the bandana into the waistband of her sweats. "Neither of our cases is worth that."

"What's that suppose to mean?"

"It means there're more important things right now than us seeing each other."

"Like what?"

Maureen sighed. "Like your job."

"Maureen, if you don't want to see me anymore, just say so. Don't make this about my job."

"What are you talking about! That's *not* what I said, and this is about your job. I'm saying--" Maureen paused as another jogger passed by. "I'm saying we can live to fight another day. Right now, you should listen to your lieutenant."

"I'm sorry, but I think I deserve a little more respect from the county's head police officer--if not as his son's friend, at least as a detective. First he asks my lieutenant about my personal life, and then he actually thinks he has the right to interfere in it!"

"You think going against his direct order is a fight you can win?"

Olivia huffed. "No way I'm letting that pain in the ass have his way on this!"

"You're taking this the wrong way, Olivia. Calm down and let's just--"

"Let's just what?! Pretend that everything is okay?! Maybe I should quit now and save him the trouble of firing me!"

Maureen pulled at her hair in frustration and said, "Damn, you're stubborn! Why did I ever…"

"Ever what?! Say you love me?!" Olivia balled up her handkerchief and threw it on the ground. "Sorry to disappoint you," she sniped and quickly walked away.

"Olivia! Don't leave like that!" Maureen followed her to her truck and blocked the driver's side door. "What is wrong with you?! I'm in love with you, and that won't change just because we have to deal with your chief's ego trip. Be patient and use your head."

Olivia hung her head and said, "It's been a long day. I'm tired and…just tired." She slowly reached around Maureen for the door handle.

Maureen, shocked and confused, quietly stepped aside and watched as Olivia sped off. She walked home, painfully feeling she was a single woman again.

\*\*\*

Pat closed the twins' bedroom door and walked back to the kitchen. She took a carton of ice cream out of the freezer and put two scoops in a bowl then placed it in front of Olivia at the kitchen table.

"Thank goodness the boys sleep like rocks," she said as she sat across from Olivia. "I'd never get them back to sleep if they knew you were here."

"Sorry again for coming by so late. I couldn't sleep." Olivia poked her spoon into the chocolate fudge scoops.

"You know she's right, Ollie. You are stubborn. You hate taking 'No' for an answer when you think you're doing the right thing." Pat got up to pour a glass of milk and get two oatmeal cookies from a jar on the kitchen counter. "And you know Roy Anderson has been a jackass for years. That's why Cliff moved away. So why are you letting him get under your skin this time?"

"Because he's wrong, Pat," Olivia said. "And I'm fed up."

"Ollie, even if he does know you're dating Maureen, defying 'Mad Max' Anderson's order is wrong. It'll only hurt you and prove whatever stupid point he's trying to make."

"I'm still pissed and tempted to tell him off."

Olivia poked at the frozen scoops again.

Pat could read her best friend like the back of her hand. This wasn't just about Chief Anderson. This was about Maureen.

"I haven't seen you this mad since Kendra broke up with you," she said.

"Don't go there, Pat!"

"I went there, Ollie!"

Olivia slammed the spoon down on the table and got up.

"Where're you going?!"

"To check on my godsons," Olivia said and walked down the hall. She really needed a minute to wipe the tears that dangled at the corner of her eyes. Pat had hit a nerve, and she was right. Olivia had been longing for years to find a woman who could help her forgive Kendra and move on. She thought Maureen could be the one.

She looked in on Jesse and Jaylon who were tucked into their black and white bunk beds. Soccer gear and comic books littered the floor and dresser tops. She watched and recalled when she bought the boys their first soccer ball. They were just big enough to pick it up and run with it into a goalie net that her dad had built for them. She then thought about Maureen and their conversation about having kids. She hated herself for losing her temper and speaking to Maureen the way she did. She never realized just how deeply the hurt from her first love had cut.

She went back to the kitchen where Pat was stirring chocolate syrup into the glass of milk.

"This stuff is seriously good," Pat said. "I put some on your ice cream."

Olivia sat back at the table. "Have I ever told you you're as smart as you look?"

"Only a million times," Pat said and bit a cookie. "What are you going to do about Maureen?"

Olivia groaned. "What can I do? I'm not allowed to call her, so I can't even apologize." Olivia pushed away the bowl of ice cream.

"Clutch your pearls, girl!" Pat said. "Olivia Ann Winston rejected a bowl of ice cream." She offered Olivia one of the cookies.

Olivia shook her head.

"C'mon, take it," Pat said. "Junk food is the cure for a crappy mood."

Olivia took the cookie, dipped it into her ice cream, and bit it.

Pat laughed. "That's the Ollie I know."

"It's not a cure, but it helps for now." Olivia dipped it again. "I wish it could tell me how to talk to Maureen without getting fired."

"She probably thinks this whole situation is nutty anyway. I know I do. Be patient like she told you."

Olivia sighed. "Patient. But hopefully not single again."

\*\*\*

Keith bit his nails and leaned against the bar inside a private Atlanta nightclub. He was having a stiff drink after spending hours looking for an attorney who wouldn't ask too many questions. He had hired legal counsel for Ronnie and was feeling burned by the high retainer. He dialed his close friend to get an update.

"Hey, man, did your girl see him?" Keith asked.

"She saw him before they moved him to a permanent cell this morning. She said he looked scared. I guess yo' boy ain't used to being on the inside."

"Be serious, man. What about the bail hearing? Is she sure it's in two days?"

"Yeah, she knows the clerk who sets the schedule."

"And the dealership?"

"The cops went through the front doors this morning."

"All right. Later, man."

Keith shoved his phone into his pocket. "Damn, this gets worse and worse." He bucked his shot of vodka and ordered another one as he tried to forget about the unwanted guest occupying the couch back at his place. He thought his loyalty to Ronnie was strong, but either his conscience or the vodka shots were telling him he'd better have an exit plan. With no return.

# CHAPTER TWENTY-SEVEN

*Ladies and gentlemen, may I have your attention. We are now making our final approach to Hartsfield-Jackson International. Please return your seats and serving trays to the upright position. Welcome to sunny Atlanta. And thank you for flying American Airlines.*

Maureen pushed up the plane's window shade and squinted at the morning light. She didn't sleep much last night as she tossed and turned thinking about Olivia. She hated not being able to talk to her, and she hated not knowing where their relationship stood. The whole thing was frustrating and made her want to climb into her hotel bed and sleep all day.

"I need a nap," she mumbled as she exited the plane and headed for the nearest snack bar. She also needed hot tea. She scrambled to find her cell phone that now beeped somewhere in her carry-on bag. "Note to self: don't pack when I'm half asleep. Hello?"

"I hope you brought your A-game this time," Sergeant Billups said. "I want a rematch."

Maureen wasn't in the mood to joke, but she played along. "You couldn't hit a free throw if I paid you. Why didn't you call me when you caught my guy?!"

"I was kinda busy breaking up a fight and writing arrest reports."

"Always an excuse. What's up?"

"We got a lead on the Virginia target. A couple of patrol units keep hearing the name 'Keith' pop up. You planning to talk to your fraud suspect soon?"

"That's the plan for tomorrow," Maureen said as she searched her bag for her wallet, "unless his attorney gets in the way. If I get the chance, I'll mention the name and let you know what happens."

"Okay. How long you in town?"

"I fly back next week."

"You coming to see the crew?" Billups asked.

"I'll swing by later and bring Gonzalez some of those energy bars she likes."

"Just what I need, more crumbs in my backseat."

\*\*\*

"Henry, you got a visitor!" The guard rattled the keys on his belt as he stood at the cell door.

Insomnia had a vise grip on Ronald Henry. He hadn't slept more than three hours since his arrest two nights ago. The food gave him constant indigestion, and there was never a quiet moment in the place. He extended his hands, and the guard cuffed him and escorted him to an interview room. He had no idea who was there to see him. He hoped it was Keith. But he knew better than to expect that. Keith could wind up in jail just like him.

A lean elderly Latino man in a tan, three-piece suit was seated at the interview table as the guard directed Ronnie in.

In a quick, southern drawl, the man said, "Ronald Henry, I'm Samuel Reyes, your attorney. I was hired by an acquaintance of yours. Don't say a word until I'm finished."

Ronnie just nodded and sat. He knew it had to

be Keith who'd sent the lawyer.

The man pulled out a file and note pad from a worn briefcase sitting on the table. He put on a pair of bifocals, combed his gray crew-cut with his fingers, and started reading from the pad.

"The State's charging you with possession of a stolen vehicle that belongs to a couple in Illinois. They claim the vehicle is part of a car cloning operation being run out of the dealership where they found your vehicle. They also claim they found a stolen sound system half installed in your vehicle's trunk. The system was traced back to a retailer in South Carolina." Samuel paused and adjusted his bifocals. "Also, they claim a Mr. Thomas Simmons, the owner of the dealership, runs a chop shop and ships vehicles out of the country. The vehicle you were driving is registered to that same dealership. And the police are looking for a fugitive who's related to you and who was spotted at the bus station where you were seen just before your arrest." Samuel looked up and removed his glasses. "To put icing on the cake, the FBI and the IRS both want to have a serious chat with you. Any questions?"

Ronnie couldn't believe the man was talking to him. Car cloning? Chop shop? "What?" was all he could get out. He looked at the note pad and at the lawyer. "You sure you got the right Ronald Henry?"

"Son, pay attention. I got the right client, and you got problems. So we need to play this smart. First, you don't talk to anybody without me being in the room. Second, we need to find out what the Feds want and what they already have.

Understand?"

Ronnie nodded again.

"Good. You got any idea what the hell was going on at that dealership?"

"Uh, not really." Ronnie knew that wasn't the truth. Keith had bragged to him about work he had done for the owner, Mr. Simmons.

"Not really? Son, either you know or you don't know. Which is it?" Samuel leaned forward.

"I might have heard something about it. But I don't know the details, and I wasn't involved in stealing cars."

"What about your vehicle being there and the sound system?"

"I dropped my car off to get a tune up. Somebody told me about a mechanic who worked there." Ronnie felt his jaw twitch as he lied. "I didn't know about the sound system."

"Really? The dealership decided to wire a brand name sound system into your vehicle without you knowing about it?" Samuel leaned back in his chair and crossed his arms. "What about the one you were driving?"

"It was a loaner from the mechanic. I didn't know it was stolen." Ronnie shifted in his chair.

Samuel leaned forward again and gestured for Ronnie to do the same. He asked in a whisper, "Why were you at the bus station?"

Ronnie couldn't think of a good, quick answer. "I was checking the bus schedule for a friend." He felt his jaw twitch again.

"Son, I have walked through bullshit way higher than what you're shoveling, even higher than the bull your acquaintance tried to shovel at me when I agreed to take this case."

Ronnie thought of Keith again. "Okay, I knew somebody was coming to town to see me. So I went to the station to pick him up."

"This somebody have the same last name as you?" Samuel whispered again.

Ronnie nodded again.

Samuel sighed and leaned back in his chair once more. "The car cloning explains why the FBI is involved. What about the IRS?"

This time, Ronnie sighed and leaned back. He slumped in his chair and looked down at the floor between his legs. "Tax refunds," he said. He looked up at Samuel and repeated it, "Tax refunds."

"I'm guessing good old 'Uncle Sam' wants his money back."

Ronnie hunched his shoulders.

"How much?" Samuel asked.

Ronnie hesitated. He shifted in his chair again and kept looking down. "About nine hundred thousand." He glanced up at Samuel whose eyes had widened. "Maybe a little more."

Samuel loosened his tie and pulled a pen from his pocket protector. He quickly started scribbling notes on the pad. "Any idea how they traced the refunds to you?"

"I don't know. I didn't even know they were watching me."

Samuel stopped writing and tossed everything into his briefcase. "Okay, looks like we need to hear from the DA and the Feds to know what they've got." He shut his briefcase and fixed his tie. "Let me give it to you straight, son. You probably won't get bail tomorrow, not with the police still looking for the other Mr. Henry. So make yourself comfortable. I'll see you at the hearing, and we'll go from there. Any questions?"

Ronnie shook his head and couldn't think of anything to ask. He was overwhelmed. "Thanks," he mumbled. He called for the guard and waited to go back to his cell.

*** 

Malley needed the cool air that blew across the balcony. He zipped up his jacket and sipped on his hot coffee. It felt like the apartment was shrinking, and the tension was thick. Two strangers cooped up together couldn't last long. Malley wanted to leave but didn't know where to go. He thought about returning to Virginia and hiding out in another county. But the chance of getting caught terrified him. The more he thought about it, the less he seemed to care that he was putting Keith at risk.

Keith opened the sliding glass door. "Hey, I'm going out to pick up some groceries. You want something?"

"No, I'm good," Malley said and warmed his hands on his coffee mug.

Keith stared at Malley for a moment. He didn't know what to make of the man or how far to trust him. "I'll be back in about an hour," he said. Keith made a mental note to buy more coffee.

Keith was on edge as he left. While at the club last night, the bouncer had told him that someone had mentioned his name to the cops. As far as Keith could tell, only his closest friends knew about

Malley, and only they knew where he lived. But it made no difference. Every moment Malley was there was one more chance that the cops could show up and kick down the door. Keith wanted Malley gone.

He looked around as he got into his car and flinched when another car pulled up beside him. It was his neighbor returning home from the gym. He put on his sunglasses, quickly backed out, and decided to drive around before heading directly to the store. He wanted to see if the cops were following him but had no idea what he would do if he did spot a tail.

***

Malley watched Keith from the balcony as he drove off. He went inside for a refill and turned on the TV. He hadn't bothered to watch the news or read a paper since he'd left Goslyn. A local morning show was re-capping the top stories including a water main break that was tying up traffic somewhere across town.

Then Malley heard, *We now have an update to Sunday night's disturbance at the local Greyhound bus station. According to police, a fight broke out between passengers who argued over who owned a designer handbag. Several people suffered minor bruises as they scrambled to get out of the way. However, no one required medical attention. The police also say they made several arrests for assault but all were released without bail, and there are no pending court dates.*

Malley's eyes were glued on the screen as a shot of the bus station appeared.

*Now for a follow up on the recent raid of a local business, let's go live to Margo Sanchez.*

*Thanks, Maria. I'm standing across the street from Simmons Luxury Rides, where the local police and the FBI have been going in and out since early yesterday morning. So far, the most authorities will tell us is that the dealership and the owner, a Thomas Simmons, are being investigated for allegedly operating an auto theft ring involving vehicles stolen from out of state and registered here in Georgia. However, an unnamed source told us that Mr. Simmons is also being investigated for allegedly running a chop shop and for allegedly shipping stolen luxury vehicles overseas.*

The camera panned to the dealership's logo sign. Malley noticed that the same logo was on Keith's license plate frame. Maybe it was just a coincidence, but he didn't feel good about it.

*The source also told us that authorities are currently questioning Mr. Simmons, but no formal charges have been filed against him. We'll have an update for the evening news.*

Malley turned down the volume and walked through the apartment. It was the first time that he focused on some of the expensive items--the flat screens, the watches on the nightstand, and a closet full of tailor-made slacks. He wondered what Keith did for a living and why Ronnie had never mentioned him. His anxiety soared, and a voice in his head was telling him to pack up and run, even if he didn't know where he was going.

\*\*\*

Keith had driven around until he found himself

stuck in a traffic jam caused by a broken water main. He had sat in traffic long enough to calm his nerves. When the jam cleared, he went across town to see one of his close friends before going to the grocery store. According to his friend, the cops were looking for him as a possible lead in finding Ronnie's brother, and Thomas Simmons was facing hard time in a federal prison unless he started naming names--*all* names.

By the time Keith had reached the store, he was beyond nervous; he was in a daze. There he was, pushing a grocery cart down the coffee aisle while the cops were tracking him. Every recent move he'd made was an amateur one--giving Ronnie a car from the dealership, letting Ronnie be the lookout at the bus station, and letting Malley stay with him. "Damn, you're stupid," he said aloud. He had always been a pro on every deal and scam he pulled, and the cops had never gotten this close to him. But he let his guard down this time and let his heart instead of his head tell him what to do. He was unprepared and rattled by the whole thing.

He pushed aimlessly up and down the aisles and reflected on the times he and Ronnie had spent together. He did care about Ronnie. He loved him. But this was too much. Besides, he had done all he could do. He had hired Ronnie a lawyer, and he let Malley crash at his place. *What else am I supposed to do?* He finally stopped and noticed that he was standing in a checkout line.

He froze when a uniformed officer came through the automatic doors and briefly made eye contact with him. She continued past the cash registers and went down the beverage aisle. Keith had a tight grip on the grocery cart handle and could hear his heart pounding in his ears.

The officer returned and stood in the express line just to Keith's right. She held a six-pack of Mountain Dew and kept tapping the top of one can with her fingernail.

Keith's knees buckle slightly, and he had an urge to look over at the officer but didn't dare. To him, her tapping sounded like a hammer banging concrete. He moved forward in the line and waited behind two customers ahead of him.

The officer's line moved quickly, and she was up next. But suddenly, she stepped toward a customer directly behind Keith. "Excuse me, sir," she said as she leaned in and reached for a pack of gum on a display rack between the customer and Keith.

Time had stopped for Keith. He heard chatter on the officer's radio and felt the air move behind him as the officer picked up the pack and returned to her line. He closed his eyes for a second and seemed to go deaf.

The officer quickly paid and was out the door.

"Sir, are you ready?" the cashier asked.

The words brought Keith back to the present. "Uh…that's okay. I forgot something." He looked at the customer behind him. "You can go in front of me, man," he said.

The customer moved aside as Keith backed up his cart.

Keith turned and headed for the rear of the store, trying to focus mentally with every step. He stopped outside the restrooms and pushed the cart into a corner. *Love ain't enough to deal with this shit,* he thought as he felt sweat on the back of his neck.

He left the cart and slowly headed for the front exit.

Once outside, he discreetly scanned the parking lot for the patrol car. It was gone. He rushed to his car with only two things in mind--get cash from an ATM and get home to pack.

He pulled out his cell phone and dialed. "Hey, Mama…Yeah, it's me. Guess what? I changed my mind about the holidays…Yeah…I'll call from the airport when my flight gets in."

***

Malley shut the cab door and shoved the forty-ounce beer into his duffle bag. He saw the driver looking at him in the rearview mirror and gave a faint smile.

"Ready?" the driver asked.

"Ready," Malley said. He was going to a motel out near the airport and planned to stay there until he could figure out what to do next.

The more he had snooped around Keith's apartment, the more he was certain that Keith was doing something that would interest the cops. The device used to duplicate car keys that he saw in the utility closet was the first clue. He then found a box in the bedroom closet with five driver's licenses--each from a different state, each showing Keith's photo with a different name. He knew it was time to go.

Malley put back on the sunglasses he had

bought from the convenience store and pulled down the brim of his cap. The look he got from the driver made him uncomfortable.

The driver turned on the radio and adjusted a card that was sticking out from the sun visor.

Malley recognized it as a meeting reminder for AA. He wondered if the driver was a member and if he was trying to tell him something.

The cab left the store and headed for the interstate, and both men listened as a local talk show on the radio discussed the latest political scandal--a decorated general's inappropriate relations with a civilian. Traffic was steady, and Malley saw some of the city's skyline for the first time. He had never been to Atlanta, and Ronnie had never invited him.

As the driver responded to a status check coming in on his dispatch radio, a bracelet dangled from his wrist. Malley had seen a similar one before. It was a sobriety bracelet with a number five medallion attached. It meant five years without a drink. The driver updated his status, and Malley noticed him glancing again through the rearview mirror.

The driver smiled and asked, "Been in Atlanta long?"

Malley wasn't in the mood to talk but didn't want to seem standoffish, especially to someone who was five years clean. "Only a few days," he said. The moment felt awkward to him. He thought he owed a better answer. "Looking for some construction work," he added.

The driver nodded.

They went back to listening to the talk show host--the general planned to resign and the civilian lost her security clearance.

The airport was in sight, and Malley could see planes taking off. He wished he was aboard one going somewhere. Suddenly, a billboard blocked his view, and it displayed a one eight hundred number to call if you needed help. Below the number was the picture of a thin, frail woman hunched over a half-empty bottle of wine. The message wasn't lost on Malley. He thought about the cold forty-ounce in his bag, and he caught the driver glancing at him in the mirror once more.

He gave a generous tip when they reached the motel, and he wanted to say something to the driver but didn't know what.

"Good luck with everything," the driver said.

The words hit Malley. He removed his glasses and offered an eye-to-eye handshake.

The driver reached out his window and gave a firm grip.

Malley watched the cab leave and turned to look at his new home.

"So this is how it is," he said, "living pillar to post and stuffing my gut with beer and burgers." He walked into the motel lobby and was greeted by a strong scent of disinfectant. *Damn, how long can I keep doing this?* He wished that he had bought two forty-ounces instead of one.

# CHAPTER TWENTY-EIGHT

Chief Roy Anderson stubbornly pushed the cell phone across the dining room table. "No. I'm not calling!" he said.

Estelle Anderson pushed it back at her ex-husband. "Call him tonight!" She drummed her red, manicured nails on the table and stroked a stray gray curl back into place.

Roy pouted and glared at her. He saw the silver-haired ex-love of his life glaring back at him. "Why?" he asked. "So he can tell me I'm interrupting his evening and hang up on me?"

"Our son wants you to call him. He said it's important." Estelle pointed at the phone.

"If it's so important, why didn't he call me himself instead of going through you?"

Estelle sighed and started to clear the plates from the table. "You know darn well why he called me. Because you're pigheaded and won't let him finish a sentence. Help me load the dishwasher."

Roy pouted again as he carried the casserole dish into the kitchen. He and Estelle still had dinner nights despite the divorce.

"The boy doesn't even bother to call me on my birthday or Father's Day," Roy said as he opened the washer. "Now he's got something important to say."

"That is so childish, Roy. Clifford gave you a birthday card every year until you told him you didn't want to be reminded you're getting old. And you haven't acted like a father since Clifford left the force."

Roy was used to Estelle's blunt comments. She was the one person he let see through his hard exterior.

"I still wanted a card," Roy griped. He clumsily loaded a wine glass next to the casserole dish and the two clanged together.

"I'll load the rest, 'Mr. All Thumbs.' You already owe me a new gravy bowl to replace the one you broke. Go call your son and don't come back in here looking for pie until you do." Estelle placed her hand on his back and gently pushed him out of the kitchen.

Roy circled the dining room table and scowled at the phone. He was ready for the short, verbal battle he usually had with Clifford whenever they tried to have a conversation. "He could've just sent me one of his smart ass e-mails."

He picked up the phone, walked out to the enclosed patio, and sat in his favorite lounge chair. He had spent many nights in that chair planning his rise to the top police position and many nights trying to figure out his son. He accomplished the former and failed at the latter.

He dialed the number but hesitated pushing the talk button. He had a twinge of fear that only his son could give him. It was a fear of rejection, and Roy suffered it every time he wanted to extend an olive branch to Clifford. Any attempt at peace always led to his accusing Clifford of throwing away his career and not being a fighter and Clifford accusing him of choosing his career over his family and of being a bully. Estelle intervened every time and calmed the waters until the next storm.

Roy pushed the talk button as he stood up and looked out into the night. "I'm hanging up after the first ring."

***

Clifford answered on the first ring before he could change his mind. He needed to do this for himself and for a good friend.

"Hey, Dad," he said with a slight crack in his tenor voice. "Thanks for calling me." Clifford heard a pause in return. He waited.

"Your mama said you got something important to tell me," Roy said.

Clifford got right to the point before things could go south. He took a deep breath and said, "I want to apologize. I'm sorry things turned out the way they did." He heard another pause. He knew he had thrown his dad off balance.

"Are you feeling all right?" Roy asked. "Do you need to talk to your mama?"

"This is between you and me, Dad. I think it's time we talk. Can we?"

"Can we what?"

Clifford held the phone away for a moment and released a frustrated sigh. This was going to be just as hard as he had imagined.

"Talk. I want to clear the air between us," he said. "Okay?"

Clifford heard his dad mumble something inaudible. He then heard what sounded like furniture being moved. Clifford suspected his dad was rearranging the patio chairs--he always did when he wanted to avoid a family discussion.

"Dad, please, I need you to sit down and listen."

"All right. I'm sitting."

"Good." Clifford closed his office door to block out the noise from his students practicing their high kicks. He loosened the black belt on his karate gi and looked out the window at the Santa Monica sun. "I'm coming back to Goslyn next week for the holidays," he said.

"You tired of eating tofu turkey with beach bums and ex-hippies?"

Clifford promised himself that he wouldn't let his dad bait him in to an argument. He grinded his teeth before speaking. "I'm finally tired of fighting--fighting about me walking away from the force." Clifford hoped for a civil response or at least an attempt at one. Instead, he heard his dad moving furniture again. "Dad!"

"I'm sitting!"

Clifford waited again as another pause followed. He thought the line had gone dead until he heard the old patio door squeak open in the background.

"Son, this was never about you leaving the force," Roy said. "It was about us not liking each other."

Clifford was off balance now. He scratched his receding hairline and sat on an exercise mat that covered part of his office floor. He listened as his dad continued.

"You know we've been on opposite ends of everything since you were tall enough to see the top of my head. If I said Up, you said Down. If I said Left, you said Right."

"Dad, I don't hate you," Clifford said.

"I didn't say we hated each other. But you're a grown man, and it's time to hear the truth. You and I are like oil and water, and I don't know what to do about it."

Clifford didn't know what to do about it either, and he was at a loss for words. He crossed his legs and hung his head.

"Do you understand why I had to leave the force?" he asked.

Roy sighed." You could've stuck it out if you had just asked me to help you."

"Dad, that's not true, and you know it." Clifford stood and looked back out the window. "I tried to tell you a hundred times that something was wrong. Even mama tried to tell you. But you buried your head in your work."

"I might've been ignorant about a lot of things. But you didn't make it easy for me, son. You treated me like I was butting into your life when I did try to reach out."

"Dad, I--"

"Let me finish. Your friends knew more about you than I did. You know how that made me feel?"

"Like I didn't love you?" Clifford asked to his own surprise. Expressing affection wasn't a strong suit of his or his dad. He waited again as the line was quiet.

"I guess so," Roy said in a low voice. "You haven't told me since I took you to your first karate class on your tenth birthday."

"It hasn't been that long, Dad."

"It has. I've been…keeping track."

Clifford felt awful. For years, he saw his dad as overbearing and intolerant. That saying "I love you" might've made things different between them seemed too simple to make sense.

"Dad, my friends didn't judge me when I told them I was too scared to put on my uniform and pick up my gun," he said. "You made me feel like it was my fault. And you took it out on me and anybody who cared about me. But…I still loved you." Clifford paced his office and opened the door to see his students lining up for their run on the beach with his assistant. They reminded him of his first lesson as his dad watched. He asked, "Can we call a truce?"

"Truce?" Roy asked. "You mean you'll answer your phone and won't hang up on me when I bring up the past?"

"I mean *we'll* stop hanging up on each other, and we'll work on the past." He heard his dad sigh.

"On one condition," Roy said. "You deliver those damn fruitcakes with your mama this year."

Clifford knew it was his dad's dry attempt at humor. Estelle and her church choir baked and gave away fruitcakes to local nursing and retirement homes every year between Thanksgiving and Christmas. Most of the recipients secretly re-gifted the cakes to a composting project at Lincoln High.

"I like mama's fruitcake," Clifford said.

"Then you can have the first bite instead of me."

Clifford laughed and heard his dad do the same. It was a sound he hadn't heard in a long time and had forgotten how it made him feel--like he was that ten-year-old kid again.

"See you soon, son," Roy said.

"Yeah, see you soon." Clifford hung up and thought, *I owed you that, Olivia.*

***

"That was strange...but good." Roy strolled around the brightly lit backyard surrounded by Estelle's blooming pink and white asters and the Virginia creepers that scaled the back fence. He felt at home even though he no longer lived there. Estelle got the house as part of the divorce but hadn't changed a thing, including Roy's favorite chair on the patio. The townhouse where he lived now still felt temporary after several years.

He heard the patio door open.

"Roy, you ready for some pie?" Estelle asked.

"Of course, woman! And don't be stingy with the slices!"

"You're lucky you're getting any at all after your last visit to the doctor." Estelle patted Roy on his stomach when he approached her at the door.

"I blame it on your cooking." Roy took her by the hand and kissed it. "Our son is coming home next week," he said.

Estelle laughed. "I already knew that."

"And you didn't tell me! I guess you also knew what he wanted to talk about?"

"Looks like you finally listened to him since you're not stomping around out here like an angry bear."

Before Roy answered, he heard sirens in the distance. On any other dinner night he would have rushed out to his car and listened to his scanner. But tonight was different--it felt different. His son told him that he loved him.

"This bear wants some whipped cream on his pie," he said and followed Estelle back into the house. He sat at the dining room table and listened as the sirens faded away.

# CHAPTER TWENTY-NINE

Maureen waved at familiar faces as she and her team member, Special Agent Abrams, entered the jail and passed through a metal detector. Her mind was off Olivia for the moment, and she was in a good mood. A search of Ronnie Henry's place had turned up a gold mine.

A guard led them down a long corridor to a locked door that had an interview room on the other side where Ronnie and his attorney were waiting.

\*\*\*

Ronnie felt worn. He hadn't slept again last night and was starving for a decent meal. The only good thing to happen was the hour he was allowed out of his cell to attend his bail hearing. But Attorney Samuel Reyes had struck out in court, and the jail was as noisy as ever. Ronnie sat next to Samuel at the conference table and braced himself for more bad news.

"I know you're disappointed, son," Samuel said as he pulled a pack of *Rolaids* out of his suit pocket and popped a tablet into his mouth. "But I warned you that you wouldn't get bail. I talked to the DA, and she won't budge an inch on anything. You were caught driving the stolen vehicle, and just about everybody who worked for the dealership is either in jail for theft or on the run. So we don't have one credible person who can corroborate your story about the vehicle being a loaner." Samuel loosened his tie and tossed his bifocals on the table. "As for the sound system, we got the same problem. There's nobody to say it was installed in your vehicle by mistake."

"What about the Simmons stuff?" Ronnie asked.

Samuel put his eyeglasses back on and thumbed through his file. "The DA and the FBI are playing hard ball. That means they want as many convictions as they can get. Mr. Simmons is the main target, but he's agreed to testify to save his own ass. He's dropping names and throwing everybody under the bus, including you and your friend, KC."

"Shit! I swear to you, Mr. Reyes, I didn't know what Simmons was doing!"

"Son, I'll give it to you straight. You were close enough to the action to make Simmons stick your name into this pile of crap. So the DA and the FBI will charge you with being part of everything. They'll threaten you with hard prison time too. But you won't say a word on my advice. Once they see they've got nothing on you, they'll let it go, but only after they put you through hell."

"Goddamn it!" Ronnie yelled. He covered his eyes with his cuffed hands. "This can't be happening to me."

"Pull yourself together. We got more Feds coming any minute now. Remember, we're not making any statements, just listening. We need to know what the IRS has. Then we'll decide what to do from there."

***

The guard opened the interview room door, and the two agents stepped inside.

"I'm Special Agent Jeffries, and this is Special

Agent Abrams," Maureen said to the two men.

The agents exchanged a cordial greeting with the lawyer and sat.

Maureen eyed Ronnie. "Good morning, Mr. Henry. We finally meet," she said.

Ronnie nodded at the agents.

Maureen placed her briefcase on the table and pulled out the Lewis file.

"Ladies, let me be clear about one thing here," Samuel said. "My client won't be making any statements. We agreed to meet only to hear what the IRS claims Mr. Henry has done." Samuel straightened his tie and brushed lint from the sleeve of his blazer.

"Fair enough, Mr. Reyes," Maureen said as she started to lay documents on the table, naming them as she went along. "Let's see. WRSouthbound95 chat room conversations, WRon95 code list from gang member, W.R. South money wire receipts, and Western Union security camera photos." She stopped and looked at Ronnie who didn't seem fazed. But that was expected. None of it tied him directly to the fraudulent tax returns and refunds, and it wasn't a crime to send money to his brother's girlfriend.

"One more thing," Maureen said. She pulled out her final piece of evidence--a sealed clear plastic bag containing a thin metal disk. "Mr. Henry, I believe this belongs to you. Atlanta PD found it in your condo last night when they executed a search warrant. It was taped underneath the kitchen sink." She held it up and let it dangle in the air. She watched closely as Ronnie's jaw twitched and saw his lawyer shoot a quick glance at his client.

"This harmless looking item," Maureen said, "is the hard drive to a laptop, and it's covered in your fingerprints. Our IT guys had one big party when they unwrapped its contents."

The contents were damning. The hard drive contained every tax refund Ronnie had gotten from the IRS along with corresponding social security numbers and untraceable bank accounts. It also showed refunds he was still waiting to receive. Payments from gangs were also included, and everything was listed under the heading WR95. It was a near duplicate of the code list found on the gang member by Atlanta PD.

Maureen stacked the documents with the disk on top. "For you, Mr. Reyes," she said as she took a separate folder from her briefcase and handed it to him. "It's a printout of the hard drive and a copy of the search warrant. I think it all speaks for itself."

Samuel slowly turned several pages and looked over at Ronnie. He closed the folder and removed his bifocals. "Ms. Jeffries, Ms. Abrams, obviously, I need some time to consult with my client in private. But in the meantime, is there any room to negotiate?"

"Mr. Reyes, as far as the IRS is concerned, we have all we need for a conviction," Maureen said. "And I hear things don't look good for your client with the State either. But...," Maureen saw an opportunity, one she had discussed with the federal prosecutor, "if your client knows where to find his brother, it could work in his favor."

Ronnie broke his silence. "Damn, I knew it would all come back to Malley." He crossed his forearms on the table and put his head down.

"Ladies, we need a few minutes alone," Samuel said.

"We'll be outside." Maureen returned the stack of documents and the disk to her briefcase and followed her colleague out the door.

"Think he'll give up his brother?" Special Agent Abrams asked.

"Turning on family can't be easy," Maureen said.

The agents waited ten minutes before Samuel opened the door and invited them back in. Ronnie was sitting on the floor in a corner. He wiped his eyes with the back of his hands.

Samuel handed Maureen a piece of paper with an address on it. "You need to look for my client's boyfriend, Keith Claiborne," he said. "He picked up the other Henry from the bus station and stashed him."

"Thank you, Mr. Reyes." Maureen then looked at Ronnie and said, "I hope you get to see Goslyn again, Mr. Henry." She was being sincere. While waiting outside the interview room, she wondered if she or Olivia had ever met any of the Henry boys years ago when they were all just kids.

Ronnie stood and sat back at the table. "Me too, ma'am," he said.

Maureen and Special Agent Abrams left the jail. On their way back to the field office, Maureen called Sergeant Billups with the Fugitive Task Force and relayed Keith Claiborne's address. She then called the federal prosecutor and informed her of Ronnie's cooperation.

Maureen desperately wanted to call Olivia next, to tell her the good news, and to hear her voice. Instead, she sent a short e-mail to Lieutenant Beal updating her on the hunt for Malley.

*** 

Gonzalez brushed her hand over the silk slacks that were thrown on the bed. "What is this guy, a male model? These must cost a fortune." She checked the closet and saw leather boots and designer slip-ons stacked high. "These shoes cost more than my whole paycheck this week."

"Let's go!" she heard Sergeant Billups yell from the front doorway. "We got another lead!"

The officers rushed out of Keith's apartment, leaving two patrol officers behind to secure the scene. According to the apartment maintenance man, Keith had left alone yesterday afternoon and was carrying a couple of suitcases.

Officers had talked to several neighbors who also recalled seeing a man come out of the same apartment earlier the same day and leave in a taxicab. The cab company confirmed that a fare was picked up, and it gave the drop-off location.

"All right, everybody. No more playing freakin' chase with this guy!" the sergeant barked. "We grab him this time and send his ass home. Am I clear?!"

A unanimous, "Yes, sir," was the response. Everyone loaded into the two SUVs and sped toward the expressway.

***

Malley drew the curtains and dropped a bag on the unmade motel bed. He turned on the TV and turned up the volume to drown out the vacuum he heard in the next room. He went to the bathroom to wash his face and was taken aback by his image in the mirror. He looked as drained as he felt even after one night of sleep.

When he finished washing up, he took a six-pack from the bag and downed half a can to satisfy the growl in his stomach. He planned to crawl back into bed and sleep rest of the day. Before settling in, he opened the door cautiously to hang out the "Do Not Disturb" sign. So far, he had avoided any contact with the maids.

As he caught the aroma from a pizza place across the street, his stomach roared, and he opened the door wider. He didn't eat last night but instead drank the entire forty-ounce and fell asleep angry at himself and at the whole situation. He didn't wake up until a couple of hours ago and was now starting the routine all over again with the six-pack from a gas station around the corner.

Someone across the street caught his eye as he savored the pizza smell. It was the cab driver from yesterday. Malley watched as the stocky, fair-skinned man wiped the windows of his cab then walked into the pizza place. He kept watching without realizing he was staring out the door in plain sight. He didn't hear the maid approaching.

"Good afternoon, sir," she said. She was standing close enough for Malley to smell the bottle of furniture polish on her cleaning cart.

Malley quickly shut the door and put the can to

his mouth. But he hesitated before taking another drink. The beer reminded him of the cab ride and the looks he got from the driver. *Maybe I should eat something first,* he thought. He set the can next to rest of the six-pack and put his jacket back on.

But reality struck hard. "What the hell am I doing? I'm a damn fugitive." He slouched down in a chair and changed the channel on the TV to some sitcom--a married couple arguing about nothing important. It reminded him of Leslie.

But he couldn't sit still. Seeing the cab driver had given him an unexpected energy. He picked up the can again and swallowed the rest as he peeked through the curtains. The cab was still there, and he decided to feed his hunger.

***

The SUVs exited the expressway and slowed as each approached the motel. Both vehicles entered the parking lot and stopped at the windowless rear of the building. The Task Force coordinated how they would approach the target.

"Gonzalez, you and Smitty check with the front desk," Billups said. "Show the target's photo to the manager, get the room number, and find out if there're any guests on either side of the target's room."

The two officers got out and headed for the lobby.

"Mullins, you and Atkins drive around to the rooms and sit tight."

The second SUV drove off slowly, trying not to attract any attention. It parked between two mini-vans, and the officers watched the maids as they pushed their carts from room to room.

***

Malley stood in line waiting to place his order. He looked around and spotted the cab driver seated in the back near a side exit. He didn't know why, but he wanted to talk to him.

He saw the driver look up from his pizza and do a double-take when he saw a man looking right at him. The driver seemed surprised but smiled.

Malley could see the bracelet and medallion again as the driver reached for his drink.

"May I take your order?" the cashier asked.

"Yeah, I'd like two large slices with everything." The order was done in seconds, thanks to heating lamps warming the morning-old pizza. Malley passed two empty tables and made his way toward the rear. He stopped to sit at a table diagonal from the driver but within speaking distance.

The driver spoke first. "My wife would kill me if she saw me eating this stuff." He poked a plastic knife at his pepperonis and onions.

"I know whatcha mean." Malley pointed to the greasy cheese and sausage saturating his pizza box.

"My name's Stanley," the driver said and picked up his drink again.

"Five years is a long time." Malley looked at the bracelet as it reflected against a metal napkin holder on Stanley's table.

"Stanley rubbed the medallion. "It's my lucky charm."

"I...haven't made it that far yet," Malley said and lowered his head briefly. He was embarrassed.

"Never too late to start again. It's a marathon

that never ends."

"Yeah. A lifelong marathon."

Stanley finished the crust on his pizza and pulled a local AA card from his coat pocket. "Here," he said as he walked over and put the card on Malley's table. He rubbed his bracelet again and said, "Got this by facing my demons. I hope you can do the same."

Malley watched Stanley walk out the side exit, and he looked at the card. It brought back memories--some good, sober ones. He quickly ate one slice of pizza and left the other in the box. When he thought about finishing it later with the six-pack, the image of the cab driver and his words replayed in his head, *It's a marathon.*

"How the hell did it come to this?" he asked himself. The chase was wearing him down--physically and mentally, and it was finally sinking in that the cops wouldn't stop looking for him.

Malley didn't know if he should catch a bus back to Goslyn to turn himself in or walk straight into the nearest police precinct. He did know that he wanted to take a hot shower, in private, while he was still a free man. He tossed the pizza box in the trash as he headed for the front exit. When he stepped outside, he looked around and couldn't imagine what it would be like to be in jail. Nor did he want to think about CJ and Ronnie already being there.

The maids were huddled around the front desk as he passed by the motel lobby. He continued down the main walkway and noticed the entire place seemed quiet, even the parking lot.

When he reached his door, the hair on the back of his neck stood up. He saw the "Do Not Disturb" sign on the ground and caught a strong scent of Aftershave musk. Then he heard a noise from inside his room and watched as the doorknob turned. He wanted to run but physically didn't have it in him. He turned toward the parking lot just as the doors of a black SUV swung open. Two men jumped out. He collapsed to his knees as the men charged at him with their weapons drawn.

"Let me see your hands!" was all he heard for the first few seconds. The officers pushed him flat to the concrete and cuffed him. Everything that followed was just a blur, as if he was watching himself on a movie screen that was out of focus.

\*\*\*

The SUVs jetted down the expressway and arrived at the jail minutes later.

Malley's eyes widened as he looked out the window at the gray-clad building that rose ten stories high and stretched an entire city block.

They drove to the rear and into a garage where they unloaded. The sergeant pushed an intercom button next to a steel door that unlocked with a loud clang. On the other side stood a broad-chested deputy who sported a red buzz-cut that brushed the top of the doorframe. He wore tight, black latex gloves that made his huge hands resemble the metal end of a sledgehammer.

"Sarge, Gonzalez," the deputy said in a deep baritone. "Who you got this time?"

"Hey, Crenshaw. We're dropping off our Virginia guy." Sergeant Billups pointed a casual thumb at Malley.

Malley saw the deputy give him a serious look-over as if to size him up.

"Welcome to Atlanta," the deputy said with a cold stare.

Malley could feel the blood drain from his face. He stepped inside and was jolted by the sound of another deputy shouting orders at inmates dressed in bright orange scrubs.

"Where do you want him?" the female officer asked.

"Right in there." The deputy pointed to a temporary holding cell that was no bigger than a closet.

To Malley, the cell looked like an up-right animal cage. *This is worse than the freakin' bus,* he thought.

The deputy opened the cell and the woman told Malley to step inside where she un-cuffed him. The door shut behind him, and he turned around to see metal bars staring back at him.

The sergeant checked his watch and scribbled something on a clipboard that the deputy had handed to him. "He's all yours, Crenshaw. See you next time."

"Next time, Sarge."

Malley watched the two officers leave and felt like he had been dropped off in a foreign country. "Damn, I knew I should've gotten drunk one last time," he mumbled to himself.

A door opened a few feet away, and another deputy appeared with an inmate pushing a mop and bucket.

"Clean up those scuff marks!" the deputy ordered the inmate. "And get around that trash can!"

The inmate, who could've been on the cover of a college brochure but for the track marks on his arms, was quick at his work as he slung the mop from side to side. He passed in front of Malley's cell and tapped the mop against the door. "What's up, ole' man?"

The deputy snapped, "No talking!"

The inmate stabbed the mop back into the bucket and went back through the door with the guard right behind him.

"Ole' man?" Malley said and rubbed the stubble on his face. He stepped back from the cell door when he saw the gloved deputy approaching.

"All right, let's get this show started," the deputy said and looked at his clipboard. "I'm Deputy Crenshaw, Mr. Henry. If you listen and follow my instructions, this'll all go smooth. Are we clear?"

Malley saw the cold stare again. He was intimidated and didn't have the strength to pretend otherwise. "Yeah, I got it," he said.

"Good. Face the wall."

Deputy Crenshaw opened the cell and handcuffed Malley. He led him to a room where he fingerprinted and photographed him. He then placed him in another room and patted him down.

"Face the wall and remove your shoes," the deputy said.

Malley complied and took off his work boots.

Deputy Crenshaw picked up the boots, pulled

271

the tongues back, and ran his hands inside. "All right. Turn around and take off your clothes including your socks and underwear."

Malley couldn't believe his ears, and he didn't move. "My what?"

"This is a full search--inside and out," Deputy Crenshaw said as he pulled and snapped his latex gloves.

Malley wasn't ready for this. He looked at the deputy as if he was waiting for a punch line.

But there was nothing funny about Deputy Crenshaw. "That was an order," the deputy said. "Strip down and put your clothes in a pile!"

Malley was dumbfounded. He couldn't wrap his mind around the idea of another man telling him to take off his clothes. "You mean here? Now?" he asked while clutching the buttons on his shirt.

"This is jail, man! Get used to it!"

As Malley started to unbutton his shirt, his intimidation turned to seething anger, and he didn't need a drink to fuel it. When he unzipped his pants, he knew immediately that he would never get used to it. He was getting out and getting a drink the first chance he got.

# CHAPTER THIRTY

Olivia pounded on the punching bag until her shoulders burned. Sweat flew off her arms and hit Marcus who had a ringside seat on a weight bench.

"Eww! That's disgusting!" he said and took off his leather blazer. "I just had this dry cleaned."

Olivia sat on the Department's gym floor and caught her breath while taking off her gloves. "Stop whining. It's just water."

"Stinky water," Marcus said and threw a towel that hit Olivia in the face. He leaned back on the bench and pretended to do a bench press.

Olivia snickered. "The day you start lifting weights is the day I give up ice cream. Why are you here anyway? I thought you were going to the shooting range before dinner."

"I did but I got bored after I emptied my first clip." Marcus sat up. "And I couldn't stop thinking about the lieutenant yanking us off the street. I don't appreciate being treated like some first-day rookie," he said and frowned.

Olivia wrapped the towel around her shoulders and hung her head. "I think this was more about me than about the case. I'm sorry you're getting hammered too."

"We're partners, Olivia. We're in this together. Besides, desk duty's like a mini-vacation for old veterans like us."

Marcus' phone beeped, and Olivia's did the same a second later. She pulled it off the waistband of her sweats and saw a text from Lieutenant Beal:

*They got Malley. You're going to Atlanta. See*

*me in the morning 9 am sharp.*

"Are you reading what I'm reading?" Olivia asked.

"Right there in black and white," Marcus said. "Did you kiss and make up with the chief without telling me?"

"I must've been sleepwalking if I did." Olivia sent a quick text back acknowledging receipt. *We'll be there bright and early.* She then thought about Maureen. Was she allowed to call her? Would Maureen even talk to her?

"Hurry up and change so we can grab some dinner," Marcus said and put on his jacket.

"I need to take a quick shower first." Olivia started toward the locker room but stopped abruptly when she saw two officers near the exit suddenly stand at attention.

Chief Anderson appeared and was tieless in an open collar shirt and dark blue suit with black loafers. He patted one officer on the back and shook hands with the other.

Marcus walked up behind Olivia and said, "This can't be a coincidence."

Olivia thought the same as she watched the chief. "First the text, then he shows up."

"Get to the shower before he sees you," Marcus said while nudging Olivia.

But it was too late. Chief Anderson was coming straight at them with both hands shoved into his pants pockets.

"Detectives, I see you're making use of our fine facilities," he said. "I could use a workout myself. "

Olivia and Marcus looked at each other.

Neither responded immediately to the chief who hadn't held a personal conversation with either of them in years.

"I prefer a good workout at the shooting range myself, sir," Marcus said. "In fact, we were just leaving before--"

"I hear you're a pretty good shot, Marcus. Do any hunting?"

Olivia looked at Marcus and saw his eyes widen. The chief had never addressed Marcus by his first name not even in the few times he had spoken to him.

"Uh...no, sir. My wife...she likes her meat without the feathers," Marcus said.

Chief Anderson's loud laughter bounced off the gym walls. "That's good, detective. I'll remember that when I'm out hunting turkey for Christmas." Chief cleared his throat and looked at Olivia. "Detective, could we have a word in private, please?"

"Yes, sir. Would you mind if I cleaned up first?" Olivia asked as she wiped her face and arms.

"It'll only take a moment," the chief said. "I'm meeting some friends at the Rotary Clubs in a few minutes anyway." He motioned toward the bleachers.

Olivia followed him and glanced over her shoulder at Marcus who mouthed to her, *Behave.*

The moment was awkward. Olivia's clothes were drenched in sweat from her venting frustrations caused by the very person who now wanted to talk to her. Part of her wanted to tell him where he could go. The other part knew she was better than that.

"Everything okay, sir?" she asked as they stood face to face.

Chief Anderson kept his hands in his pockets and jingled together what sounded like coins.

"I just hung up with your lieutenant about Atlanta," he said. "Despite all the property damage and publicity, I've put you back on this case because…well…your work is good." Chief took his hands out of his pockets and crossed his arms. "But this doesn't mean I'm entirely happy. Our job, detective, is to serve and protect, not to make breaking news on the front page of the local paper."

"Sir, with respect, I don't look for attention when I'm working my cases," Olivia said. "I'd be happy if there were no crimes to report at all. I do understand your point, sir." But she didn't understand why the chief needed to have a private chat. She suspected there was more to it and wasn't afraid to ask. "Sir, it's rare we speak to each other, may I ask why the personal visit?"

Chief Anderson put his hands back into his pockets and twisted his lips. "I see why my son thinks so much of you, detective. You're sharp without being insubordinate. Represent us well in Atlanta." Chief turned to leave but threw his final words over his shoulder. "By the way, he's coming home for the holidays." Chief was out the door just as suddenly as he had appeared.

"Cliff's coming home?" Olivia said aloud. Then a light bulb went off in her head. *That explains it.*

Marcus walked over and tugged at the towel

around Olivia's neck. "What was that about?" he asked.

"You were almost right," Olivia said.

"About what?"

"Kissing and making up. I think Cliff puckered up for me."

"He's behind all that special attention we just got? How'd he know we were catching hell from his dad?"

"I don't know," Olivia said. "Let's enjoy the moment and hope it lasts." She threw her sweaty towel at Marcus. "You're buying dinner this time, 'Mr. Sharp Shooter,' and don't complain about me ordering extra spring rolls."

"Who's complaining? It's Thursday, coupon night."

\*\*\*

Maureen opened the new e-mail displayed on her phone as she lay across her hotel bed. She'd been hoping for a reply since yesterday. Lieutenant Beal was subtle again. She wrote that Olivia and Marcus, due to a "workload re-adjustment," were back on the case and would be coming to Atlanta Monday morning. Maureen was dying to know the real story and keyed up Olivia's number on her phone. Should she call? Why hadn't Olivia called her?

She got up, pulled the covers back, and got into bed. But she was starving.

"I should've gone out with Abrams," she griped to herself. She wasn't good company right now though--not with Olivia crossing her mind every five seconds. Room service wasn't even a

277

good option; the menu didn't have a single tomato dish on it.

She clicked the TV on, and it was tuned to a cooking channel with ice cream as the main course--fried ice cream, ice cream sundaes, and gelato with a honey glaze.

"Olivia would be in dessert heaven if she saw this." Maureen buried herself under the covers and hoped to drift off before her stomach reminded her that she had skipped dinner.

The room phone rang, and she rolled over to answer it. "Hello?"

"Miss. Jeffries, this is the front desk," the clerk said. "We have a package for you."

"A package?"

"Yes, ma'am. Should I have someone bring it up, or will you pick it up in the morning?"

"Do you know what it is?" Maureen asked as she sat on the edge of the bed.

"Looks like a present, ma'am."

"A present? For me?"

"Yes ma'am, the manager from our gift shop delivered it this evening. I can have it sent now if you like?"

"Okay." Maureen hung up and slid a pair of sweats over her boxers. "This must be one of Billups' goofy jokes."

She heard the elevator bell a minute later followed by a knock on her door.

"Hotel service, ma'am."

Maureen looked through the peephole and opened the door.

"Good evening, ma'am," the young bellhop

said with a smile. "Here you go." He handed Maureen a bag that must have weighed a pound. "There's a note inside. Good night, ma'am."

"Thank you." Maureen shut the door and dug a yellow card out of the bag.

*I'm so sorry. Can we talk?* it said. It had Olivia's name at the bottom.

Maureen rushed over to her cell phone on the bed and hit the talk button. After two rings, she heard Olivia's voice and got goosebumps.

"Hello back at you, detective," she said.

"Maureen, I apologize a thousand times for acting like that. I never meant to lose my temper. It was so immature."

"Was that about your chief or about us?" Maureen asked. She heard a pause.

"It was about me. I felt like he was taking something away from me that I deserved. And I just blew up. It sounds childish when I say it out loud, but it's how I felt."

"We're grown ups, Olivia. No one can dictate what happens between us unless we let them. Do you doubt the way I feel about you?"

"No, I don't…but when we argued you said--"

"When we argued, I was going to say why did I ever think I could stay on my case after I knew I was falling for you. I could've handed the lead over to another agent to make things easy for us." There was another pause on the other end. "You still there?"

"Yeah…just picking my face up off the floor," Olivia said. "God, I was so…so--"

"Stubborn?" Maureen said and picked up the

gift bag. "Olivia, somebody once told me that life goes on after your first love leaves. Do you believe that?"

"I do since I met you."

"Then you have to let go of the past and embrace the present."

"I've been trying since our first date," Olivia said. "Guess I need to try a little harder."

"You think it'll get better after a few more dates with me?" Maureen heard Olivia laugh.

"Maybe after a few more sleepovers."

Maureen looked in the bag and took out a yellow wrapped box. "Is this a bribe for my affections, detective?"

"Only if it works."

Maureen tore the paper off. "You already know me too well. I'm so hungry!" She opened the box of Godiva mint chocolates and bit half of one. "Mmm…that works, Olivia."

"Hey, save some for me!"

"I'll try but I don't know if they'll survive the weekend." Maureen popped the other half into her mouth.

"I don't know how I'll survive the weekend without you. I'm in love with you, Maureen."

"I'm in love with you too, Olivia." Maureen curled up under the covers and put the box on the pillow next to her. "You want to hear about my interview with Ronald Henry?" she asked.

"I'm all ears," Olivia said. "Then I'll tell you about my new bosom buddy--Chief Roy Anderson."

# CHAPTER THIRTY-ONE

The AA counselor checked Malley's name off in his appointment book. "You got a lot off your mind," he said. "Are you ready for the trip home?"

Malley sighed and scratched his chin stubble. He was ready to get out of there by any means necessary. He asked to see the counselor not only to help him deal with his withdrawal symptoms but also to get away from a cellmate who sat too close and asked too many questions.

"I've got all day and night to think about it," Malley said. "I wish I could fall asleep and wake up in my own bed."

"It's one day at a time, Malcolm. Don't look too far ahead." The counselor signaled to the guard and handed Malley an AA pamphlet. "Good luck."

"Thanks again for seeing me on short notice. I appreciate it."

Malley walked a step ahead of the guard. His talk with the counselor was a chance to clear his head before he was to see Ronnie. They hadn't been face to face in months, and he was nervous. He didn't know who had arranged the meeting with his brother and didn't care. It was just one more opportunity to be out of his cell.

He walked the long hallway, forced to take short steps because of his ankle cuffs. He turned the corner and entered a room with the guard close behind.

"Damn. No doubt you both got the same daddy," the guard said when he saw Ronnie.

The crude comment made Malley smile. But

the older brother immediately saw the strain in his younger brother's face. Ronnie looked thin and tired. It shook Malley as he pictured himself looking the same.

"Gentlemen, you got ten minutes," the guard said and stood by the door.

"How you holding up?" Malley asked as he looked at Ronnie.

Ronnie leaned back as he sat on a steel bench and showed his cuffed hands to Malley. He looked down at his feet that were cuffed to the floor. "How does it look like I'm holding up?" He clinched his fists.

"I know it's rough," Malley said and held out his own cuffed hands. He sat on another bench across from Ronnie. "We made some wrong turns, and it all caught up with us."

Malley saw an expression on Ronnie's face that combined anger and fear. He couldn't blame Ronnie if Ronnie wanted to reach out and strangle him. He knew he was the reason his younger brother was sitting behind bars and facing hard time. If he had stayed away from Atlanta, Ronnie would be a free man.

"Mal, I had to give you up to the cops. I got my back up against the wall, Mal. I didn't know what else to do."

"Stop, Ronnie. What's done is done." Malley felt a pang of guilt. He glanced over his shoulder at the guard. "You know I've said and done plenty of stupid shit to you in the past. I'm sorry about that and about Keith leaving. I could tell he cared about you."

Ronnie shrugged. "At least he got me a lawyer. I guess that counts for something."

The brothers sat for a long minute without speaking. The sound of a cell door slamming in the distance broke the silence.

"You think you'll see CJ when you get back?" Ronnie asked.

"I don't know. I just hope he's clean since he got locked up. Damn, he was a mess."

The brothers spent the last minutes reminiscing about better times when they felt like a family and took care of each other--when they had shown their love for each other.

"Time's up, gentlemen," the guard announced.

"This is it, huh?" Ronnie asked.

"Maybe. You know I like to go down swinging, right?" Malley smiled at Ronnie and kissed him on the top of his head. "Take care."

The guard followed Malley back down the hallway and toward the cellblock. The closer they got, the stronger was the smell of musty, male body order.

The guard removed Malley's cuffs inside the block and told him he could sit outside his cell in the common area. "Your roommate's decorating again," he said.

Malley walked to his cell door and saw his roommate tearing articles out of a newspaper and sticking them to the wall with toothpaste.

"Hey, roomie. Just keepin' up with my investments," Charlie Ward said.

*Idiot,* Malley thought. He looked at the stock market pages stuck on the walls. "Charlie, stop bullshittin' me and get your paper off my bed."

Malley had been Charlie's cellmate for only a couple of days but could tell he was a life-long conman. Everything that came out of Charlie's mouth involved his spending other people's money. It was known throughout the jail that he was awaiting trial for running a Ponzi scheme that had duped retired cops out of their pension checks.

"I'm on the up and up," Charlie said. "I got a thousand shares in Microsoft and another thousand in Apple. My girl's gon' sell 'em for me and post my bail."

"Right. And I own Walmart." Malley gathered up the loose pages from his bottom bunk and dropped them on the metal desk welded to the cell wall. He sat on his bunk and looked at the AA pamphlet before tossing it on top of the pages.

Charlie whispered, "Hey, man, I can get you some jailhouse wine. They call it 'pruno' in here, and it's crazy strong--like hard liquor."

Malley was desperate for a drink but not that desperate. His hands still shook, and he got nauseous when he ate. But he was a beer man and didn't have the stomach to gulp down some concoction that had fermented in some inmate's footlocker. Nor did he want to get caught by the guards.

"Nah, man. My gut's already screwed up."

Malley scooted back on his bed and leaned against the wall. By tomorrow afternoon he'd be sitting on a bed in the Goslyn County jail and thinking exactly what he was thinking now--*How do I get out of this?* He looked at Charlie but tuned him out as Charlie rambled on about business associates who worked on Wall Street. Was Malley looking at his future? Was he a Charlie Ward--a man who treated jail like a second home? Not if he could help it. After all, he wasn't guilty of anything--not of burglary, not of attacking Bertrand Lewis, and not of making meth.

He got up and pulled out a plastic bag from underneath his bunk. It held copies of his extradition papers he had signed on advice of his court-appointed lawyer. The lawyer told him he'd be wasting the court's time by fighting the extradition, and that he'd probably do something stupid the longer he stayed locked up in Atlanta.

The lawyer was right. Malley just couldn't see himself spending day after day caged like an animal that was told when to sleep and when to eat. He tried to tell himself that he would have his day in court--a chance to explain that he didn't do anything wrong. He even told himself to man up and be an example for his brothers. But it didn't work.

He flipped through the court papers that he had already read a dozen times and thought about the flight home.

"Do I still have a home?" he mumbled.

"Huh…you say somethin'?" Charlie asked as he wiped toothpaste on his shirt and sat next to Malley.

Malley shoved him away with a forearm. "Damn, man, give me some room!"

"My bad. No disrespect. So they takin' you back tomorrow?" Charlie hopped back up and started pasting articles again.

"Yeah, tomorrow." Malley lay on his bed and stared at the wall. He tuned Charlie out again and tried to plot his next move and when to make it. He closed his eyes for a moment and thought about his girlfriend, Leslie. When he opened his eyes, Charlie was in his face and flashing a devious-looking grin smudged with toothpaste.

"How bad you wanna get out of here?" Charlie whispered.

Malley jumped up and dropped his court papers on the floor. "What's your fuckin' problem, man!"

"Shh!" Charlie put a finger to his lips and peeked out the cell's steel door then pulled it shut. "Chill and listen, man. I know somebody who can show you a way out. Understand?" Charlie winked.

Malley was furious and ready to punch his cellmate in the mouth. It took him a minute to process what he'd heard. "Who?" he asked.

"That mop slinger who looks like a boy scout. You know the one who called you 'Ole' Man' at breakfast this morning."

Malley picked up his court papers. "Do I look stupid to you? That boy's got a bad habit. I wouldn't trust him to tell me the time of day." Malley sat on his bed.

Charlie moved closer but backed up when Malley stood up again.

"I'm serious, man," Charlie said. "He's been planning to get out of here for months. But he needs a second man."

"Then why the hell don't you go with him?" Malley caught the embarrassed look on Charlie's face.

"That's not my style, man. I prefer to talk my way out of here in front of the judge. And I, uh … owe that mop slinger some money I invested for him in a deal that went bad. If I find somebody to do the break with him, all is forgiven."

"So you offer me up like a piece of meat, right?" Malley stared at the conman.

"It's your choice, man. I doubt a judge back in Virginia will cut you slack since you high-tailed it across state lines. Besides, it's harder to catch two rabbits on the run than to catch one."

Malley still wanted to punch Charlie. He sat down again and thought about it--him breaking out and disappearing into the night. Was it better than being dragged back to Goslyn in handcuffs? Was it worth never seeing Leslie or his brothers again? Malley looked at his hands as they started to tremble. He clinched them together as if he was praying for an answer. *God, I need a drink.* "Let's do it," came out of his mouth before he knew he had said it.

Charlie flashed another devious grin. "All right. I'll set it up."

# CHAPTER THIRTY-TWO

"Hey, beautiful." Maureen kissed Olivia and took her carry-on bag. "How was your flight?"

"Thankfully short," Olivia said. "Marcus had an iron grip on my hand the whole time."

"Where is he?"

"Thanking the pilot for landing the plane safely. He hates flying."

"Ladies, there's nothing like standing on solid ground," Marcus said when he stepped off the ramp and into the concourse. He bent over and pretended to kiss the ground. "So where's our man?" he asked Maureen.

"At the main jail with his brother."

Olivia shook her head. "Three brothers, all of them locked up. This whole thing is so sad."

"At least Malley waived extradition," Maureen said. "That's one less headache. What time do you take him back?"

"Seven a.m. on the dot." Olivia checked the time on one of the airport monitors and set her watch.

The three made their way through the busy terminal and headed for the airport's parking garage. Along the way, the terminal brimmed with holiday reminders--from free turkey flavored bagels offered by one café to turkey sausages with gravy offered by another.

"It's hard to believe Thanksgiving's just three days away," Marcus said. "I can't wait for my wife's sweet potato pie."

"Which reminds me, do we have any special

plans?" Maureen asked Olivia.

"You mean you haven't heard?" Olivia laughed and held Maureen's hand as they walked. "Your Aunt Lena and my mama have made plans for us."

"Get ready for this one, Maureen," Marcus said.

"Oh no. Olivia, what did they do?" Maureen looked genuinely frightened.

"We've been drafted to help cook Thanksgiving dinner."

"Cook! Are you kidding? I'm still learning how to fix grits!"

"That's why your Aunt Lena drafted you," Olivia said. "Somehow word got around that Rita May Jones' granddaughter is dating a woman who doesn't know a pot roast from a pot pie."

Marcus snickered and ducked into the backseat when they reached Maureen's rental car.

"My aunt hates for people to be in her kitchen!" Maureen said. "She won't even let me boil water at her place."

"Don't worry about it. Stick with a dessert and you'll be fine."

\*\*\*

Maureen flipped her phone shut and set it next to her empty glass. "There's a conspiracy against me, Olivia," she said as she slipped off her shoes under the restaurant table and wrapped her feet around Olivia's. "Even my dad knew about this cooking nonsense."

Olivia licked chocolate from her lips and wiped her mouth. "Against you? What about me? I have no idea what my mama wants me to cook."

"You're better in the kitchen than I am, and you have a secret weapon--your grandma."

"It'll be easy. You can borrow my secret weapon anytime." Olivia took another bite of cake.

"All right. But if I have to make anything from scratch, we'll be eating takeout for Thanksgiving." Maureen nibbled on her own cake and gestured to the waiter for a water refill.

She and Olivia were capping off the long day with spicy calamari and spinach lasagna. Olivia and Marcus had spent most of the afternoon reviewing security procedures with jail officials and the airline. Maureen had been tied up in meetings until well after five. After work, she had given Olivia and Marcus a quick tour of downtown Atlanta. Marcus was more impressed with the sixty-inch flat screen in the hotel's bar. That's where Olivia left him when Maureen picked her up for dinner.

"This double fudge cake is incredible," Olivia said.

"So was that lasagna sauce. I love coming here when I'm in town."

Maureen looked at Olivia and realized she still hadn't thought of a good Christmas gift to give her. An MP3 player just didn't seem romantic.

"Olivia, any idea what you want from Santa?" she asked.

"A good-looking woman about five-nine who loves tomatoes. I asked Mrs. Claus for the same gift next year too."

Maureen blushed. She reached across the table and took Olivia by the hand. "You flirt as much as I do."

"I had a good teacher this year. What about you? What's on your wish list?"

"Mrs. Claus already delivered--an attractive, kind woman with a great sense of humor."

"Speaking of kindness, it was kind of you to ask the jail if the Henry brothers could see each other."

"What the heck. It's the holiday season, and they're from Goslyn."

"That deserves a kiss." Olivia leaned forward, and Maureen met her halfway.

"Mmm, sweet," Maureen said.

The waiter approached and cleared his throat.

"Pardon me, ladies. Will there be anything else?"

"I'd like an extra dessert in a takeout container, please," Olivia said.

"For Marcus?" Maureen asked.

"He's got a serious sweet tooth just like us. I bet he cleaned out the free mints at the hotel bar."

***

Olivia stood in the doorway of her hotel room. "I would invite you in, but I know that's a bad idea."

"What's bad about it?" Maureen asked. "I'll keep my hands to myself." She pulled Olivia closer.

"No you won't, and neither will I. I'm traveling with a fugitive in the morning. That means bedtime for me."

"Okay, but one more kiss before I go." Maureen made it a long one and whispered in Olivia's ear, "I'll dream about you, Olivia."

"Make it a good one." Olivia wrapped her arms

around Maureen and stroked her back.

A persistent beep from Maureen's cell phone interrupted the moment. She looked at the caller ID. "I better take this now."

"Hello?" Maureen scowled as she listened. "Crenshaw, are you freakin' serious?! When?!"

"What's wrong?" Olivia asked.

Maureen hung up and sighed. "Malley Henry is missing!"

"Missing? From jail?"

"From the jail infirmary. They took him there after a guard found him doubled over in his cell. The doctor had to pump his stomach after Malley told him he drank some jailhouse liquor."

"Let's go!" Olivia said and rushed for the elevator.

"Where? The jail's on lockdown--nobody in, nobody out. The best we can do is wait outside the building."

"I don't care, Maureen. I'm not leaving Atlanta without seeing Malley Henry--not after I've kissed and made up with my chief."

Maureen ran to catch up. "Okay, you grab Marcus, and I'll meet you at the car."

\*\*\*

Malley's knees were throbbing as he crouched in an alley behind a mom and pop service station. His body hadn't been through this much since his last construction job lifting and hanging drywall.

The back door opened and the mop slinger came out carrying two oil-stained jackets and two pairs of black khakis. He shoved a jacket and a pair at Malley.

"Here, ole' man, we got to cover up these ugly ass jail scrubs," he said.

Malley was trembling all over from the fall temperature that cooled the sweat running down his chest and back. "You didn't tell me you were going to break into the place," he said as he struggled into the clothes that were one size too small.

"Stop bitchin', man. I told you my buddy works here and left the side door unlocked. But the bastard forgot to leave some cash in the register."

Malley looked at the young man and immediately hated him. He didn't even know his real name and didn't want to know. He just wanted to get away from the mop slinger before he robbed somebody to get a fix.

Malley crouched down again when he heard sirens pass in front of the building. He hadn't envisioned this part of the breakout--breathing in garbage stench in a dark alley with a smart-ass junkie talking to him like he was a nobody. He rubbed his throat that still hurt from the pruno he threw up in the infirmary.

But the pruno was the easy part of the plan. Once Charlie Ward got a half-pint of the brew for him, Malley drank the entire thing straight. Minutes later, his stomach cramped so bad that he couldn't stand up. After a stomach pump and a cold pack in the infirmary, the nurse left him alone to rest. Then the mop slinger appeared and started emptying the trash cans and sweeping the floor. Malley knew that was the signal for him to ask to go to the bathroom. The nurse gave permission just as another inmate patient intentionally stumbled out of bed, knocked over his IV pole, and fell to the floor.

Malley went to the bathroom where the mop slinger was waiting. They quickly jimmied the toilet away from the wall to reveal a hole that the mop slinger had punched out weeks ago. He had stuffed it with two thin mattresses. They climbed in and crawled between cell walls toward a vent that opened out into a mechanical room. The room had an unbarred window ten feet from the ground. They dropped the mattresses out the window and jumped. They were free and on the run.

"I need to find some money fast, ole' man," the mop slinger said as he wiped his nose on his jacket. "You go your way, and I'll go mine." He walked to the end of the alley and disappeared around a corner.

Malley zipped up the tight jacket to hide his orange shirt. He looked down at the cheap prison sneakers on his feet and felt a draft between the toes on his left foot. The sole on the sneaker was badly ripped, and the black khakis were above his ankles and pinched his crotch. He stuck his hands in the jacket pockets and pulled out a wad of paper. It was five dollars. "Damn, five bucks and a busted shoe."

He followed the mop slinger to the end of the alley and turned in the opposite direction.

*** 

Marcus sat in the backseat of Maureen's car with the rear door open. "We have had the worst luck on this case," he said as Olivia handed him a cup of coffee.

Olivia stood by the rear door and massaged the back of her neck. "We haven't had *any* luck on this case. Our guy is on the loose, and we're sitting in a Waffle House parking lot three days before Thanksgiving." She looked through the Waffle House window at Maureen who was on her cell phone and waiting to buy hot tea. "I got to admit, it's been good for my love life though," she said.

"Hey, watch how you talk in front of me," Marcus cracked. "I've got virgin ears."

Olivia sighed. "You got any more of those hotel mints?"

"Nope. I'm all out."

Olivia sighed again. "I wish we could do something! I feel useless waiting here."

"The last thing Atlanta PD needs is two out of town cops running around their city looking for an escaped fugitive," Marcus said. "Could you imagine the headlines on that?"

"Could you imagine if it happened in Goslyn? Chief Anderson would lose his mind."

Olivia watched as a police cruiser sped toward an adjacent intersection and stopped. She saw the officer inside look at her and Marcus then look around the connecting streets before speeding off.

"I guess there's no update," Olivia said.

Marcus let out a big yawn. "This coffee's not strong enough. I should've brought that double fudge slice you gave me."

"Why don't you ask your wife to bake--" Olivia stopped as she looked down the street. "Orange pants," she said.

"Orange *what*?"

"That older guy walking there." Olivia pointed discreetly at a crowd that was coming out of a movie theatre and huddling around a bus stop. "Check out his pants and shoes."

\*\*\*

Malley couldn't decide if he should keep walking or wait for the next bus. His knees felt better after he had sat for ninety minutes watching a cheap dollar ninety-nine cent movie. As he tried to blend in with the crowd, he felt his pants leg slipping from underneath his khakis. His torn shoe leaned to one side and flapped each time he took a step.

\*\*\*

"No news from the Fugitive Task Force," Maureen said as she returned to the car. "What're you looking at?"

Olivia nodded toward the crowd. "Watch the guy facing away from us--the short-haired one in the mechanic's jacket," she said.

At that moment, more people poured out of the theatre, and a city bus came around the corner and blocked the view.

"Come on. Let's get closer," Maureen said.

They drove up behind the bus, and Olivia and Marcus got out on foot.

"Hey, no confrontation unless necessary," Maureen said as she leaned over and looked out the passenger window. "I'll call it in."

Olivia and Marcus walked toward the crowd and watched people get on and off the bus. They didn't see the man until Olivia looked farther down the street.

\*\*\*

Malley mingled in with another crowd as it

headed toward a bar and grill. He wanted a beer but couldn't afford one unless somebody took pity on him. He first needed to tuck the orange pants legs back under his khakis.

As he stopped and leaned against the security gate of a closed store, a couple bumped into him from behind. The woman's purse spilled on the ground, and the man dropped his cell phone. Malley immediately bent down to help the woman but suddenly jerked back up. Both pants legs were showing.

"Crap!" the man said. "Honey, you okay?" he asked as he stooped down.

Malley mumbled an apology over his shoulder as he hurried off.

"Thanks a lot, asshole!" he heard the man yell.

Malley passed the bar and grill's entrance and ducked in between it and a tattoo parlor. He tucked the pants legs back up, but the shoe was hopeless. He looked on the ground and saw a half used roll of surgical tape covered in tattoo ink.

"You lucky bastard," he said and wrapped strips of the tape around his shoe and around the cuffs of his pants. "Okay, now where the hell am I going?"

The couple was in his face the second he stepped back onto the sidewalk.

"You raised in a barn or somethin'!" the man said. "You could've helped my girl pick up her stuff. And you scratched up my phone!"

The woman held up her purse and slurred, "And you broke the strap on my bag. You know how much this cost me!"

Malley could smell alcohol on both of them. "Sorry, man, sorry." He tried to step around the couple, but the man put a forearm in his chest.

"Sorry, my ass! My phone was brand new!"

"He's just some homeless dude, babe," the woman slurred again. "Let's go."

But the man wouldn't move, and Malley saw a look in his eyes that he had seen many times in the eyes of his drinking buddies who had had one too many--that cocky "I can whip this guy's ass" look.

Malley slapped the man's arm down and glared at him. He started to walk off just as he spotted an armed security guard standing two doors down outside a sushi bar. He turned the other way and immediately zeroed in on a woman who was looking right at him. He thought he recognized her.

\*\*\*

"That's him. That's Malley," Olivia said.

She and Marcus picked up the pace, and she signaled to Maureen who was following them in her car. Maureen sped ahead and was instantly stopped by a parade of jaywalkers and another city bus pulling out into traffic.

Olivia rushed through the crowd when she saw a woman swing her purse at Malley and kick him in the shin.

"Police, out of the way!" Olivia yelled.

\*\*\*

Malley stumbled back between the buildings and rubbed his leg. "Lady, are you crazy!"

An ambulance siren was approaching, but Malley mistook it for the cops. He looked down the path between the buildings and saw stairs leading up to a second story door of the tattoo parlor. He ran up the stairs and pulled on the door handle, but it was locked. There was no place to go. Then a side door of the bar and grill swung open and out came a waitress who lit a cigarette and sat on a beer crate. Malley thought he could slip inside and hide among the staff and patrons.

Before he could take a step, he heard, "Police, stop!" He looked toward the sidewalk and squinted. Then it clicked. *Damn, that's the cop from the trailer fire.*

"Don't move, Malley!" Olivia yelled. She put her hand on her gun but didn't draw.

Malley's eyes dotted around the tight space. The waitress sat motionless with a terrified look on her face.

"Put your hands up and come down now!" Olivia ordered.

Malley looked at her, heard more sirens, and saw flashing blue lights behind her. He was trapped.

But his bravado or fear wouldn't let him quit as he again looked down to the bar and grill door. He could jump and rush inside. The officer wouldn't dare take a shot at him with the waitress between them. Or would she?

He eyed the officer's hand on the butt of her gun and slowly raised his hands and pretended to surrender. He looked at the waitress and saw the cigarette go limp between her trembling fingers. He had to make his move now.

He quickly dropped his hands and took a step back to get momentum to jump over the stair railing. As he grabbed the metal bar with both hands, he heard a loud thump from the other side of the door behind him. He made the mistake of hesitating for a split second. The door flew open and smacked him square between the shoulder blades. He remembered seeing the waitress' eyes roll back in her head as he flipped head first over the rail.

When his eyes fluttered open, the smell of cooking grease flooded his nostrils, and he lay atop a heap of trash. Straight up was a man in a long, black, leather jacket pointing a gun down at him.

"Show me your hands," the man said, "or get shot!"

Malley stretched out both arms before blacking out.

Marcus kept his gun pointed as Olivia checked the waitress who had fainted. Two Atlanta PD officers struggled to drag Malley off the trash pile. They barely got a grip as the cooking grease smeared his jacket. They cuffed him and left him facedown.

"Is she all right?" Marcus asked as he came down the stairs.

Olivia checked the waitress' breathing and touched her forehead. The waitress sat up and stuck the cigarette back into her mouth.

"Yeah, she's good." Olivia helped her stand, and one of the officers escorted her back inside the bar and grill.

"You got him!" Maureen said as she arrived with the Task Force Unit.

Marcus rolled Malley over. "Finally."

"And no burning building this time," Olivia

said.

Malley coughed and mumbled something when the Task Force officers stood him up and patted him down. He mumbled again but louder. "You came?" he asked. "You came for me?"

Olivia deliberately faced him toe to toe and said, "All the way from Goslyn, Mr. Henry. Just for you."

The Task Force placed Malley in an SUV and whisked him away with an entourage of police units following. The crowd that had gathered to see the action, slowly dispersed into the Atlanta nightlife.

"All in a day's work," Marcus said. "And I seriously need a sugar fix."

Maureen dug into the pocket of her blazer and held out a handful of mints from the hotel. "How 'bout these until we get back?" she handed them to Marcus.

Marcus looked at Olivia and said, "I think you've found your better half." He took the entire handful and swatted Olivia's hand when she tried to grab one. "See you back at the car." Marcus hurried off like a kid ready to tally up his Halloween swag.

"One day I'm going to trade him in for a new partner," Olivia said.

Maureen laughed. "Where're you gonna find a *Shaft* replica these days?"

# CHAPTER THIRTY-THREE

Lieutenant Beal was surprised at Chief Anderson's reaction--or lack of. She thought he was taking the Atlanta news far better than she had expected. She had called him late into the evening, but he insisted on a meeting at her office to be briefed. He arrived wearing an old two-tone nylon jogging suit and a pair of high top Chuck Taylors. He plopped down in Beal's guest chair.

"The detectives did have to chase down the suspect, sir," Beal said.

"Are they all right?" the chief asked as he sat surrounded by the lieutenant's aroma candles.

"Yes, sir. They fly back tomorrow, but the suspect will have to stay in Atlanta to face the escape charge. And the detectives could be called to testify about his capture unless he takes a plea." Beal looked at the chief who appeared relaxed.

"I think I should touch base with Atlanta PD's chief in the morning," he said, "just as a courtesy. Are we still on good footing with the IRS?"

"As far as I know, sir. They're cutting a deal with their suspect and plan to make more arrests related to the Lewis tax files." Beal knew why the chief had asked. He and several Board Supervisors were still hoping for that new federally funded response center even though the plan was no longer secret thanks to the local watchdog group.

"Good. Is there anything else?" the chief asked.

"No, sir. I'll have my official report by end of tomorrow." The lieutenant swiveled around in her desk chair and hit the return key on her computer.

"No hurry. I'm clear on everything," the chief said.

Beal watched as Chief Anderson straightened his posture and brushed his baldhead with his hand as if he had hair.

"I think I owe you...an apology, Lieutenant. I've overreacted more than once on this case, and I want to commend you for keeping your composure. You're an asset to the Department."

*Wow, that call to Clifford really paid off*, the lieutenant thought. "Thank you, sir."

The chief stood and zipped up his jacket. "I should get home and change. My son put me through a pre-holiday workout."

Lieutenant Beal quickly eyed the chief up and down. "Sharp outfit, sir," she said while trying to keep a straight face.

"Yeah, right. If I were going to a break-dancing contest thirty years ago. It was the best I could do on short notice." Chief Anderson looked around the lieutenant's office at the candles. "Lieutenant, have you considered a nicotine patch?"

Beal smiled. "I have, sir. But I kind of like the smell of a spring garden. It gives the place a feminine touch."

Chief Anderson shrugged. "If you say so. I'll see you in the morning, Lieutenant."

\*\*\*

Olivia picked up the Christmas catalog and lay on her couch. "When did Tuesday start feeling like Monday?" she said.

"Tell me about it." Maureen dried her hands on the dishtowel and turned off the kitchen light. "I'm glad we're both off tomorrow. I would love to sleep late." She turned on the CD player and stretched out face up on top of Olivia with her head on Olivia's chest.

The music started, and Luther Vandross, Olivia's favorite singer, crooned "Wait for Love" through the speakers.

"Where did we stop on your list?" Olivia asked and turned several pages.

"Let me think. I've got a new nine iron for my dad, a tool belt for Uncle Frank, and a Yankees jacket for Wallace. That leaves Elijah."

"How about a small train set?" Olivia asked and showed Maureen the page.

"Nah, too many moving parts for a two-year-old."

"How about…this? A teddy bear. It dances while rapping the alphabet. And it giggles."

"That'll work."

Olivia dog-eared the page. "Who's next?"

"Aunt Lena wants something for her kitchen, and Gloria wants something for her salon."

Olivia flipped through more pages. "Here's a stainless steel cook set and…a pair of professional hair clippers."

"Perfect. Mark those pages, too," Maureen said.

"What about your co-workers?"

"That's way too many people to think about right now. I'll still be shopping on Christmas Eve. What about you?"

"Nothing says 'I love you' like a gift card," Olivia said as she shut the catalog and dropped it on the floor. "It's quick, easy, and people can buy exactly what they want."

"That's no fun, Olivia," Maureen said and turned over onto her stomach. "You have to buy real gifts so people are surprised on Christmas Day."

"Tell that to Marcus who hates the sweater I gave him last year and my grandma who's never even turned on the flat screen I bought her."

"So you're a gift card Scrooge?"

"I'm not a Scrooge. I'll give gifts--plastic cards with a pre-loaded dollar amount."

Maureen laughed and laid her head on Olivia's chest again. "Whatever you say, Scrooge. What's the plan for tomorrow?"

"I talked with my secret weapon, and you're good to go. I'll play interference with my mama to keep her out of the way while you get a cooking lesson."

"Listen to us. We sound like we're planning a bank heist."

"If your aunt is anything like my mama, you don't ever want to mess up in the kitchen. My mama won't let me forget the time I burned the stuffing when I was fifteen."

"I love the holidays regardless of  kitchen duty."

Olivia brushed her finger against Maureen's cheek. "I'll love the holidays with you."

Maureen slid up and kissed Olivia. "Wanna finish what we started in the hotel?"

"Let's start with a shower."

Olivia led the way to her bathroom after

turning up the volume on Luther. She pushed back the shower's glass door and set the controls to massage.

Maureen was right behind her when she turned around. She kissed Olivia, and pulled Olivia's sweater up and off. She then unzipped Olivia's slacks and ran her hands inside Olivia's panties. "You won't need this," she said as she went up Olivia's back and removed her bra.

Olivia pulled at the front and back of Maureen's oxford and started to unbutton it from the bottom while Maureen unbuttoned the top. Her hands moved down to Maureen's zipper where she slid one hand farther passed the metal strip and gently pressed her fingers against Maureen.

A quick kiss was Maureen's response and off came her oxford and bra.

Both stepped nude into the shower's warm stream.

Maureen caressed Olivia's breasts and said, "I love touching you." She kissed Olivia on her neck, and turned her around to face the pulsating water that ran down to her short dark curls. With a hand still on Olivia's right breast, Maureen massaged Olivia's mound with her other hand.

Olivia guided Maureen's hand to her clitoris and held it there. "Right there," she said.

Maureen started a slow rub with her fingers and pressed herself firmly against Olivia. Olivia swayed her pelvis forward against Maureen's fingers, and back against Maureen. She moaned out loud, reached around, and palmed Maureen's behind. They quickly fell into a long, slow groove.

Eyes closed, Olivia started to come, and she used both hands to hold Maureen's hand against her clitoris. It was a warm climb with a cool climax.

As Olivia came down, she felt Maureen still firmly against her. She opened her eyes and turned. "Let me do that for you," she said. She wrapped one arm around Maureen, gently found Maureen's clitoris with her other hand, and softly stroked.

Maureen entwined her fingers in Olivia's braids and embraced her.

Olivia felt the muscles tighten in Maureen's back and between her legs. She gave a final stroke that raised Maureen to her tiptoes.

Maureen's body slowly relaxed against Olivia's, and she kissed her. She nibbled on Olivia's earlobe and asked, "Did you hear that?"

"Hear what?"

"Your bed calling us. It wants to know if you're ready for more."

Olivia laughed. "I do hear it." Olivia licked a drop of water from the tip of Maureen's nose and kissed her back.

"I'll take that as a yes," Maureen said.

They exited the shower for the bedroom, expecting little sleep and at least two more rounds.

# CHAPTER THIRTY-FOUR

"Pat, see if the boys are done washing their hands. Harold, Eric, put those Christmas decorations down. We're ready to eat."

Like soldiers at roll call, everyone followed Mama Winston's orders and gathered for the Thanksgiving feast. Grandma Rita took her place at the head of the dining room table as Olivia, Maureen, and Mr. Brooks sat on one side. On the other side, Pat seated the twins in between her and Eric.

"Got room for more turkey?" Olivia whispered to Maureen as Mama Winston rushed back to the kitchen to get extra napkins for the twins.

"Plenty," Maureen whispered back. "I skipped Aunt Lena's dessert for this."

Maureen had also skipped the potato salad at Aunt Lena's where she had introduced Olivia to her dad. Olivia said she saw where Maureen got her good looks, and Mr. Jeffries beamed when he boasted to Olivia about both his daughters' careers. He insisted that Olivia sit next to him at dinner because he wanted to get to know the woman who made his daughter smile in a way that he hadn't seen in years. During dinner, Mr. Jeffries tried to talk Olivia and Maureen into a round of Sunday golf. Maureen nipped that offer in the bud when she reminded her dad of the last time she played with him. They never found the nine iron that he had tossed into the local course's pond after a double-bogey.

Maureen's attention was brought back to her

second Thanksgiving dinner as Mama Winston returned to the table.

"Let's take a moment, everybody, to send up a silent prayer," Mama Winston said as she sat opposite Grandma Rita.

They held hands and bowed their heads. Maureen squeezed Olivia's hand and kissed her on the ear. She caught one of the twins spying on her, and she winked at him. His giggles got an evil eye from Pat.

"Settle down, young man," Mama Winston said. "Okay. Let's dig in!"

Mama Winston stood and starting carving the turkey as Mr. Brooks took the first roll and passed the bowl to Maureen. Eric went for the collard greens while Pat filled the twins' plates with gravy-topped stuffing. Grandma Rita couldn't resist fixing Olivia's plate for her. She piled on macaroni and cheese and a little bit of her homemade cranberry sauce--the only kind that Olivia would eat.

"Maureen, I hear you're quite the cook," Grandma Rita said with a smile. "We'll have to trade recipes sometime."

"Yes, ma'am. I've got a good one for candied yams." It was Grandma Rita's secret recipe that Maureen had used to impress her family at Aunt Lena's.

*** 

Mama Winston's clock chimed at ten, and the twins were sound asleep on the living room couch. Maureen and Eric had cleared the table and were loading the dishwasher while Mr. Brooks joined Mama Winston and Grandma Rita on the front porch to untangle Christmas lights. Pat and Olivia were on the back porch swing eating their second slices of German chocolate cake.

"I eat like a maniac every Thanksgiving," Olivia said.

"Me too," Pat added as she licked her fork and lips. She sat her empty plate down on the porch between her and Olivia. "How was dinner with Maureen's family?"

"Really nice. It was fun talking to her dad." Olivia set her empty plate on top of Pat's. "Are you and Eric taking the boys to see your parents for Christmas?" she asked.

"Not after that last bitter winter in Ohio. In fact, my parents dropped hints about moving back here. I think they miss being close to us."

"Are they finally tired of harassing your poor brother?" Olivia asked.

"I know Milton hopes so. They made it their mission to find him a wife so he could give them more grandchildren. Mama even posted signs all over Central State campus that her professor son was single and available."

"Have you and Eric thought about having more kids?"

"We don't have the energy, Ollie. We both lie awake at night and talk about the day the boys leave for college," Pat said. "Aren't we horrible? We plan to throw ourselves a block party that whole week. What about you? You reconsidering since you met Maureen?"

"I'm okay with being the coolest godmother in the world for now. But … it could happen." Olivia thought about the two Collins kids.

Pat curled up on the swing and pinched at Olivia's sweater. "Feels good to be in love again, don't it, Ollie?"

"It does. I guess good things happen if you let them."

Pat checked her watch. "Speaking of good things, let me get my two musketeers home while they're too tired to do anything but sleep. Give me a hug, you goofball."

The best friends hugged.

Pat got up and opened the storm door just as Maureen was approaching.

"Coming back for more?" Maureen asked.

"No thanks. I'm stuffed to the gills and ready for bed."

"Leaving already?"

"Yeah, it's past the boys' bedtime. It was good to see you again, Maureen."

"You too, Pat." Maureen stepped out onto the porch as Pat held the door open then went inside.

"Finished with kitchen duty?" Olivia asked as she motioned for Maureen to join her on the swing.

"It wasn't that bad. The dishwasher's doing all the work."

Olivia pulled Maureen closer and put an arm around her shoulders. "This is still my favorite spot in the whole house."

"It's peaceful," Maureen said and looked out into the night. "I see your grandma turned on her Christmas lights." She pointed to the house in the distance.

"Yeah, but don't be fooled by that woman's

holiday cheer. She'll work us to death in that garden next spring."

"Oh, it'll be fun. We'll sleep together on Friday nights, and go play in the dirt the next morning."

"I guess there is an upside," Olivia said and picked up the empty plates. "I'll wash these before we say good night."

"Should we offer to hang your mama's Christmas lights?"

"Don't bother. My mama intentionally tangles those same lights every year so she can spend all night gossiping on the front porch with those two."

"You know, the more I learn about the women in your life the more I like them."

"Let's go back to my place, and I'll teach you more about me."

# CHAPTER THIRTY-FIVE

Spring returned in full bloom, and gardening started every Saturday morning at sunrise despite Olivia's attempts at a labor strike.

Olivia leaned back in a lawn chair that she had set under a tree a few yards away from the garden. She fanned herself with one of Grandma Rita's magazines and sipped from a glass of lemonade.

"Ollie, what are you doing over here?" Maureen asked as she approached and threw her garden gloves at Olivia.

"A silent protest," Olivia said and threw the gloves back.

"Will you stop joking around and get up and help me plant the flowers?"

"I warned Grandma that if I had to dig one more hole without getting paid, I would take action."

"You're too much!" Maureen said. "I'm not getting in trouble with you."

Maureen turned to go back to the garden, but Olivia grabbed her around the waist and pulled her down on her lap.

"Ollie, your grandma will embarrass both of us out here!"

"Don't worry about it. I hid her broom when we got here this morning. Just lean back and enjoy the shade."

"You do realize we're the only ones goofing off?" Maureen nodded to the neighbors who were on their hands and knees in the yam patch.

"I asked for volunteers, but everybody wimped

out."

"Gee, I wonder why!" Maureen said and turned to wrap her arm around Olivia's neck. "How long you planning to protest?"

"Until Mr. Brooks tattles on me. Right now, he's too busy showing off his chicken eggs to the twins."

"I see. Am I supposed to strike with you?"

"Have I ever led you astray? Trust me, I can handle Mrs. Rita May Jones. But keep your ears open for the back screen door. She's famous for sneak attacks."

"So we're sitting ducks?" Maureen asked.

"Yeah, but it's a nice place to sit, don't you think?" Olivia raised her eyebrows and rubbed Maureen on her thigh."

"Don't get any ideas, sexy. I'm not getting caught making out under the tree with you." Maureen kissed her anyway.

"See, striking has its advantages," Olivia said.

Maureen kissed her again. "You can relax when we're done," she said as she slid her index finger in and out of a gold Venus ring that hung from a thin, gold chain around her neck. Olivia had given it to her to celebrate the one-year anniversary of their first date.

"Are you sure you like it?" Olivia asked.

"Of course I like it. Do you still like your gift?"

"I do. The twins say it makes me look cool." Olivia flexed her right wrist and looked at the braided leather wristband. It had a stainless steel charm in the center etched with the equality sign.

"I'm getting back to work before that screen

door opens." Maureen finished off Olivia's lemonade and put her gloves on just as Grandma Rita stepped onto the back porch. She held a basket in one hand, a glass of ice tea in the other, and a magazine tucked under her arm. "You're on your own, Ollie," Maureen said and waved over her shoulder as she went back to the azaleas and the mums.

"Traitor! See if I help you again when you're babysitting Elijah!"

Olivia watched Grandma Rita weave her way through the garden, giving instructions as she went. When Olivia knew she was spotted, she pretended to be asleep. She could feel the taskmaster sneaking up on her.

"Olivia Ann Winston! If you don't get out of that chair, I'll put you across my knee!" Grandma sat the basket on Olivia's lap and swatted her on the knee with the latest issue of *Soap Digest.*

"Sorry, ma'am, but I've been advised by my union rep not to speak with management."

"You silly child. Give me that chair and start snapping those string beans."

Olivia, with a pout, gave up her seat and sat on the ground.

"I think I deserve a dollar for each string bean I snap," she said.

"You sure you don't need to check with your union rep first? He may want a cut." Grandma snickered and stirred her tea.

"Very funny, Grandma. You and Mama should be comediennes."

"Did you talk to her this morning?"

"Yes, ma'am, and all is well. She showed my baby pictures to her class yesterday."

"Because she's proud of you, Ollie. You're still her little girl."

Grandma took a sip and started humming the theme song from her favorite soap opera.

Olivia had suffered through several episodes of the show and dubbed it *The Mean and the Desperate*. She knew her grandma hummed the tune every time she brought up the subject of marriage and grandchildren.

Grandma didn't disappoint. "Mrs. Thompson's granddaughter is getting married next year," she said. "And her youngest daughter just adopted her second baby. Would be nice to have a wedding here in the garden some day."

Olivia rolled her eyes. "Grandma, Maureen and I just had our first date anniversary. Give us some time."

"I'm not rushing anybody. I'm just thinking out loud. You know what they say: you can't get what you don't ask for."

"Talk about pressure! Maybe we should run out and adopt a puppy for practice!"

"Couldn't hurt. You'll learn plenty about the three Ps--pooping, peeing, and puking."

Olivia didn't respond. She just kept snapping beans.

"I'm only joking around," Grandma said as she fanned with the digest and sipped again. "But I am serious about one thing, Ollie--your happiness. I know you're a grown woman, but your mama and I felt your pain too when you learned being in love can hurt. We're both glad to see you give it another try." Grandma patted Olivia on the head.

"Thanks, Grandma. I love you."

"I love you too. Now give me that basket and get your sly self over there and help Maureen plant those flowers."

Olivia sighed. "I knew that was a set-up. That's what I get for talking to management." Olivia got up and handed her the basket.

"Stop whining. I'll make it up to you at Sunday dinner."

"Roasted turkey with coleslaw and string beans?"

"Just the way you like!"

"And royal fudge ice cream for dessert?"

"Uh-huh, and a chocolate cake for Maureen."

"You're the best boss I know, Grandma." Olivia kissed her on top of her head and left with a spring in her step as she joined Maureen.

Maureen pushed the shovel into the fresh, soft soil. "Just in time," she said. "I think my little helpers are allergic to work. They ran off to teach a trick shot to Mr. Brooks."

"I'll dig, and you can set the azaleas in first," Olivia said.

"Okay." Maureen passed the shovel and asked, "Any words of wisdom from Grandma Rita?"

"How'd you know?"

"I've been paying close attention this past year."

"She thinks we should get a puppy. But I told her it's too soon for that."

"Oh. I've heard the same thing from Gloria."

"Really? You think it's another conspiracy?"

"I wouldn't be surprised if Gloria's been working behind the scenes with your grandma. She's very good at plotting."

"Are you ready for a so-called 'practice puppy'?"

Before Maureen could answer, the twins' soccer ball flew by, and the boys followed in hot pursuit. They just missed stepping on a row of cabbage heads as they tripped over each other and landed right in front of Grandma Rita.

Maureen scratched her head. "How about a couple of practice goldfish instead?"

"Good answer," Olivia said. "But Grandma doesn't give up easy. She plans to soften you up tomorrow with her cooking."

"More cake?"

"And ice cream."

"Heads up!" Somebody yelled.

Olivia and Maureen ducked as the soccer ball zipped passed them going the other way this time.

The twins charged over. "Sorry, Aunt Ollie. Sorry Miss Maureen," Jesse said with a twinkle in his eye.

"Yeah, sorry," Jaylon repeated with a smile brightened by his braces. He dashed off and around the house after his brother.

Olivia looked at Maureen. "Maybe one practice goldfish, and we'll work our way up from there."

Maureen laughed. "Throw in a tomato plant, and it's a deal!"

CPSIA information can be obtained
at www.ICGtesting.com
Printed in the USA
LVHW081212070821
694638LV00009BB/710

9 781515 323099